WILLIAM'S PROGRESS

William has a twelve-year-old boss bent on his destruction; the interior design duo from hell redecorating his bathroom; and an angry ginger midget with a mean right hook on his case. Then there's the flood. And the village full of Machiavellian nutters. On the plus side, he also has a gorgeous wife and an adorable new son — and he loves them both. It's just a shame that parenthood doesn't stop him doing the wrong thing at precisely the wrong time, with catastrophic results for his small — and increasingly exasperated — family. It's very nearly too much for one man to handle. And that man is William Walker.

Books by Matt Rudd
Published by The House of Ulverscroft:

WILLIAM WALKER'S FIRST
YEAR OF MARRIAGE

MATT RUDD

WILLIAM'S PROGRESS

Complete and Unabridged

CHARNWOOD
Leicester

First published in Great Britain in 2010 by
HarperPress,
an imprint of
HarperCollins*Publishers*, London

First Charnwood Edition
published 2011
by arrangement with
HarperCollins*Publishers*, London

The moral right of the author has been asserted

Illustrations by Simon Spilsbury

This novel is entirely a work of fiction. The names, characters and incidents portrayed in it are the work of the author's imagination. Any resemblance to actual persons, living or dead, events or localities is entirely coincidental.

British Library CIP Data

Rudd, Matt.
    William's progress.
    1. Fathers- -Fiction. 2. Spouses- -Fiction. 3. Diary
    fiction. 4. Humorous stories. 5. Large type books.
    I. Title
    823.9′2–dc22

    ISBN 978–1–4448–0727–1

Published by
F. A. Thorpe (Publishing)
Anstey, Leicestershire

Set by Words & Graphics Ltd.
Anstey, Leicestershire
Printed and bound in Great Britain by
T. J. International Ltd., Padstow, Cornwall

This book is printed on acid-free paper

To Freddie and Felix

JANUARY

'Somewhere on this globe, every ten seconds, there is a woman giving birth to a child. She must be found and stopped.'
SAM LEVENSON

Tuesday 1 January

I am a father.
 I have a son.
 My son is alive.
 My wife is alive.
 My son and my wife are both alive.
 I am alive.
 We are all alive. Happy new year.
 I am a father. Right now. As of forty-three minutes ago. For forty-three minutes, I have been a father.

★ ★ ★

It must have been the cold air hitting me when I stepped out of the maternity ward. Not just the

1

cold air, of course. I am perfectly capable, under normal circumstances, of not fainting in the face of cold air. There were other contributing factors, too. Lack of food, for instance. I hadn't eaten for forty-six hours. You lose your appetite when your wife is groaning at you and the midwives are barking at you and no one's dilating quickly enough and everything's going wrong. For forty-six hours.

The only sustenance I'd had during the whole debacle was a gulped whisky during the small hours of the first night of the two-night labour when it was only me and Isabel (and the bump). The whisky was purely medicinal. We'd been 'in labour' for a good eighteen hours by then and I needed something to stiffen my resolve and prevent me from running, screaming, from the house. What a huge mistake that was. Running, screaming, from the house would have been a far more sensible course of action than staying for the full *Reservoir Dogs* experience. Isabel and the bump would have managed fine without me.

Lack of sleep: that's another of the extenuating circumstances leading to my fainting in a bush next to the ambulance bay. I have never stayed up for forty-six hours in my life. Hardened SAS men give up sensitive military secrets if they are kept awake for that long. But I'm not a hardened SAS man, and I wasn't allowed to sleep. Or I might have been allowed, but I never dared ask: one doesn't want to appear unsupportive during these (many) hours of need.

As it turns out, the first eighteen of the forty-six hours, the ones in the run-up to the whisky, weren't *actual* labour. They were only pre-labour, a sort of softening-up phase God threw in so that everyone would be completely exhausted gibbering wrecks by the time the proper labour began.

I didn't enjoy the pre-labour. I'm pretty sure Isabel didn't, either. She was having are-you-sure-this-isn't-the-actual-labour contractions every fifteen minutes or so. And when I say contractions, I mean proper on-all-fours, groaning and screeching and spitting like the possessed girl in *The Exorcist*. With me, frantic, helpless, stroking her lower back like they encouraged in the prenatal classes. And her saying, 'What the fuck are you doing?' and me saying, 'It's okay, darling. Swearing is a good release. They said that in the NCT class.' And her saying, 'Okay, well stop fucking tickling my back or I'll fucking kill you,' and me saying, 'Yes, darling'. And then her head spinning around 360 degrees.

That was the pre-labour. Eighteen hours, punctuated only by a midwife coming round and saying, 'Well done, dear,' before leaving again. And me, about halfway through, saying, 'Are you sure you want to stick with the whole home-birth plan, because we could go to hospital like everyone else? They have nice monitors and tubes and drugs there and stuff.'

And then the whisky. Thank God for the whisky. For a minute, a beautifully precious minute, peace and quiet. Nerves settling. The clock saying 1.30 a.m. and me wondering whether I could sneak in forty winks since we all seemed to be relaxing into this whole giving-birth thing.

3

No. Oh no. The moment of tranquillity evaporated as soon as Isabel gave out a real, proper, blood-curdling scream. It was a new noise altogether, a noise that, if you heard it in the distance while you were sitting in a safari truck halfway through a night drive in the Okavango Delta, would prompt you to immediately ask the ranger to drive you back to the camp. It was a noise that would chill a man to the very core, make him drop to his knees and pray, even though he doesn't believe in God, to make this all stop happening.

MY PRAYER

Dear Lord,
If you can get us through this thing, this terrifying thing, I promise never, ever to have unprotected sex with my wife or anyone else ever again. I promise to give my life to you and spend my days wandering the world preaching your gospel. Without shoes on and everything. Make the next few hours pass as quickly and painlessly as possible, oh, Mighty One, and I shall never, ever be a twat again, I really, really promise. And I'll bring up the bump in the Christian faith, rather than encouraging him down a more logical humanist path. I promise.

Amen

. . . and that was it: the start — only the *start* — of the 'real labour'. All systems go. 'This is Houston,

4

you are cleared for liftoff,' I said to Isabel in an attempt to sound excited and positive.

'If you say anything else that makes me feel like a space shuttle, I will kill you,' she replied. 'Now call the midwife back and tell her to get round.'

The midwife arrived. Four centimetres dilated, she said. Only four? Six whole centimetres to go. *Six!* Jesus. I mean, blimey. Sorry, God. I started another prayer, but the midwife interrupted, telling me to make myself useful by pumping up the birthing pool. Yes, of course, the birthing pool. Must pump up the birthing pool.

BIRTHING POOL: INSTRUCTIONS FOR USE

1. Important: make sure you unpack the birthing pool and inflate it prior to use to ensure that you are familiar with the equipment and there are no faults. Aquasqueeze Ltd will not offer a refund if any pool malfunctions are only discovered during the birthing procedure.
   (Frankly, it was a miracle I even read the instructions on the day, let alone prior to use. I mean, seriously, as if it's necessary to have a trial run of a glorified paddling pool.)

2. Plug in pump.

3. Pump.

Why didn't I do a trial run for the paddling pool? It's childbirth, for goodness' sake. You don't muck about with childbirth. But it was one of several things I hadn't done. I hadn't read any of the baby books Isabel had asked me to read. I hadn't got in an awful lot of lie-ins. I hadn't painted the bathroom, the horrible old bathroom with its horrible old paint. I *had* painted the nursery, but badly. The birthing pool was the least of my worries. Except, it wasn't.

It took forty minutes to inflate the pool, during which time the foot pump and I fell out on several occasions. I twisted one ankle and had room spin twice. Shouldn't have had the whisky. It took another ninety minutes to fill the pool with water using a complicated, improvised, ever-so-slightly panicky siphoning system I devised with the garden hose, a colander, a plastic bag and the bath. Why hadn't I worked this all out earlier? Idiot, idiot, idiot.

The leak was discovered at approximately 0400 hours, long after the helpline at Aquasqueeze Ltd had closed. Mind you, they were probably closed for the entirety of the Christmas period, anyway. That's the trend these days, isn't it? No one's going to turn up for work at a birthing pool company on New Year's Eve, even though it's a Monday. Even though people still might be giving birth. That would be far too much to expect, now wouldn't it?

Only once the pool was full did the pressure begin to force water through the until-then-unnoticeable tear right at the base. From then on, it was like a crack in a dam in a 1970s disaster movie. It got bigger and bigger and bigger. I was already too tired and dehydrated to cry proper tears, and Isabel and the midwife were too busy doing grim things in the front room to notice.

I put a finger over the hole and looked around the dining room. Why we had decided that Isabel should give birth in the dining room and not somewhere one might find the necessary equipment to mend a leak, I have no idea. Next time, we're doing it in the garden shed. Plenty of appropriate mending equipment in there. Back in the dining room, all I could reach was masking tape. Masking tape is porous, but it bought me enough time to find the Sellotape. Which bought me enough time to explain to Isabel, between contractions, that the pool was ready, but that she couldn't bounce around in it or anything because, well, it was a touch, erm, faulty, darling . . .

She didn't like this idea.

'I told you we should check the effing pool out before I — bbleeeaaaaaaaarrrrrrrrrrgggggggggggghhh-hhhhhh'.

There are at least some advantages to regular strong contractions. You can only get shouted at for the ever-decreasing periods in between.

7 a.m. Six centimetres dilated. Could it go any slower?

10 a.m. Seven centimetres. But maybe still six because things are getting a bit swollen down there.

'Keep going, darling, you're doing wonderfully,' I told her, while reflecting that God really could pick up a bit more support if he answered the odd agnostic's desperate prayer every now and again.

By midday, we were on to our third midwife and the pool was starting to sag. Sellotape can only go so far.

By 4 p.m., I had given up trying to keep the water in the sagging pool at a comfortable temperature because Isabel was now roaming around the house like an injured animal. Absolutely no point sitting in the dining room with a thermometer and a kettle when your wife is in a dark corner of the bedroom growling at anyone who tries to offer her a biscuit. And then it was 10 p.m., and the two latest midwives had decided that she was eight centimetres, but Isabel had had enough.

'I've had enough,' she said quietly and I had to look away because I didn't want her to see how frightened I was.

So we went to the hospital . . . her in an ambulance with blue flashing lights and everything, me following in the Skoda without blue flashing lights, the baby bag, a change of clothes or anything. Idiot.

Drugs, gas and air, epidurals, something that sounded like Sanatogen, more slow progress, baby in distress, mother in distress, me shaking my fist at bloody non-existent God for the ridiculous, stupid, impossible nature of child-birth. And then, suddenly, at 5 a.m., I hear the phrase 'fetal distress'. Isabel is barely conscious. The bump is in trouble.

'We have to get this baby out. You've been going long enough, dear,' said a no-nonsense mid-wife with arms like beanbags. And Isabel burst into tears of sheer exhaustion and resignation.

I can't remember much about the Caesarean, except that it was quick and there were slurping noises like when you're at the dentist and the assistant sticks the vacuum cleaner down the back of your mouth and you try to keep it away from your epiglottis because you were already very close to gagging but she's not paying attention because it's almost lunch and she's bored, and, oops, a little bit of breakfast has come up and now the dentist doesn't like you, which is annoying because it wasn't your fault, it was the bored assistant's.

At the point of incision, Isabel had to tell me to stop squeezing her hand so hard because it was hurting. Then the doctor made a joke and I made a joke and Isabel had to tell us all to stop joking. 'Gallows humour,' I said and immediately regretted it. Three or four seconds or minutes or hours later, there was a piercing, gurgly scream from behind the turquoise curtain: our boy, beautiful, grumpy from all his efforts to escape Isabel. My turn to burst into tears.

And that was forty-three minutes ago. Now I am lying in a bush and an old lady is prodding me with her Zimmer frame and I'm laughing and crying at the same time.

★   ★   ★

I phone the families. They are equally pleased that we are all alive.

Isabel's dad says, 'Bloody home births. Bloody ridiculous. This isn't the Crimean War.' And I have to explain, not for the first time, that these

9

days women are empowered to make choices and that Isabel didn't want to give birth in hospital. He points out that she did in the end. I point out that he's right and I don't care . . . the main thing is that everyone's alive and he is now a grandfather.

'A grandfather? Yes, I suppose I am,' he replies more warmly. 'About time, too. I was beginning to think Isabel was past it. Everyone leaves it so late these days. I mean, in my day, you got married and you got on with it. None of this work-life balance nonsense. As slow as a giant panda, but you got there in the end. Well done, my boy.'

I then have the same conversation with Dad before he puts on Mum, who is immediately hysterical and then tells me her birth story, which I've heard a thousand times before and don't want to hear this morning. Not now that I have my own which is just as gory.

'I have to go, Mum. I need to check on Isabel and the bump.'

'You can't call him 'the bump' any more. Doesn't he have a name? Please tell me you've decided on a name. Please tell me it's not something trendy.'

'Not quite. But you'll be the first to know.'

THE HORROR OF NAMING A CHILD

There is much responsibility attached to having a baby. This much we know. But by far the worst aspect of it is giving the child a name, particularly if it's a girl. Every girl's name that Isabel thought was sweet was a porn name. Chloe. Jessica. Ella. We may as well just call her Pamela. Or Paris.

'What about Sarah?' Isabel had suggested, reasonably.

'No, I snogged a girl called Sarah. We were only fourteen and she let me touch her breast. Not appropriate.'

'What about Susannah?'

'Everyone snogged Susannah.'

'Maybe you could give me a list of girls' names that have no sexual connotations for you.'

'Okay, Beatrice.' Because Isabel isn't the only one who can make reasonable suggestions.

'*Beatrice?!*'

'Yes, or Bea for short.'

'Don't be ridiculous.'

This went on for months and all we agreed on was that we shouldn't go for an 'interesting name', like Apple, Moon Unit or Prince Michael II. You are not, as the axiom goes, more interesting because your children have interesting names.

'What about Electra?' she suggested while we were failing to choose a pram at John Lewis.

'Are you making these preposterous suggestions simply so I have to say no a lot so that when I make sensible suggestions in return — like Mildred — and you say no, you don't appear unreasonable?'

'Electra was my grandmother's name.'

I only realised she was joking when we got back to the car. You can lose your sense of humour with the whole girls' names fandango.

On boys' names, we had narrowed it down to

11

thirty. My favourite was George, but because her favourite was Albert, which is French and makes me think of pierced foreskins, I had to agree that we would cancel out favourites. Next was my Kit (after the car in *Knight Rider*, thereby guaranteeing my unborn child a life of success and coolness of which I could only ever have dreamed), knocked out by her Finbar. Neo and Ralph went the same way, but for a long time we found common ground on Elijah.

'Elijah,' I had announced proudly to Johnson in the pub. 'Elijah Walker.'

He'd looked at me coldly, looked at his pint forlornly and said, 'Poor kid. Poor, poor kid, with his poncey parents and his ridiculous name that will follow him through life ruining any chance he ever had of not being judged. Another pint?'

That left us with deadlock, so we decided to put the whole terrible matter on hold until nearer the time. And then we got nearer the time and were no closer to resolution. Then the time came and went. And now we are the proud owners of an unnamed child and the grandparents are appalled.

Back in the ward, Isabel is sleeping. So is Bump. Ahhh, they are so sweet. Look at him with his little head. His tiny little head. Is it *too* little? It looks very small. So do his arms. His arms are too short. Oh, God, a short-armed son. Didn't Hitler go off the rails because of his short arms? I can't remember. I'm so tired.

'Darling, you're hurting my stomach.'

'What? Who? How? Oh, God. I'm sorry.' I had nodded off on the chair and slumped forward on to the recently dissected stomach of my wife. 'I'm so, so, so, so, so sorry. Are you okay? Should I get the doctor? Shall I press that emergency button?'

'It's fine. I'm fine. Look at your beautiful son'.

And there he is, looking straight at me. Possibly. Hard to tell, though. He has a glazed expression. He looks a bit dopey. Oh, God, is he simple? Will he still be living with us when he is forty, in an anorak, untouched by women, untroubled by a career, enthused by nothing but trains and their sequential numbering system. Oh, God.

He hiccups and there is a flicker of alertness. No, it's fine. Everything is fine. And we are all alive. 'I love you, darling. Happy new year.'

'Darling? Darling? DARLING!'

'What? What happened?'

'You fell on my stomach again.'

'Oh, God. I'm so, so, so, so — '

'Why don't you go home, have a rest, get the bag of things I told you not to forget last night and come back? Bump and I will be fine.'

She's right. I must stop falling on her recently severed stomach. I must go home and hunter-gather. I shall return in no more than two hours with clothes and Innocent smoothies and flowers. A thousand flowers for my amazing wife. Fear not.

And I was gone.

13

Our front door. I'm standing looking at our front door. Marvelling at it, at its familiarity. It looks the same, but everything is different. This house is now a family house. My family will live here. Nothing will ever be the same again. The thought — combined with a new wave of tiredness and hunger — overwhelms me. I can hardly find the energy to fumble through my coat pocket for the keys.

Inside, it's *Reservoir Dogs*, the leftovers. There's the birthing pool, its water congealing nicely. I take a closer look and remember the moment, the very specific moment, when the pregnancy ceased to be fun.

THE SPECIFIC MOMENT WHEN HAVING A BABY CEASED TO BE FUN

October 27. 10.44 a.m. Second baby-group meeting. Isabel was excited but nervous. I was nervous but excited. We were running through the list of things we'd need for the birth: the nappies, the breast pads, the wet wipes, the snacks for daddy, the sanitary towels, the pumps, the nozzles, the pointless homoeopathic pills and the million other items that were all absolutely essential if things were to go smoothly. The longer the list went on, the less excited and more nervous Isabel looked and the more strongly I felt like hugging her and telling her everything would be all right, list or no list. Hugging didn't seem appropriate, so I gripped her hand and gave her a reassuring smile. She smiled back and if, at that second, a lion had jumped over the hedge and attacked her, I would have fought it off with my bare hands. Or at least had a jolly good go. I felt like I would do anything to protect her, anything at all.

But then we got to the very last item: an old sieve.

That's what it said. Not simply, 'Sieve', but 'Old sieve'.

'Why old?' asked one of the more inquisitive mothers-to-be.

'Because you don't want to use your newest sieve to get all the bits out of the birthing pool, do you?' came the matter-of-fact reply. And in that instant, I didn't feel like everything was going to be all right and I didn't feel like I could protect Isabel from anything at all. I wanted to smile and shrug calmly at my wonderful, brave, nervous, pregnant wife — but I couldn't. I needed fresh air. It wasn't so much that I was squeamish about bits in a birthing pool. It was more that it was going to happen to Isabel, and there was nothing we could do about it. In fact, it was normal. Having an old sieve on a list of things you need for a water birth was normal.

'Are you sure you're okay?' she asked during the break. 'You look a bit pale.'

'I'm fine. Absolutely fine. Just a bit airless in here.'

That is all over now. Now we are postnatal. We are, as I have mentioned, all alive. And now I am here, looking at the birthing pool that never was, thinking about the old sieve we never needed. I

15

make my way upstairs, finding more detritus of the previous two nights: half-drunk cups of camomile tea ('It's making me feel sick'), wet flannels ('Get that flannel away from me'), massage oil ('Stop rubbing me'), CDs of whale music ('William, will you turn that racket off? I already feel bloated enough without having to listen to the mating rituals of a blue whale'). In the bedroom, I find the bed. Which I shall just lie in briefly. Forty winks, as instructed. That is all . . .

Wednesday 2 January

'I can't believe you left us for a whole day. I'm still wearing the same nightdress I came to the hospital in. I've had to borrow some sanitary towels from the nurse.'

'I'm so, so, so, so, so, so, so sorry. I got home. I had a quick liedown. The phone was still unplugged from when you told me to unplug that ('fucking') phone. Then it was 11 p.m. I called the hospital. They said you were asleep. I called your mobile. It was off. I'm here now. I'm so sorry. Look, I bought a cranberry, yumberry and blackcurrant smoothie. It's very high in vitamin C.'

'Thanks. Now, go and change Jacob's nappy.'

'*Jacob*?'

'Yes, he's called Jacob. I had to call him something because the midwives were about to call social services and report us for neglect. You had gone AWOL. So I decided on Jacob. We can

16

always change it later.'

Ahh, the old we-can-always-change-it-later trick. Isabel has been using this all year. We can't agree on a colour to paint the baby's room. I want a good, honest, sensible yellow. She wants a pinky-white, which is ridiculous if it's a boy, but she says, on the contrary, it's perfect because she intends for our child to have a non-gender-specific upbringing. Halfway through the standoff, she paints it pink while I'm at work. I come home and look angry. She says, 'We can always change it later.' *Kapow!*

Also while I'm at work, she pays a proper handyman to come round and hang pictures where I don't want them on the grounds that we've been in this house for over a year and she's tired of looking at bare walls. The same happens with the placing of plant pots, the reorganisation of the kitchen and the moving of all my clothes to the bottom drawer of the small cupboard in the spare room (to make room for all the cloth nappies). But it's okay, we can always change it later . . .

We will *never* change it later. We could barely be bothered to change it in the first place.

This is fine when it comes to the feng shui-ing of a living room or the buying of a girly tree for the front garden, but not so fine for the naming of a first-born.

Jacob.

I'm not sure. I knew someone at university called Jacob. Did philosophy. Smoked drugs. Now lives on a beach in Bali. How much of that is because his parents called him Jacob?

17

It does have a ring to it, though. Jacob Walker. You probably wouldn't get an astronaut called Jacob Walker, but equally, you wouldn't get a shoplifter. It didn't sound prime ministerial, but there was a certain gravitas. Broadsheet newspaper editor, perhaps. Barrister. Surgeon. Discoverer of (a) the cure for old age, (b) life in another solar system or (c) the ark of the covenant. If they haven't discovered that already. I can't remem —

'William! The nappy.'

THE DADDY NAPPY

Well, I missed that one. We had given over ten minutes of the prenatal classes to the treacly first nappy. Turns out I could have skipped that bit on account of having rather tactically skipped the whole of day one. I got day-two nappy instead and, frankly, I don't see what all the fuss is about. It went absolutely fine until Jacob (see, I'm already calling him that) decided to have a wee the second, the very second, I'd finished cleaning him up. No drama. I changed him again — and that was less fine because he was screaming. And the screaming is very hard to cope with when you're trying to work out which way around the nappy stickers go and how you wipe the poo off without getting it on the (pink, why is it pink?) babygro. Still, the smell was bearable, the trauma minimal. All trauma will appear minimal now that I have witnessed the miracle of childbirth.

Thursday 3 January

One more night in hospital on account of the whole dissection thing. This has worked out very well. Now that I have slept — and we have put the whole missing-the-first-day-with-Jacob debacle behind us — I am finding the routine of being a new dad quite acceptable. Wake up, drive to hospital, fuss over amazing mother of my child for a few hours, marvel pathetically every time child moves ('Look, look, look, he moved his hand, ahhhhhh'), go home, watch DVDs, drink beer, watch more DVDs, go to bed.

Today, we introduced Jacob to both sets of grandparents. We had to prise him from the claws of both mums, but other than that — and a slightly disgusting moment when Jacob tried to suckle Isabel's mum and Isabel's dad said, 'Hang on now, old chap, there's only one of us allowed to sup at that particular cup these days' — everything went smoothly.

Until the flowers arrived from Alex, Isabel's best friend.

WHY ALEX IS STILL ISABEL'S BEST FRIEND

Alex very nearly ruined my marriage. He spent the first year of it spying on us and trying to break us up. He gate-crashed our romantic weekend away. He faked photographs of me having sex with my ex-girlfriend, Saskia (the Destroyer of Relationships). Worst of all, he

19

found out I was getting Isabel's parents some cheese knives for Christmas and he got them better ones. How could anyone be so devious?

I had assumed the answer was simple enough: he loved her, she didn't love him, he turned into a nutter. But after the dust had settled, after Isabel and I had repaired the damage he had done, after he had cried a lot and begged for forgiveness, it became clear that it wasn't quite so simple after all.

'Isabel. William. I have something else to tell you.'

You're moving to Indonesia? You're becoming a Trappist monk? You're —

'I'm gay and I'm in love with an interior designer called Geoff.'

I don't know why we were even still talking to him at all, let alone talking to him about this exciting new revelation, a revelation which, frankly, if he'd revealed it to himself a bit earlier, could have saved us all an awful lot of hassle.

'Wow,' exclaimed Isabel charitably.

'Couldn't you have worked that out a bit earlier?' I asked as patiently as possible.

'I know. I'm so sorry. I always knew deep down. You just do, don't you? But I was too frightened to admit it to myself, let alone to anyone else. I think that's why I spent all my time chasing a woman I knew I could never be with.'

'And hiding a camera in her bedside lamp.'

'Yes, well, I was in denial. And denial led to confusion. And obsession. And . . .'

'And psychotic behaviour?' I was only trying

20

to help him finish his train of thought, but Isabel gave me a look. Despite everything, Alex was still her friend and she would still support him, a fact which I found intensely annoying. Given the lengths to which he had gone to spoil our wedded bliss, announcing he was gay was about the only way he could insinuate himself back into Isabel's affections. Which is exactly what happened. He went from, 'Sorry for nearly ruining your lives' to 'I can't wait for you to meet Geoff, you're going to love him' in the space of five minutes.

A week after that, contrary to Alex's prediction, I found that I didn't love Geoff. Geoff loved the sound of his own voice too much for there to be room for any other love. 'William. Hi. Heard a lot about — Blimey, I hope that rug was a present, or are you being ironic? Maybe the latter, I've heard you're quite dry and, my God, what a bold statement you're making putting that picture against that wallpaper. Bravo. Anyway, sorry, where was I? So good to meet you. I was thinking on the way here that — '

The only time anyone else could speak was when he had food in his mouth. The rest of the time, he monopolised the conversation with long, fanciful stories about how brilliant he was and how awful everyone else's taste in home furnishings was. I don't know why he thinks he's so brilliant. He's only an interior designer who was on daytime television once.

'You know, he used to be on television?' whispered Alex when Geoff gave us all a break by going to the toilet. 'And he wants me to work with him. He loves my style. He thinks I could be an interior designer, too. Isn't that exciting?'

'Yes.'

No.

So now Alex is back in our lives. He has chucked in his old pretentious job and got a new pretentious job. He is now an interior designer. And we have to have dinner with them at their annoyingly designed flat. And they have to come to dinner and make annoying comments about our normally designed house.

And, clearly, he still can't help upstaging me on the present front. First cheese knives. Now flowers. His bunch would embarrass the head gardener at Kew.

'Isabel, I thought you disapproved of out-of-season flowers. Because of the food miles, or whatever it is.'

'Yes, but aren't they beautiful?'

Friday 4 January

The baby seat. My God, the baby seat. Even when I'd read the instructions (birthing pool: lesson learned), in four languages, I still couldn't work it out. You have to feed the seat belt through several different holes, loops and clips, all at the pace of a snail to prevent the very touchy seat belt from locking up. If there are any slight twists or kinks in the seat belt, YOUR BABY WILL DIE. You have to get a floaty orange thing lined up with another floaty orange thing, or YOUR BABY WILL DIE. Even though the orange thing is a sort of spirit level and it only lines up when our car is on the road, not the drive. You must then clip one clip into another clip, even though the clips don't reach one another, or YOUR BABY WILL DIE. If the air bags go off, YOUR BABY WILL DIE. If you have the headrest angled wrong, YOUR BABY WILL DIE. If you don't follow points 1 to 97 of the health and safety section of the policy document of the car seat, you will be a child killer.

Before leaving for the hospital, I managed to get the seat into the car in a relatively non-lethal way. It took twenty-five minutes and an awful lot of swearing, but I did it. As long as I put it in when the car was on the road, not the drive, it was safe. But when I got to the hospital, they wouldn't let us carry Jacob out in our arms — against health and safety regulations. So I had to unravel the seat, bring it into the hospital, put Jacob in it, take it and him back to the car and then tell the hardcore hospital traffic warden to back off because, even though I was in a ten-minute loading bay, I was dealing with baby seats as well as a baby and would be more than ten minutes. The traffic warden backed off.

Putting a baby-filled baby seat into a car is much harder than putting an empty seat in. Eventually, I gave up. I told Isabel, sitting in considerable pain in the front seat, that all was well, smiled at Jacob, cursed the fact that Alex's flowers had to be brought down to the car in two separate journeys, then drove all the way home at no more than four miles per hour so that OUR BABY WOULD NOT DIE.

Ahhh, home. Start of the babymoon. We are all alive. We are all at home. None of us appear to have contracted a hospital superbug. Although I can no longer get away with watching DVDs or drinking beer, I am feeling very, very happy — as happy as someone who thought everyone was going to die and then found out they weren't. As long as I don't make Isabel laugh at all in the next two weeks (her stitches forbid it) and as long as we never want to drive anywhere ever again with Jacob, we will be fine.

Saturday 5 January

Well, that was interesting. I think I slept about nine minutes in total. In one-minute bursts. Jacob was in a crib next to the bed. He didn't like that, so Isabel brought him into the bed. Co-sleeping, they call it. By the time I came to bed (very late, after trying to recover from eight hours of constant waitering), Isabel was fast asleep and Jacob was in the middle of the bed stretched out in a star shape.

He looked very, very small. Easily squashable. Isabel says that a parent, so long as he or she is sober, is perfectly in tune with his or her baby and wouldn't squash it in a million years. She's read that in a book. But in the small hours, with Jacob snuffling away next to me, a half-remembered horror story about a giant panda

24

squashing its offspring creeps into my head. I think it was a panda, but it could have been a Glaswegian. No, it was definitely a giant panda.

So I lay there trying to work out if giant pandas aren't comparable because they are animals, not half as intelligent as humans, and they have the sort of fur that would easily suffocate their offspring. Or if they are comparable because even if they aren't as intelligent, they're probably more in tune with their instincts than we are. And one of their instincts is bound to be, 'Don't crush your offspring.'

Every time I succeeded in rationalising the giant-panda issue and began to nod off, Jacob would emit what sounded an awful lot like a final death rattle. Then he would stop breathing. I would pull up the blind so the streetlight would illuminate his face. I would peer at him closely, listening for signs of life. There would be none. Was he going blue? Were his tiny lungs packing in? Should I not be reacting? React, man, react! This child, this poor helpless child, is dying of some rare and undetected condition and you're not reacting! And then a millisecond before I started shaking Isabel awake, he would make another gurgling noise, as if back from the brink, and carry on breathing.

An hour of giant-panda analysis would pass before I felt even remotely calm enough to nod off again.

Another death rattle.

And repeat.

Until 6 a.m. when he wakes up and looks at me. Or looks in my general direction. I put my

25

finger into his wrinkly little hand for reassurance and he grips it tightly. I know in that moment that I will do anything for Jacob for ever . . . sleep permitting.

Sunday 6 January

7 a.m. Breakfast in bed for Isabel, who is in a lot of pain but pretending that she isn't to make me feel better. I ask her if she can remember anything about the sleeping habits of giant pandas and she starts laughing and then shouts at me for making her laugh, which was the last thing I was trying to do, what with her liable to split open at any second. Which I tell her and that makes her laugh again and so I get shouted at again. As punishment, I spend the day slogging around getting this and that for Isabel. Another night of total sleep deprivation.

Monday 7 January

'This is why Ali and I never had kids,' says Johnson, my second-best friend, when he phones to apologise for not sending flowers — even though Ali actually had.

'I thought it was because you didn't want to risk having a girl because girls are manipulative and controlling and you have enough of that in your life already?'

'Yes, that as well. But mainly because you don't sleep for years and you become a domestic slave. I'm delighted for *you*, of course. You ignored my advice about marriage and now you've ignored my advice about procreation. You have no one to blame but yourself, and I shall enjoy seeing you fall to pieces over the next few months. Pub tonight?'

'No.'

'Thought as much.'

The problem now is that I'm so tired, I'm worried that if I do manage to nod off, I'll sleep so deeply that I wouldn't have any anti-child-crushing instinct. Isabel says this is nonsense. I point out the case of the panda. She says this is nonsense: I am not a giant panda. On the plus side, she and Jacob are sleeping brilliantly and I only have two more weeks of paternity leave before I, too, can sleep brilliantly, back at my desk.

Tuesday 8 January

I love Jacob. I really do. But he's so very, very small and fragile. Because of the whole stomach-slicing style of birth, Isabel can't carry him around easily. So I have to. Every time I take him up or down the stairs, I have resolved in my mind that if I slip, I will cushion him, rather than put my own arms out to break the fall. I may kill myself, but Jacob will survive. This is what I am prepared to do.

At lunch, which I have made because Isabel still can't do very much in the way of chores and because she seems to spend most of the day breast-feeding, I sit watching my pasta get cold because I am holding Jacob. Every time I put him down, he cries.

'He needs a feed,' I say hopefully.

'I fed him five minutes ago. I'll take him in a second. And anyway, you can hold him with one hand and eat with the other.' Isabel is way ahead of the curve on this whole parenting thing. Despite being sore, tired, pale and red-nippled, she is already putting things into perspective, behaving rationally, becoming supermum.

'No, I can't. I might drop him.' I'm not quite there yet.

'No, you won't. Just relax.'

So I relax, take a mouthful of pasta and Jacob's head lolls unexpectedly, striking the edge of the table. It takes ten minutes for him to stop crying. It takes ten hours for me to stop freaking out at my own stupid stupidity. Isabel says it's only a little bump. I say he could have been killed. And even if it is only a little bump, he still has a bruise.

And the health visitor is coming tomorrow.

Wednesday 9 January

The health visit is compulsory. Society does not allow people to vanish into domestic anonymity without first double-checking that they are not doing horrible things to their newborn children.

This is unfortunate because the bruise looks epic this morning. It looks like I've punched him. I look like a heroin addict because I haven't slept for three nights. We will be flagged as an abusive family. Jacob will be taken away from us and raised by horribly strict foster parents who, at least, will never try to stuff their faces with pasta while holding an eight-day-old infant. Years from now, Jacob and I will be reunited, perhaps on a television show presented by Esther Rantzen. And I will try to explain that I hadn't meant to bang his head on the table, I just hadn't realised how floppy a newborn child's head could be. And the crowd will boo. And Jacob will tell Esther how, despite his strict Christian upbringing, he finds it hard to forgive me.

* * *

'Morning. I'm the health visitor.'

'Morning. Hi. Come in, come in. How are you? Can I get you a cup of tea? Or something stronger? No. Silly. Of course not. Don't know what I'm saying. Tea? Yes, right away. Isabel and Jacob are in the front room. Okay. Fine. Right. Okay.'

Brilliant. The same guilty ramblings I spout when I'm going through customs. Which is why I always get searched. And now why this health visitor is going to take Jacob away from us.

'Here's your tea. Hahahaha. Can't remember if you said white. Or black. So I've brought both. I mean milk. I've brought milk.'

Calm down, you idiot.

The health visitor tells Isabel that she shouldn't co-sleep. It's dangerous.

Isabel tells the health visitor that it isn't and that it's up to her how she raises her own child.

29

The health visitor makes a note.

This is going badly. I explain, apropos of nothing, that the bruise was an accident. She makes another note. Isabel rolls her eyes really theatrically at me, as if to say, 'Why on earth have you mentioned the bruise?' I throw back a 'What?!' face, as if to say, 'What?!' The health visitor makes another note, so I pretend I have some e-mails to answer.

Ten minutes later, the coast is clear and Isabel reveals that the woman asked if I was abusing her. Apparently, they have to ask. Apparently, Isabel saw it as a good opportunity to make a joke about our marriage. 'Only mentally,' she had answered, laughing. And instead of laughing, the health visitor had made another note.

Saturday 12 January

I think we have a routine. Bed at 8 p.m. Awake at 5.30 a.m. Naps at 11 a.m. and 3 p.m. This is fine. This is survival, at least. And Isabel and Jacob seem to be sleeping rather beautifully together. I know this because I still can't relax. It's not just the whole panda thing; it's the responsibility. The sheer mind-blowing responsibility of having a baby totally dependent on you. Well, us. Well, her. But at least we have a routine.

Sunday 13 January

We don't have a routine.

30

Monday 14 January

The routine is that I have to get up at 5.30 a.m., even though I haven't slept, and read Thurber to Jacob while Isabel sleeps. She's still recovering. He prefers Thurber to Hardy — I can tell by the way he dribbles faster. Isabel reckons I should stick with *The Hungry Caterpillar* but Jacob finds the inevitability of the caterpillar's descent into teenage obesity depressing.

Tuesday 15 January

I can't do it any more. I can't go shopping, tidy the house, change eight thousand nappies, make tea, make coffee, bounce Jacob to sleep, bounce myself awake, tidy the house again, attempt to write thank-you letters to all the people who have sent us chintzy flowers, lurid babygros and mindless, noisy, cluttery plastic toys. I can't then tidy the house again, make breakfast, lunch, dinner, a second dinner (because, as I think we've established, Isabel is breast-feeding and needs all the energy she can get, even if this means matching the caloric intake of an Olympic decathlete) and a midnight breakfast, and tidy the house again. I can't do it.

I love being a dad. I'm delighted we're all alive and that Jacob appears to be not just growing but taking an interest in serious literature. Honestly, though, this is even worse than the third trimester, when Isabel was at her itchiest, her most disconcertingly oversexed, her most bloated and her most intemperate all at the same time.

Thursday 17 January

It's not worse than the third trimester. I have slept. Hallelujah, I have slept. True, I have been forced from my own bed, but this is understandable. They need each other. I need sleep. The sofa bed: my new salvation.

Friday 18 January

Isabel's mum has decided that Isabel's decision not to buy a pram because she wants to carry Jacob everywhere is a silly one. 'You are not a hunter-gatherer. You are not toiling in the harsh conditions of the African bush. You are in Britain. Your mother didn't escape from the tyranny of Communist Poland and marry your fine upstanding English father in order to produce offspring that behave like they live in a hut. So, darlink, I have been to John Lewis and have spoken with the lady who is expert in prams, and I have bought you a Bugaboo.'

The Bugaboo is the four-by-four of the pram world: excellent for pushing up a mountain, but something of a handful if you have a small house and you confine most of your pram-pushing to standard-width pavements. Still, it looks cool. And Caroline, the most vocal of the NCT baby-group mums (yes, they have formed a gang and she is the leader), has a sister who claims her children are five centimetres taller than all the other children at her nursery solely because she used a Bugaboo. This, pontificated Caroline, is because it's the only buggy that allows the child to lie flat. This helps their bones to stretch. When I pointed out that it might be genes, she replied that it might . . . but was it really worth the risk? Was it really worth having a buggy — or a sling — which could stunt the growth of a baby?

'I bet the Hunchback of Notre Dame's parents didn't use a Bugaboo,' said her husband, in an attempt to diffuse his wife. And then the conversation moved on to torn perineums.

Saturday 19 January

Only two days until I go back to work. Bravely, I volunteer to take Jacob out for an hour on my own to give Isabel some morning 'metime'. I aim for the park, proud new dad pushing quite grumpy baby. Grannies smile as I lift him out of the buggy to show him what our local trees look like. In a few months, he'll be on those baby swings. In a couple of years, he'll be on the next swings up. Then he'll be on the big slide. Then he'll be snogging another teenager over there. Then he'll be smoking cigarettes behind the hut over there. Then he'll be sitting on this bench with his own baby, thinking about the future.

This is it now. This is my life. It is all mapped out. My plans to resign from my boring office job, retrain as a sailor and enter the Vendée round-the-world yacht race have been put on hold indefinitely. Ditto resigning and moving to a yurt on the Mongolian steppe. Or resigning and moving to Buenos Aires to drink heavy red wine and master the tango. Adventure and unpredictability have vanished, or rather, they have been condensed into the child looking up at me right now. I think this is probably fine.

'Are you looking for salvation?' A man in an anorak is peering down at me through milk-bottle glasses.

'Sorry?'

'You look sad. Are you looking for salvation?'

I notice he is clutching a pile of pamphlets entitled *Let Jesus Save You*. Right now, this seems unlikely. Can't a parent sit in peace mulling over lost freedoms without being God-bothered? I tell him I'd love to be saved, but I have a nappy to change and it's going to be a big one. So he leaves.

Sunday 20 January

Alex, newly gay and newly full of *joie de vivre*, has popped round with Geoff to give us our baby present.

'Surely the tropical rainforest you sent over was ample?' I ask innocently.

'Don't be silly, dears. This is the greatest moment in your lives — ever. Flowers alone would not suffice. Geoff and I have been talking and, well, we've decided we would like to give you something very special indeed.'

Oh, God.

'Something to mark this wonderful time in your lives.'

This is going to be bad.

'Your three lives.'

He grips Geoff's hand, and then Isabel's. Like he's Madonna about to walk on stage.

'Geoff and I would like to design your bathroom for you.'

'But —'

'No buts, babes. You wanted it done before Baby arrived, but Willy was too busy at work to do it. We can do it for you. Geoff and I. This country's newest and hottest interior design team. And I know you're going to say it's a bad time, but I promise you won't even notice the work going on. You'll blink and it will all be done.'

'But —'

'Didn't I say no buts, babes? You've done the nursery yourselves, and look what a mess *that* is. I simply can't let you ruin the bathroom, too. Now, here are the catalogues. I'm thinking this bath. And these taps. And Geoff was thinking an LED mirror with a built-in sensor, weren't you, Geoff? You twenty-first-century designer, you.'

And that was Geoff's cue. Until then, he'd been uncharacteristically quiet, but he made up for it now with a twenty-five-minute speech on how our bathroom would be the bathroom to set the new standard for all bathrooms. And then he just started saying random words. Light. Space. Air. Movement. Energy. Calm. Length. Girth. Swirling vortex. Drip. Drop. Drip. Movement.

'You already said movement,' I point out.
'Movement. Movement. Movement,' he continues.
Nothing good will come of this.

Monday 21 January

Don't tell Isabel. Nobody tell her, for goodness'
sake. This must be our little secret. But, oh my,
the joy! The joy of leaving home, of bidding
farewell to my beloved wife and my beloved
three-week-old child, of strolling to the station
on a crisp winter morning, buying a coffee,
boarding a train and sitting unmolested for
forty-five whole minutes — no, more than
forty-five minutes because the train is delayed
due to the late running of an earlier service. No
crying. No screaming. No panicking.
Bliss.
Let the train be delayed all day. Let me sit
here in this railway siding, staring into space,
dribbling a bit like a baby but not with a baby
that I have to worry about all the time. Even
when the pointy-faced little woman sitting next
to me still doesn't move her bag on to her lap
when I ask politely, I refuse to let the bliss
dissipate. I simply open my paper as unthought-
fully as possible, allowing its pages to encroach
on her personal space. I have had enough
practice of commuter one-upmanship to remain
unflustered in the face of pointy-faced rudeness.
The bliss lasts until the minute I get to work.
Even though he only sits two desks away,
Johnson sends me an e-mail: 'Welcome back.

And by the way, I don't know if you've been keeping up to speed with the Media *Guardian* and I'm sorry I didn't mention this before, though I was being thoughtful because you were having a baby, but did you know that Anastasia has been made Editor?'

'Corridor. Now,' I reply.

He isn't joking. Anastasia, who was work experience less than eighteen months ago, has been appointed the youngest-ever editor of *Life & Times* magazine. The teenager over whom I once threw a cup of (cold) tea because she was so irritatingly efficient is now the boss. I start strangling the water cooler.

'Not having anger-management issues again, are we, Walker?'

It's her: our four-year-old boss.

'No, no, he isn't,' mumbles Johnson. 'He was telling me how much fun being a dad is. Turns out not much fun at all. Hahahaha.'

'Johnson, a baby is a lifestyle choice. We mustn't feel sorry for people who opt to procreate. Even idiots could grasp the fundamentals of a condom if they wanted to. Now, conference in fifteen minutes. And I want some fresh ideas for front of book. It's looking tired. Tireder than poor Walker here.'

I go back home that evening wondering how best to break it to Isabel. In the end, I opt for the direct approach.

'Isabel, I'm afraid I have to resign. Anastasia has become Editor.'

'Oh no, you don't. You have a family to

support. We can't live on my maternity leave. Now take Jacob. I've had him all day.'

And the matter is closed.

Thursday 24 January

It has occurred to me that now I am a dad with a bitch for a boss, the train is the only place where I can relax. At home, I appear to have developed a sensor on my arse that triggers an order from Isabel. Every time I sit down, no matter how gingerly, I set off the sensor: 'Darling, I'm breast-feeding. Could you pass a muslin?'

I get up, I get the muslin from all the way upstairs, I come back, I sit down and I trigger the sensor again.

'Sorry, darling. And a glass of water.'

Repeat. 'And another cushion.'

Repeat.

'Could you not group your requests in some way?' I ask. And this makes her apologise and so I feel terrible. But, really.

At work, Anastasia is on my case. She breaks up a group of people ahhing at the new baby photo on my desk. She barks at me every time I look like I'm about to drop off (which is frequently, because the sofa bed doesn't provide quite the blissful night's sleep I had initially hoped for). She criticises my poor grammar, even though it isn't poor at all. Not really.

The train is all I have left. No one can bark at

me on the train. And the sensor on my arse is out of range. And this is the reason why I won't let the pointy-faced woman who keeps hogging one and a half seats on my carriage annoy me. She is short. She is ginger. Life cannot have been easy for her. This is her way of getting her own back on the world. I won't rise to it.

Saturday 26 January

Today marked our first social occasion as a mobile family unit. It was only lunch at Isabel's parents who only live a ten-minute walk away, but it was still something of a milestone. We hoped, I think, that it might have gone better, that it might have been enjoyable, but even with military-style planning, it didn't and it wasn't.

We asked Isabel's mum to have lunch ready at midday because, if we have managed to establish any kind of routine — which we haven't — it was that Jacob tends to need bouncing to sleep from 2 until 3 p.m., or he screams until 8 p.m.

We arrived at 1.20 p.m. because we were about to set off an hour earlier, but then Jacob needed a feed. And a change. And another feed. And another change. Then it started to rain and I couldn't remember where I'd put the waterproof buggy cover, even though Isabel had expressly asked me to leave it somewhere handy. By the time I did find it, the rain had passed but Isabel had hunger-anger. It comes on quickly in breast-feeding mums. So she demanded toast

39

even though lunch was but a ten-minute walk away. Until, at last we set off.

Frankly, Sherpas bound for the summit of Everest carry less. I had at least nine bags containing everything from nappies and wet wipes to toys, changing mats, breast pads and nipple cream, arnica, snack bars, babygros, backup babygros, backup-backup babygros and a kitchen sink. I walked ten steps behind Isabel and Jacob all the way to the in-laws.

We had roast chicken accompanied by a relentless monologue about timekeeping from her mum and advice on no-nonsense parenting from her dad. Isabel had no appetite because of the toast. Then we set off back to base camp, me with the nine bags plus four Tupperware containers of some kind of Polish stew and, inexplicably, a very large photo album from when Isabel was a baby. By the time we returned, Isabel needed more toast. I needed a lie-down.

'You can't lie down. Jacob needs changing.'

'Seriously, how many times can one human being need changing in one hour?'

'Darling, you are at work all week. You can't complain about a bit of light parenting at the weekend.'

It has begun. The thing I had been warned about. Mothers, completely understandably, complaining about how much easier it is for fathers because at least they can escape to the office.

Which, praise be to the Lord, they can.

Monday 28 January

I escape to the office. On the train, the lovely train. Again, the bliss was not ruined by the pointy-faced woman, even though she was sitting opposite me this morning and had a laptop. Even though she then angled the laptop's screen well and truly into my airspace. And then typed very loudly, as if her laptop was a percussive instrument, as if by typing very loudly she was demonstrating that the thing she was typing was more important than the things the rest of us would be typing when we got to our offices. Even though it wasn't because I had a peek on my way off the train and she was only playing Tetris.

So I really wasn't already in a bad mood when I arrived five minutes late and Anastasia told me not to be late again. I may have to confront her: I think she still holds the throwing (cold) tea incident against me.

Wednesday 30 January

First proper argument of parenthood. Isabel wants me to take another week off and rent us a cottage in Devon. This is madness on two counts.

1. I can't manage a whole week off again so soon after the previous three.

2. How on earth are we going to get all the way to Devon if we almost killed ourselves going to visit her parents who live in the same town?

I only mention point two to Isabel, but she reacts badly. 'We'll be fine'/'I need a change of scene' / 'It's all right for you. You get to go to London every day'. I react badly back, even though she's right. I do get to escape on a daily basis, even though it's only to a horrible office with a boss half my age who hates me. Now that we have both reacted badly, Jacob bursts into tears. 'Now look what you've done,' says Isabel, and I suddenly realise how tired she looks. So I apologise, spend the rest of the evening feeling like an arse and worrying that we will be the kind of parents who do lasting damage to their offspring by fighting all the time in front of them. I then agree to a week in Devon in just under three weeks' time. On a farm. In February. Just what the doctor didn't order.

Thursday 31 January

Anastasia frowns when I ask for a week's holiday, makes a barbed comment about lack of dedication and storms off to her lunch interview at the Ivy with the Dalai Lama. I storm off to lunch at the pub with Johnson, but I am momentarily perked up by a text from Andy, best friend but strangely busy for the last six weeks. Can he join us for lunch?

'Hello, stranger,' I say when he walks in.

'Congratulations,' he replies, but he isn't looking me in the eye, which is unlike him. People say that on becoming a parent, you lose friends, even best friends, because all you can talk about is nappies, sleep routines and birth stories. Friends without children have very little interest in these things. In fact, some of them would rather not hear anything about it at all. They would prefer to remain in denial about the whole messy topic until as late as possible. I assumed that the reason Andy hasn't been in touch at all since the birth was because he doesn't want to know what may await him if he ever goes out with anyone long enough to marry them and have children. And I don't blame him. If he would rather steer clear of me while all I can talk about is Fallopian tubes and nappy rash, so be it.

But here we are in the pub — him, me, Johnson — like old times. And he isn't avoiding. He's just oddly nervous.

'I have some news of my own,' he says after I've tried hard to have a whole conversion without mentioning tubes or rashes. 'I have a new girlfriend.'

This is hardly news. I'm convinced Andy, an incurable but dastardly romantic, only forged a career in the diplomatic service so that he could fall in love with as many girls in as many different countries as possible.

'This time, it's serious. I think she might be the one.' He has said this before, many times, which Johnson and I point out in unison.

'Yes, but this is different.'

' . . . because you and she share a bond, even though she speaks only Farsi and you speak only nonsense?' asks Johnson.

' . . . because you and she transcend the

boundaries of simple geography, even though you live in Tooting and she lives in Islamabad?' I add.

'No, because it's Saskia,' he whispers into his pint.

FEBRUARY

'The biggest thing I remember is that there was just no transition. You hit the ground diapering.'

PAUL REISER

Friday 1 February

Punch, punch, punch, punch, first day of the month.

Of all the women in all the world, Andy had to fall in love with the one who very nearly destroyed my marriage. It's not like he didn't have warning. She's not called Saskia, the Destroyer of Relationships for nothing.

She had been the most exciting girl I had ever met. She had strolled into a party several years ago, informed me that we were leaving and then pretty much forced me to have sex with her on Hyde Park Corner. It was every man's perfect fantasy but, after a few more casual encounters, it turned to a nightmare. The fling finished because that's what flings are supposed to do. I

45

fell in love with Isabel and married her and thought nothing more about Saskia or her long legs or her short skirts, until the day she coincidentally moved into the flat below ours in Finsbury Park. Except, it wasn't coincidental: she had joined forces with Alex, back when he wasn't gay, to help ruin my marriage. He wanted Isabel. Saskia wanted revenge. Apparently, the fling from years before hadn't been a fling after all . . . I was the first person Saskia had ever loved, she said, and I'd discarded her without a moment's thought.

That was how she put it, anyway. She was Glenn Close; I was Michael Douglas. The pet rabbit was my marriage and it very nearly got boiled to death.

Once Alex and Saskia admitted to their plot — and Isabel and I had managed to start trusting each other again — Saskia vanished. And now she was back.

'What do you mean, 'She's back'? I thought you killed her,' joked Isabel.

'She's, umm, going out with Andy.'

'What?!' stuttered Isabel. Jacob, who until that moment had been happily sucking away on a breast, started to cry. Perhaps the milk had curdled.

'They met by chance in a bar in Islington. Andy was going to avoid her, but she and her friend were getting hassled by a group of yobs. Andy stepped in. The yobs threatened him and got thrown out by bouncers. Saskia and Andy got chatting and now they're madly in love. The end.'

'Blimey.'

46

'I know.'

'Can you make me a camomile tea?'

Saturday 2 February

The weekend. It's hard to say whether it's worse than the week. Obviously, it doesn't contain any work-related horror, but equally, it doesn't contain any work-related loafing, either. It is much easier to give the impression that you are busy in an office than it is at home. You sit at your desk and you do pretend typing. You dial some nonexistent telephone numbers and have some non-existent conversations about non-existent articles you aren't really writing. A whole afternoon can pass with the minimum of brain activity. Not so at home. Pretending to change a nappy, make tea, cook dinner, unload the dishwasher and make decisions about what type of bathroom suite we want is easily detectable by an overly tired wife.

'Have you unloaded the dishwasher?'

'Yes.'

'Are you lying?'

'No.'

'Are you sure?'

'No.'

I'm wondering if they'll let me go into the office at the weekend as well.

Andy texted to see if I wanted to go out with him and Saskia for a tension-breaking drink. Tonight. Even if we ignore the fact that I have a new baby and a very tired wife and I'm an hour from London, we can't ignore the fact that my best mate is going out with my worst ex. So no, I can't.

He texts back: 'Saskia wants a chance to talk to you. To explain.'

I don't reply. Instead, I sing soporific nursery rhymes over and over again, right through the Lottery show (my only chance to get the money I need to hire a full-time nanny) and *Casualty*. Jacob loves my singing. Point-blank refuses to miss any of it by going to sleep.

Sunday 3 February

My parents come round with lots of blue clothes for Jacob. Isabel explains her desire to give the poor chap a non-gender-specific upbringing. Dad rolls his eyes and bites his tongue. Then they leave.

Alex and Geoff come round minutes later. Isabel has failed to dissuade them about the bathroom. They are still promising it will be done in a jiffy and that we will hardly notice and I only just manage to stop myself pointing out that I have already noticed them because they're here on a Sunday prattling on about bath shapes. And it's Jacob's nap, the only time of the day when I can lie catatonic on the sofa and pretend to read the newspaper.

Geoff likes egg-shaped.

Alex likes roll-top.

Isabel is split between the two.

When they leave, at last, I look stroppy. Isabel asks why I look stroppy. I tell her it's annoying that our Sundays have to be intruded on by Alex and his very overbearing boyfriend.

'Darling, I know he's a bit crazy and I know he did all that horrible stuff last year but, well, he's still trying to make amends. I thought you liked baths. Aren't you excited about having an egg-shaped one?'

'No, it will be too steep at the top. I like the one we've got.'

'It's yellowing and you complain about it all the time.'

'I'll paint it.'

'You can't paint a bath.'

'I'm sick of Alex. Why can't he leave us alone?'

'Why can't Saskia leave us alone? At least Alex is gay. *And* sorry. Which is more than can be said for that tart.'

I give up. 'Cup of camomile tea, darling?'

Monday 4 February

CONTENTS OF MONDAY MORNING INBOX

1. Three e-mails from Andy apologising for falling in love with the Destroyer of Relationships, but also saying that Saskia is completely misunderstood and isn't a Destroyer of Relationships at all.

2. Two e-mails from Isabel, the first delighting in the fact that Jacob is sleeping properly, the second, much shorter, lamenting the fact that he isn't. And that the house is virtually

uninhabitable. And can I please get home early, if possible.

3. One e-mail from my mum asking if I could check if it has a virus atta — oh, bugger.

Thursday 7 February

Jacob smiled. And just when I was beginning to wonder if he had the same syndrome as the boy on the Channel Five documentary — the one who had to have nine operations in order to smile, or was it the boy with the face-eating bug who had the full nine? I can't remember. But the point is, we hadn't seen a smile yet, and Isabel's mum's greengrocer's daughter's baby smiled after the first month. I was beginning to wonder whether I'd passed the stress of an unreasonable boss, a traitorous best friend and a psychotic but newly homosexual bathroom designer on to our precious child. But it was definitely a smile. And it came at 4 a.m.

4 A.M.

This used to be the time when you would be sound asleep or possibly clubbing or hosting a terribly good party or, very occasionally, having sexual intercourse. Used to be. Now, it is the hour of the zombie parent. It is said, although no one has reliable statistical evidence to back this up, that at least 20 per cent of traffic on the M25

50

at 4 a.m. constitutes exhausted parents trying to drive their insomniac babies to sleep. The figure could be far greater. It is certainly the time I am out pushing the goddam four-by-four Bugaboo round the block under the quite possibly inaccurate assumption that cold air makes our insomniac child sleepy. I loop the block twelve or fourteen times, singing nursery rhymes as boringly as possible. Why won't he sleep? Doesn't he know I have to pretend to work in the morning? And finally, he closes his eyes.

And then opens them again.

And this is the point, the horrible dark point, in that horrible dark hour, when you think, is this really worth it? Would adoption be such a bad thing? Maybe I could leave him in a cardboard box outside the gates of the hospital? With a blanket, of course.

Then he smiled — a beautiful smile right at me — and it was all worth it a million times over. I had the energy for another few hundred loops of the block. Or the M25.

And when he finally did nod off, I went back inside to find Isabel, anxious, in the front room. She never sleeps properly now when Jacob isn't with her.

'He smiled!'

'Did he?'

'Yes. A proper smile. It was beautiful.' And Isabel didn't look like a zombie parent any more, either. She looked happy, happy for me and happy for Jacob. We hugged and she took him off to bed while I checked the NHS handbook. Three months, they're supposed to start smiling.

Three months! Not five weeks. We have a genius on our hands. Cancel the Channel Five documentary. Phone Channel 4. We're making *The Child Who Smiled Seven Weeks Early.*

Friday 8 February

Isabel, having read an article about the plight of the bumblebee, has signed us up as members of the Bumble Bee Conservation Trust. This despite the cost of nappies (the initial outlay for the cloth ones, plus the recurring outlay for the horrible plastic ones that will sit in a landfill for a thousand millennia because, as I had predicted, we really haven't managed to keep up with the cloth-nappy washing demands), baby clothes, prenatal wardrobe, postnatal wardrobe and the Barn Owl Conservation Society she made us join last year when she read about barn owls being combine-harvested or something.

As sole breadwinner in this house, excluding paltry maternity leave, I have been forced to put my foot down. From now on, barn owls and bumblebees will receive our support and sympathy. All other endangered animals will have to fend for themselves . . .

Saturday 9 February

. . . except, perhaps, for coral and red squirrels. And a certain type of parrot that only eats mangetout. I have conceded additional species on the understanding that I can go to the pub this evening, but only between the hours of 7 and 9 p.m.

It was Andy's idea that they come all the way down to my local pub because I have a baby. He's clearly trying to get back in my good books. Johnson isn't. He arrives grumbling about it being a long way to go for a couple of hours, seeing as they both live in London and I live in the sticks. Despite Andy being a bastard and Johnson being miserable, I am delighted. I am in the pub. I am a free man.

The first pint vanishes in twelve seconds. The next two go almost as quickly. I should probably hold back: I am a dad now. But Johnson explains that it is important to wet the baby's head, even if the baby isn't here. And besides, I have to leave in an hour and they've come all this way, so we have another two pints in quick succession. We talk about nothing in particular, largely because baby talk is boring and talk about women would involve mentioning Saskia, which none of us feel like doing, given that we only have two hours.

None of us, except Johnson.

'Andy?' he asks after a long draw of lager. 'Do you find it weird sleeping with a girl with whom your mate has already slept? It's only, I did that once, back when life was fun, and the image of my mate, naked, kept popping into my head every time we shagged. It got to the point where I had to stop mid-coitus every time because it got all strange and homoerotic. I had to dump her because it felt like being in the wrong sort of threesome.'

Andy looks first at Johnson, then at me. He sips his pint thoughtfully and says, 'Saskia and William. It was almost five years ago. I think we can all assume it's water under the bridge.'

This is not the case. Saskia is still Saskia. Andy is still Andy. But the pub is still the pub, so after explaining that I'm fine with it as long as I never have to talk to Saskia, I have another quick pint and then another one. Then I suggest they come back because I have beers in the fridge.

'And a baby in the living room,' says Johnson. 'We'll leave you to it.'

This proves to be a sensible decision. I zigzag home, open the door to the blissful domestic scene of Isabel still trying to make herself dinner, half undressed because she had momentarily given up on dinner and tried to go to bed, Jacob screaming in one arm, a soup spoon in the other, the kitchen looking like it has been ransacked by angry chimps.

'Forget the coral and the parrots. You're never going out again,' she says. And she is only half joking.

Sunday 10 February

Everyone has decided on an egg-shaped bath. Everyone, except me. It will take four weeks to be delivered from Sweden or Denmark or whichever other design-obsessed country it is made in. Alex promises the bathroom will be started mid-March and finished mid-March.

Thursday 14 February

Even though we both disagree with Valentine's Day, even though it is a stupid American invention designed to keep us as impoverished slaves of the capitalist system, even though I spent eight million quid at Budding Ideas last year (motto still: 'Flowers for that special occasion or just because you want to say I love you.' Spew), I have no choice but to return and spend another eight million quid this year on a dozen long-stemmed red roses.

Then we have an argument because twenty minutes after I present them to her, I discover them in a vase in the bedroom . . . with the long stems cut off.

'I wanted to use this vase.'

'The short one?'

'Yes, the short one.'

'So you cut off the long stems?'

'Yes, is that a problem?'

'Well, I could have saved seven and a half million pounds if I'd known you were going to cut the stems off.'

'Do you want me to get the stems out of the bin, or can I enjoy the flowers you gave me in the way I want?'

Eight million pounds out of pocket and an argument for my troubles. But I decide to remain circumspect. We are both very tired and very ratty. It is no wonder that little things are triggering arguments more than usual. I must remain calm. I must remain calm because this is the first step on the long Zen Path to the Mastery of Parenting.

THE ZEN PATH TO THE MASTERY OF PARENTING

Step one: you must remain calm in the face of petty marital discord and not let it develop into a proper argument as it may have done in the time before children. Arguments take energy. You do not have energy. Whereas before, you could afford to spend days bickering about Marmite toast, bathroom usage and unappreciated long-stemmed roses, now you must centre yourself and allow these minor annoyances to wash away.

Step two: you must remain calm in the face of stressful situations as well. If you get a parking ticket, you must accept it and move on with your day. If someone, that someone being Isabel, spills red wine on the expensive white rug you bought for Christmas, you must shrug and volunteer to clean it. If you find yourself in Sainsburys still wearing your pyjama bottoms because you were halfway through getting dressed when your child woke up and started screaming (and if there's one thing you've learned, it's that you can only stop the screaming if you get to the child in the first ten seconds), but in your head, you've finished getting dressed and you only remember you haven't when the checkout girl gives you a funny look, you must simply close your eyes, imagine a calm place, a garden perhaps, full of recently sprayed orchids, then pay the bill and leave quickly before anyone can call the police.

Step three: you must remain calm, even when it makes no sense to do so. Like when you haven't slept continuously for more than an hour in six weeks, when you get home from work and have four hours of tidying to do before you can have dinner, which you can't have because it's then your turn to take the baby because your wife is exhausted and then you find the only way to get your child to sleep is by jogging around with him in a tight anticlockwise circle while reciting 'The Owl and the Pussycat' backwards in the voice of Barry White. For an hour.

I am still struggling with step one.

Friday 15 February

I have asked Isabel to start packing now for our incredibly ill-conceived trip to Devon on Saturday. She has agreed to do what she can.

This turns out to be very little because Jacob has a fever. Not a wink of sleep — not a single wink — mainly because I can't stop myself taking his temperature every hour or so through the night to check it's still only 99.8°C, not 101°C or 102°C. God forbid it gets to 102°C, even though Isabel phoned her doctor mum, who told her that babies get high temperatures and it doesn't necessarily mean Jacob is going to die a horrible feverish death. 'It doesn't necessarily mean' is not good enough for me. He is still tiny. His little body shouldn't have to have a temperature. I'm not taking any chances.

Saturday 16 February

Not going on holiday today on account of Jacob's temperature, even though it's gone down and it looks as if he might survive. The snowstorm sweeping across the country isn't helping, either. I am not saying 'I told you so'. It is enough that, for once, I am right about something. She knows it. I know it. Jacob knows it.

Sunday 17 February

Still not going on holiday because the snow has turned to black ice and Isabel's mother and my mother have both phoned and pleaded for us to wait until it is safe to drive. Even the bloody weatherman warns us not to travel anywhere unless it's absolutely essential. I preferred it in the old days, before the Met Office missed the hurricane. They were more inclined to throw caution to the wind, so to speak. I say, 'I told you so,' because I simply can't hold it in any longer.

Monday 18 February

And so, two days late, the first Walker family holiday begins. It will be the first of many. Over the next two decades at least, we will explore the world together. We will drive across Europe in campervans, we will sail narrow boats across England, we will explore exotic cultures in an educational and adventurous way. And we are starting with Devon. If we get that far. We woke at 6 a.m., a lie-in, and I suggested our ETDIAAHP (estimated time of departure if at all humanly possible) should be a very conservative 10 a.m. We left at 1 p.m., which isn't bad when you consider that we had to take the entire house, the whole of Waitrose and a large section of Halfords with us, and that we'd only had five days to pack.

Twenty minutes in, against all odds, Jacob fell asleep. For the first time in seven weeks, Isabel and I had a conversation. It was leisurely. It had no sense of urgency about it. It was trivial and no child's life depended on it.

'Nice coffee,' I said.

'Do I get points for bringing it, dearest?'

'Yes and no. Which would you like first?'

'I may have to kill you, but purely out of interest I'll start with the yes.'

'Yes, because you've used proper milk, not devil's spawn goat's milk, and there's enough sugar for once and we won't have to spend £972 on crap motorway service station coffee.'

'Right. And the no?'

'No, because bringing a flask on a car journey is the beginning of the end. Only middle-aged people do that. Have you got some travel sweets in the glove box, too? Oh my God, you have. I rest my case.'

'I hate to tell you this, but you're already middle-aged, sweetheart. You planned the route three days ago.'

'I didn't.'

'You did. You phoned Johnson and had a conversation with him about it. Only middle-aged people can spend more than twenty minutes discussing whether the M4/M5 is quicker than the A303.'

'Well, Johnson was talking rubbish. Everyone knows the M4/M5 is best if there aren't roadworks.'

'I love it.'

'Love what?'

'Being middle-aged.'

'Really?' For a minute, I'd thought she was having me on, but she wasn't.

'Yes. We're settling. We know what we're doing. We know where we're going.'

'Do we?'

'Yes. Apart from this whole parenting thing . . . which I think we're doing all right at, don't you?'

'Well, you are. You've been brilliant.'

'You're doing all right as well. I think we make quite a good middle-aged couple, all things considered. And here we are, going on a lovely holiday as a family with our beautiful sleeping boy.'

She paused, smiling, and looked out the window. I smiled, too, because perhaps everything was going pretty well. And there was no denying it: we were going on holiday. A family holiday. It might even be fun.

Except then Jacob woke up and needed a feed. The fourteen miles to the next service station were the longest fourteen miles of my life. It's bad enough listening to babies crying in general, but when it's your baby, it has an extra piercing quality. It cuts straight into the very centre of your brain. It is almost impossible to do anything but deal with that noise. This is very clever: Mother Nature's way of ensuring the offspring isn't left abandoned in its hour of need. Except Mother Nature didn't take into account the fact that we were going on holiday to Devon in the driving rain of bleak midwinter with a seven-week-old child. And that I might need to be able to concentrate on driving.

. . . and breathe.

THE ZEN PATH TO THE MASTERY OF PARENTING (CONTINUED)

Step four: you must be able to drive a car at high speed in the rain while a child is screaming and the petrol gauge is on empty and your wife is saying, 'Hurry, he needs changing and it's still ten miles to the next service station,' and you know he needs changing and you know it's still ten miles to the next service station and, oh Christ, there's a police car and, oh Christ, he wants me to pull over and, oh Christ, should I keep going because it's now only five miles to the service station and he can give me the ticket there.

I pull over. Isabel climbs into the back to feed Jacob while I face an interrogation.

'Good afternoon, officer, Can I start by saying how sor — '

'Do you know what the national speed limit is, sir?'

'Seventy miles an hour, officer. But this is our first-ever — '

'And are you aware of how fast you were travelling?'

'Too fast, officer. But you see Jacob was — '

'Ninety-eight miles an hour,' he interrupts again, peering into the back of the car at Isabel, who is trying to change Jacob.

'Seriously? Oh God. I'm sorry. We're new to this whole parenting — '

'How old is your child?' he interrupts for a fourth time and I begin to wonder whether the police computer is connected in any way to the health-visitor computer because we're bound to be flagged on the latter so a flag on the former might constitute two flags on aggregate and I wonder how many flags you're allowed before they take your child away. Probably no more than three.

'Seven weeks,' says Isabel. 'And I don't think we're going to be doing any more long journeys for a while.'

The policeman hesitates and shakes his head. 'Tell me about it. Mine's three months old and we still can't make it beyond the M25.'

'If you arrested me and carted me off to prison, I would be grateful,' I say, in an attempt to build on our shared pain. 'Anything to escape the nappies.'

'I'd love to, but I can't,' he replies. He is no longer a police officer. I am no longer a felon. We are new dads together, trying to make the best of

62

a crazy world, a world of tears and stress and sleep deprivation and a necessity, every now and again, to drive at ninety-eight miles an hour.

'I can only issue a ticket.'

'But — '

'If you pay in the next fourteen days, you won't need to appear in court, but you will get three points on your licence and this will affect your insurance premiums. Another two miles an hour and you'd have got a ban.'

'But I thought you were — '

'There's no excuse for driving so fast on a motorway. You'll get yourself killed. And your little kiddie there, too. And perhaps someone else's kiddie. Like mine.'

Unbelievable. He knows about the piercing scream that cuts straight to the very core of your brain but because he's a copper with an annoying high-vis jacket and a Taser and a hat, he thinks he's above the laws of parenting.

'But he is right, darling. You shouldn't really be driving so fast,' says Isabel, astonishingly, as we pull away, but I know better than to try to argue. She's tired. I'm tired. We must get through it. I shall content myself with muttering all the way to Devon.

Why would anyone pay good money to stay in a house that is more rubbish than their own? Because it looked nice in the picture? Because they automatically but inexplicably drop their standards while they're on holiday? Because holidays are supposed to be rubbish? And because if they weren't, it would be unbearable to go home at the end of them?

The cottage is what an estate agent might call rustic but what I might call uninhabitable. The drive and garden are submerged in five centimetres of what an estate agent might call locally sourced, organic yard cover but what I might call mud. The puddle by the front door into which I drop the seventh bag, the one containing all Jacob's baby clothes, is a metre deep, although no one could have foreseen that until a bag had been dropped in it. An estate agent might call it a well-appointed plunge pool.

The heating system is what an estate agent might call an original fixture, the logs for the fire are what the lying bastard might call slightly damp. The oven has the remains of someone else's pizza in it. The microwave doesn't exist. There are many beds scattered around the top floor, but none of them are comfortable. The windows open, but they don't shut. The bath has a pink and brown shower curtain slouching bacterially over it. The pink is its original colour, the brown a modification over years. Or vice versa.

If we put the quarter-kilowatt electric shower on at the same time as the kettle, the television, the radio or the baby-listening monitor, we have a power cut. To re-trip the switch, I have to walk across the swamp to a shed in which the mains electrics are housed.

The television, in direct contrast to every other television in the land, only gets Channel Five.

Unfortunately, the farmer is very friendly. He describes himself as an artisan. He grows not enough pigs and not enough cows and sells them to people like Isabel at posh farmer's markets at vastly inflated prices. And people like Isabel can't help feeling sorry for him, this last protector of the land, even though he's conned us out of £400 for an outbuilding on a farm he is clearly struggling to keep going.

I refuse to feel sorry for him. He could always stop being a farmer and condemn himself to a life of office radiation and zombie commuting like the rest of us. He could be an accountant. Isabel claims that, without him, a way of life will be lost for ever. And the bumblebees and barn owls would go with it. We must use this week to live the good life . . . conversation round a candle, reading a book, playing backgammon, listening to the drip-drip-drip of the leaking roof.

There is nothing for it but to go to bed.

So I go to bed.

And Isabel goes to bed.

And Jacob starts coughing.

It is this damp shed's fault. Pursuing a dream of rural existence that vanished in the nineteenth century, we are dooming our tiny, defenceless baby to a nineteenth-century cough.

Tuesday 19 February

I have caught the cough. The one time I thought I might go on holiday and not immediately get sick ('It is your body relaxing, darlink,' says Isabel's mother every time it happens), I get sick.

It is raining so hard that we abandon going outside altogether.

Wednesday 20 February

Isabel has also succumbed to the pleurisy-type disease Jacob and I are struggling with. They don't mention this in the 'Welcome to Devon' pamphlets that lie curled and ageing in the top drawer of the only piece of furniture in our damp and smelly living room, so I burn them. And unless our chipper farmer produces some dry wood in the next hour or so, I'm going to burn the chest of drawers they came in, too.

Thursday 21 February

There is nothing worse than having a sick baby, except when you are sick yourselves, except when, instead of being at home, you are in mid-Devon, about a thousand miles from a chemist, and bloody wildlife is keeping you awake at night. Last night, in the precious minutes when Jacob wasn't hacking his way through an illness he wouldn't have if we were in a nice centrally heated house, a barn owl, a bloody barn owl, was hooting away in the adjacent bloody barn. Isabel, the barn owl conservationist, didn't notice. She had a pillow over her head. This was a shame. Even she, the great farm-loving romantic, is beginning to see that there are advantages to the twenty-first century and that perhaps farm holidays aren't right for (a) this time of year, (b) a young family and (c) enjoying oneself in the slightest bit, ever, at all. If a bloody barn owl had kept her awake all night, too, she might have also seen that (d) barn owls aren't worth conserving.

Friday 22 February

I have made an executive decision. We are leaving. We are leaving one day early from the holiday we started two days late. I don't care about the money. I don't care about offending the friendly farmer. I am tired. I am damp. Most of Jacob's clothes, the ones I dropped in a muddy puddle, are still not properly dry. The bloody goddam barn owl was at it again last night with his infernal hooting, so much so that I woke Isabel to complain. She then had the temerity to shout at me because I'd woken her up.

When she had finished shouting at me, she listened to the barn owl and then said, 'Wow, it is a barn owl. You're right. How amazing,' and immediately went back to sleep, content that our annual subscription to the Barn Owl Conservation Society was money well spent.

I went downstairs to make a Lemsip and, because I'd forgotten to turn the bedside clock off first, fused the lights. I then stepped in the three-foot-deep puddle on my way to the shed. I then locked myself out. I then threw stones at the bedroom window, but Isabel didn't hear me because she presumably had the pillow back on her head and it had begun to rain noisily on the tin roof.

She noticed when the last stone I threw broke the window. And that was when we had the argument that ended in my executive decision. It began like any normal middle-of-the-night, exhausted-parent shouting match, only with one of us standing outside getting wetter and wetter, and the other one shouting through a nice new hole in the window. But like a migraine, it developed into something darker, something more poisonous and unshiftable. It became one of those arguments in which horrible lurking disputes that were supposed to be long ago forgiven and forgotten rise to the surface.

'You're always negative.'

'No, I am bloody not.'

'You were negative when we lived in Finsbury Park.'

'That's because it was dangerous. And our neighbours were crazy. And that man with a knife tried to kill me.'

'A boy who said he had a knife said he might try to kill you. That's not the same thing.'

'It is in this day and age.'

'You're negative about living outside London.'

'That's not true. I love it. I love our suburban existence with our curtain-twitching neighbours, our soon-to-be-ruined bathroom and the relentless commute.'

'You see, that's just it. *Relentless commute?* You told me the last time we were arguing that the commute was the only time you could sit quietly without being ordered around by me or that work-experience girl who is now your boss. You're negative about everything, even the things you are positive about.'

'I am not.'

'You were even negative about our wedding.'

'Let's not go there again. I wasn't negative. I was emotional. It's not the same thing. The fact that Alex tutted all the way through it was a bit of a dampener. Especially after he turned up with all those horses. You'd think he wouldn't have bother — '

'If we are going to survive this whole parenting thing — and we probably should, don't you think, for Jacob's sake at the very least — then you are going to have to get a grip.'

'I *have* got a grip. You are the one who thought it was a good idea to go on holiday to a bog in February.'

'Is everything all right?' It was the chipper farmer, peering out of his probably properly insulated window across the yard.

'Yes, everything's fine. Just another power cut. Sorry to disturb,' I replied, pausing only for the slightest second to marvel at how, even in this terrible crisis, I am still so English that I will apologise to the person largely responsible for it. Would I apologise to a tailgater if he crashed into the back of our car? Would I apologise if someone spilled my pint? Would I apologise to a hoodie for getting his knife covered in my blood? Probably.

'Can we continue this discussion inside, dearest? I am now soaking wet and I have bronchitis.'

69

She let me in. How kind. 'Where were we?' One thing you become quite good at as a parent is continuing conversations over many interruptions. It works particularly well with arguments.

'This bog. February.'

'Oh, yes. Right. Well, I have two things to say: one, we're never coming to Devon again; two, we're going home tomorrow. How's that for negative?'

In the cold light of day, we packed in silence. I thanked the farmer for a lovely stay, apologised for breaking the window and offered him £20 to cover it, which he accepted. I then spent the whole return journey furious with myself for paying someone £20 because their dodgy electrics trapped me outside in the rain at 4 a.m. when I already had early-stage triple pneumonia. The whole journey, that is, minus the time spent driving at ninety-eight miles an hour to a service station because we mistimed Jacob's feeds again and even the prospect of another speeding ticket won't make me put up with that screaming a second longer than I have to. And minus the time spent queuing outside the only baby-changing facility on the whole M4. And minus the time spent queuing outside the same baby-changing facility again because Jacob always likes to poo twice when he knows there's a queue for the changing facilities.

Saturday 23 February

We are all friends again.

Jacob, who hadn't smiled for a week — and

who could blame him — has been grinning away all morning. So much so that, by midday, I was wondering if he was grinning too much. Have they done a Channel Five documentary called *The Boy Who Couldn't Stop Grinning*?

Isabel is as relieved to be home as I am. We apologise to each other, we cuddle, we kiss. I can't remember the last time we kissed . . . certainly not last week. But that was probably because of the hacking coughs. Maybe the week before. I think we might have done it then.

We haven't had sex since Christmas Day when she was forty weeks pregnant, frightened and frightening. I do not intend to have anything approximating sex with Isabel until she is completely and utterly recovered from childbirth. My benchmark for this is a full month after the last time she says 'Owwwwwch' and clutches her stomach when trying to pick something up. If it takes six months, that is fine. Or a year. Or ten years, even. (Well, maybe not ten years.) But kissing . . . we always kiss. Or we always did.

HOW MUCH ARE YOU SUPPOSED TO KISS ONCE YOU BECOME PARENTS?

I always assumed that kissing each other good night was the absolute cornerstone of a healthy marriage. Kissing in the morning went out the window soon after the honeymoon, but if you don't even bother to kiss each other at bedtime, then you may as well accept that your relationship has become entirely platonic. An affair is more or less inevitable.

I assumed wrong. Since having Jacob, kissing, even at bedtime, has become intermittent at best. It is enough to be alive and/or dressed in the daytime. Other things previously considered essential, such as teeth-brushing, tea-drinking, shaving more than once a week, going to the toilet and not falling asleep while standing up, are now very much optional luxuries. Kissing is going this way, too.

Does it matter? When I ask Isabel, she says it hadn't occurred to her that we hadn't been kissing although now that I mention it, I'm right. But then again, we have other priorities, like not killing each other. Ha ha. And anyway, we'll have plenty of time to kiss when we're in our rocking chairs. Ewww. 'Darling,' she says, reassuringly, 'right now, going to the shops not wearing my pyjamas is a more important target to aim for.'

All the same, we make a point of kissing each other good night. The kiss is awkward, toothy, self-conscious. We bang our noses together. It's like we're teenagers again, except with an unmanageable mortgage, a nearly unmanageable baby and a vague memory that we have sworn we'll spend the rest of our lives together in sickness and in health.

This is my fault. I have ruined kissing. I don't even need a barn owl to keep me up worrying about it.

Monday 25 February

Johnson says he still kisses Ali at least twice a day, but (a) they don't have children and (b) the kissing is now so utterly devoid of emotional meaning that he could be kissing the postman. Like he reckons she does every time he goes to work. Not for the first time, I wonder why on earth Ali puts up with Johnson.

I ask my seventeen Facebook friends how much they kiss. Most of them are people I haven't seen for years and will probably never see again. They are virtual friends and I can ask them virtually anything I like but I immediately wish I hadn't. The one I used to play clarinet duets with when I was fourteen, who now has three children, a dog, a goldfish and a husband who is in the army, kisses her husband all the time. Except when he's on tour (and presumably when she is Facebooking, which also appears to be all the time). I Facebook back asking how long he's away at a time, which is annoying of me. I am being further assimilated into a system of social networking that will ultimately destroy face-to-face human interaction, leaving us controlled by computers, plugged into a mainframe, devoid of legs and fed through tubes.

'Nine months,' she Facebooks and then does some random punctuation :(which I'm given to believe is teenage shorthand for a sad face. This is good news. Not for her but for me. I think Isabel and I would kiss all the time if I had been in Afghanistan for nine months. Maybe I should sign up? The adverts look quite exciting.

Building bridges out of oil drums, jumping in and out of helicopters and so forth. Of course there's the shooting and the bombing, too. That's a given. But it does have its pluses. No nappies to change, for example. Quite a lot of kissing and so forth when I was back. And no unfeasibly young, over-promoted, man-hating boss who still holds a grudge against me because I once, almost accidentally, threw a cup of tea over her. They wouldn't allow that sort of nonsense in the army.

'Shouldn't you be a bit too busy catching up after yet another week off to have time to muck around on social-networking sites?' says the unfeasibly young, over-promoted, man-hating boss after a particularly fast pass through the office. 'Everyone else is striving to make *Life & Times* a great magazine once again. It would be nice if you could at least pretend to help.'

Right, that's it. I'm joining the army.

No, I'm not. According to the stupid website, I am too old. Even though the army is desperate for recruits, someone in their very early thirties, someone at the very peak of their physical and mental condition, is too old.

To make matters worse, Andy, my only real friend on Facebook, has posted a picture of him and Saskia tonguing each other in Paris. Underneath, it reads: 'Paris in the winter: it's like being in a film, a beautiful film. The romance is illicit. You steal each other's kisses.'

It has always been important to keep Andy grounded when it comes to women. Johnson and I think of ourselves as his emotional anchor.

Every time he starts talking rubbish about romance, we have to take him for a pint and suggest that he calms down, cancels his plans to emigrate to Santiago with the secretary from the Chilean Embassy and maybe first goes for dinner with her a couple of times. After that, things usually sort themselves out. Saskia is a different prospect: emotionally manipulative with very long legs. It may prove harder to keep him on an even keel.

Happily, there is a small text box below the photo inviting comments. I type, '*Pass le sac de vomit*,' and hastily log off before Anastasia can make any more sarcastic comments.

Tuesday 26 February

Andy's e-mail: 'I found your comment on my Facebook page upsetting.'

My e-mail: 'Lighten up.'

His e-mail: 'You need to get over your hang-up with Saskia.'

My e-mail: 'I have, but do you really expect to post a cheesy picture of you and my ex on the internet and not get the slightest reaction?'

His e-mail: 'You didn't go out with her. You had a fling with her and you dumped her. Callously. You should move on, man.'

I decided not to dignify that with a response. For about five minutes. Then I e-mail back saying how disappointed I am in Andy, that he was there when we discovered what Saskia had been up to with Alex, that I can't believe he is being so easily manipulated. No reply. Loser.

Wednesday 27 February

THE THREE TERRIBLE THINGS THAT HAPPENED TODAY

1. Isabel woke up at 5.30 a.m., snuck down to my sofa bed, woke me up and said, 'Jacob's asleep,' before starting naughty kissing. Having been asleep, I was still half asleep when I began naughty kissing back. Then, before I could stop and think what I was doing, Isabel was saying, 'Gently,' and we were having post-op sex. Less than two months after the Caesarean. And then Isabel was saying, 'I think we need to stop. It's hurting.' And I suddenly remembered that I wasn't going to have sex with Isabel until she was a thousand per cent recovered. How had this happened? We stopped and that will be it for a while.

2. Saskia is trying to become my Facebook friend. I can't say no because she'll know and Andy will know and that will seem childish. And I can't say yes because then I'd be Facebook friends with Saskia.

3. When I got home from an entirely miserable train journey during which the ginger woman filed her nails and *flossed her teeth* right opposite me, I found a large half-egg-shaped package in the midst of our living room.

'Hi, darling,' said Isabel, as if there wasn't a large half-egg-shaped package blocking our view of each other.

'Hi. How are you?' Was I the only person who could see it?

'Oh, fine. Jacob is playing up but nothing out of the ordinary.' Maybe I was imagining it. Maybe I had suddenly developed a half-egg-shaped cataract.

'Darling?'

'Yes.'

'I think I've got cataracts.'

'What?'

'Either that or the bath, which was supposed to arrive in two weeks' time, has arrived already.'

'I know, it's exciting, isn't it?'

'Does this mean we're going to have a bath in our living room for the next three weeks? Or is there the slightest chance that Geoff and bloody Alex are starting earlier than expected?'

'No, they can't, unfortunately. They're going to Barbados. And they want to be around when the work begins. Because of the filming.'

'*The filming?*'

'Yes. In order to cover the costs of the whole installation, they're going to have a small camera crew doing a little television thing. It's only a daytime thing. *Spruce Up Your House* or something. Geoff and Alex are the presenters. It's a big deal for them, but it shouldn't affect us. Didn't I mention it?'

'No.'

'Oh right, sorry. It's not going to be a big deal, so don't worry.'

'But — '

'I should also mention that there's been a slight change of plan re the colour.'

'Why are you talking like someone at a call centre?'

'It's lilac.'

'What is?'

'The bath.'

'What do you mean?'

'The bath is lilac. Only a bit. You'll hardly notice. It's like a lilac-white. They just thought it would match the colour scheme better and be more relaxing.'

'We have a pink bath?'

'Lilac. Lilac-white. Do you want to see?'

'No.'

MARCH

'I think that I see something deeper, more infinite, more eternal than the ocean in the expression of the eyes of a little baby when it wakes in the morning and coos or laughs because it sees the sun shining on its cradle.'
VINCENT VAN GOGH

Friday 1 March

REASONS TO BE HAPPY

1. I am a father.

2. I am still alive.

3. Isabel is still alive.

4. Jacob is still alive, he is two whole months old already and no longer looks so fragile that he might not make it through the night. According to the health visitor, who appears to have accepted that we are, in spite of

79

everything, not about to end our child's life at our earliest convenience, he is now above average in height and weight. If we play our cards right, this means he will be a successful rugby player and I will get tickets for Twickenham internationals through his club.

REASONS TO BE UNHAPPY

1. Due to the pressures of modern life as well as the relentless marketing that children are exposed to from a very early age, we won't have a chance to play our cards right and Jacob will become one of the nine out of ten children who are morbidly obese by their fifth birthday.

2. We have a bath in our living room. This means I can't open the sofa bed. This means I can either sleep back in the bedroom with a fidgety baby and a fidgety wife or I can sleep in the bath.

   The bath, due to its annoying egg shape, is uncomfortable to lie in.

   And it's pink.

   The 'present' Alex and Geoff have given us comes with a television crew attached, so it wasn't really a present at all.

3. And I am not talking to my best friend.

4. Every time I think about sex with Isabel, I feel terrible because she's the mother of our

baby. She's vulnerable. She wants protecting and looking after and help with the whole mother-baby thing. Not sex. She says otherwise, but I'm pretty sure she's pretending to make me feel better. It's confusing.

5. This is having an effect on kissing, too. And I was already worried about the kissing.

6. I only have seventeen Facebook friends, only one of whom is a real friend and he's gone to Sudan for two weeks while we're in the middle of an argument.

Saturday 2 March

We still have a bath in the living room. It is still pink. I am sleeping in it.

Sunday 3 March

Isabel's mum has volunteered to baby-sit for a couple of hours to give us a break. This seems very early in Jacob's life, but frankly, the thought of two whole hours without a child makes it worth the risk. Isabel has borrowed a breast pump from Caroline. I don't know how I feel about this. Weird, probably. All the same, it is astonishing how long Isabel's nipple becomes when she uses the pump. I find myself wondering if the same is true of Caroline's nipple.

'Couldn't we buy our own nipple pump?'

'I want to try it out first. Some people find they can't use them. And it's a breast pump, not a nipple pump.'

'Right. Doesn't that hurt?'

'Yes. Now pack the bags. We need to leave at 12.47 p.m.'

We arrive half an hour late, which is some sort of record. We've never done it in under an hour before. Isabel then spends another half an hour filling her mother in on every last detail of Jacob's life, before handing over the expressed milk. She then asks me to explain how the Bugaboo works to her dad. This is difficult because I don't fully understand it myself and her dad is too busy giving me a lecture about how, in his day, a pram was a pram, not a designer accoutrement. We then give them nine different emergency numbers and leave.

We are free. And elated. We are late for our lunchtime reservation at our favourite pre-Jacob café, but they have kept our favourite table for us. We order our favourite wine. We smile. We hold hands. And we talk about Jacob. How amazing he is with his little hands and his little eyes and his little smile. How much more amazing he is than all the other children in our baby group with their horrible little hands and pokey little eyes and crooked little smiles. And how lucky we are that he isn't one of those children that sleeps all day and all night, that although it is, at times, challenging, we are much better off with a child who is expressive.

We are maybe twelve minutes into lunch

82

before I say, 'Shall we call to check he's okay?' and Isabel says, 'No, he'll be fine. Mum would call if they were having a problem.' And it is maybe another seven minutes before Isabel suggests that perhaps a quick call wouldn't hurt, and it is my turn to pretend I don't think it is necessary. By the time our main courses have arrived, we have still spoken about nothing but Jacob and can stand it no longer.

'Hi, Mum. Sorry to call. Just check — . . . right . . . right . . . right. Okay. Speak to you later. Thank you. Bye.'

'What happened?' I ask. 'That sounded bad. Is he all right? Has something happened?'

'He's fine. He's had the milk. He's had four stories read to him. They've taken him for a walk round the block and now he's asleep. She says there's no need to rush.'

'Was it just once round the block?'

'Yep. Went straight to sleep, she said.'

'With singing?'

'Didn't mention any singing. Now, eat faster and let's go home and have a cuddle.'

★   ★   ★

Two things ruined my enjoyment of the remaining time we had free.

First, I could not believe that Jacob had chosen the one time neither of us was looking after him to behave angelically. All the exhaustion, the shuffling through the first two months of parenthood with that haunted, hunted look in our eyes, the desperation, would now seem to Isabel's parents like we were simply making a meal of things. I could hear it now: 'Jacob was a little treasure, my darlinks. He is charming. We will look after him again any time.' Annoying.

Second, the cuddle. She meant it as a euphemism. She was talking about sex, which she now very definitely does want and she says there isn't time to worry about whether it's a good idea or not. So we had to race home, take off all our clothes and 'cuddle'. Really quickly, though, because nipple-pumped milk can only go so far.

Is it fair, with all this going on, to expect me to perform at the drop of a hat or, in this case, a rather stylish pencil skirt? Was it reasonable to demand sudden sex, given that we were worrying about whether Jacob was still all right? Women seem capable of worrying about things *and* having sex.

What if the scar bursts open?

What if Jacob runs out of milk?

'I can't do it,' I blurt out. 'I can't do it in such a small window. I'm not a performing seal.' And with that, I got up, dressed hurriedly, checked the clock and set off to fetch our son. Now it's my fault we haven't done it. I have post-traumatic sex syndrome.

Monday 4 March

Johnson has sixty Facebook friends — three times as many as I have — and I have a syndrome. It's a terrible start to the week.

Tuesday 5 March

Maybe I should talk to Isabel about it. The syndrome, that is. Not Facebook. I don't care about bloody Facebook. I know it's not a real indicator of social importance.

Wednesday 6 March

The new work experience girl with 500 Facebook friends also has 600 followers on Twitter, which she can update from anywhere in the world via her WAP phone. I don't know what a work experience thinks she's doing being able to go anywhere in the world. Let alone in possession of a WAP phone, whatever that is. Whatever happened to good honest impoverished workies? Is it possible to have a workie without a double-barrelled name and an ambition to rule the world before their twenty-fifth birthday? Please.

She also has a blog. Johnson, who is Facebook friends with her, says the blog is very funny.

Thursday 7 March

Isabel has only got twelve Facebook friends. Hahahahahaha. But she's a new mum and she only joined it yesterday. But still, hahahahaha.

Friday 8 March

Isabel now has more Facebook friends than me. I ask her how that's possible given that she's always saying she doesn't have a second to herself at all. She gives me a scary don't-mess-with-me look, one that is getting much scarier as she develops into a proper mother. We are, I can tell, only months away from a full mum look, the sort of look that can stop a boy spooning yoghurt on to the wall-paper at fifty yards. I decide this is a bad time to discuss the failed attempt at sex and go to work.

The work-experience girl is now on a six-month contract. She has been given her own column to write about technology. I still don't have a column. I have been here for almost two years and I've only had one big interview shot (which didn't happen because apparently Hillary Clinton had to fly somewhere and host some peace talks, thus simultaneously solving a humani-tarian crisis and scuppering my big break). I had a column at *Cat World* within two months of starting. Yes, it was called 'Good enough to eat?' and involved me tasting actual cat food. But you got used to it. And it was a column.

Sunday 10 March

Alex called from Barbados to say how surprised he was that the bath had arrived early and that it was almost certainly a good omen. He and Geoff fly back tomorrow. The team will start on Thursday. The team and the crew.

Monday 11 March

I am now avoiding Isabel when Jacob is asleep, just in case she wants another 'cuddle'. To the pub at lunch with Johnson. He says he has a friend who looked over the curtain during the Caesarean through some misguided sense of duty. Bursts into tears every time he and his wife start kissing.

If it was him, Johnson says, he would have refused to attend the birth full stop. All you need to do is make the woman think it is a decision based on some spurious ancient tribal nonsense. Women love that sort of stuff.

'Darling, I'd say. Darling. Sweetness. Sugar pie. About the birth, I was thinking that we should do what the Amazonian tribespeople do. Women in the birth hut. Men outside praying to the gods. I will be there in spirit, but I won't be there in person. This is because my biorhythms are incompatible with the mystical process of labour. Let's try it like that and, if you feel you do need me, text me and I'll be there in ten minutes.'

Sometimes, amid all the dross, Johnson speaks the truth. Only sometimes, though, and usually when it's far too late to be of any use.

Wednesday 13 March

Isabel, who now has twice as many Facebook friends as me and counting, has also managed to find the time to reorganise our wardrobes. All

Jacob's clothes now occupy the small chest of drawers and all Isabel's clothes now occupy the top four drawers of the large chest of drawers. My clothes are now confined to the bottom drawer and a large bag which I am to check through before it goes to charity. In it, I find my favourite trousers, bought with my first proper pay cheque ten years ago from Donna Karan, no less. I also find my favourite T-shirt, the one an Australian girl had once said I looked muscly in. There is also my favourite shirt and my favourite jumper, both birthday presents from my mother. This is nothing short of a fashion coup d'état.

'This is nothing short of a fashion coup d'état,' I say as Isabel chops carrots and Jacob watches me suspiciously. He is part of it, I know he is.

'Darling, you never wear any of those clothes.'

She always calls me 'darling' when she's trying to bend me to her will. But I won't be bent. 'That's because you shrank them.'

'Darling, I shrank one shirt once. And it was that ridiculous Italian one that made you look like a Frisbee.'

She continues with the carrots. And I continue to protest: 'I love this T-shirt.'

'Yes, you told me. An Australian girl said you looked muscly in it. And she was right, darling. It's like a magic muscle T-shirt. But it has holes in it now. It's almost a metaphor.'

She takes the T-shirt from my hand and stuffs it into the duster drawer to join my favourite pair of pants, which had gone in a previous cull. I'd loved those pants, too. Sure, the elastic had gone and they sagged in all the wrong places and didn't in all the right ones, but they were comfortable. And comfort is rare in pants. By the time I had noticed, they had already been used to polish shoes. I had cried for those pants. Why should I cry for the T-shirt, too? I begin to protest but she interrupts, smiling sweetly.

'Darling, we have limited space. We have to make room for another man in the house.'

Hmmm. Fair enough, I suppose.

'And besides, we need to tidy up. The television crew is coming tomorrow for a recce.'

Hmmm. Not so fair enough, but Jacob gives me a look that says this conversation is over. I retreat to the front room sulkily, nursing a Scotch and dry in one hand and the T-shirt in the other. I sit in the bath, because this is now the only way I can see the television. I flick through the channels looking for something monotonous to watch, and there are Alex and Geoff in a trailer for their new show. It isn't called *Spruce Up Your House*. It's called *Alex & Geoff to the Rescue*. I really don't think our bathroom is that bad.

Thursday 14 March

The producer of the show does. The three of them — he, Alex and Geoff — came round this evening and said lots of nasty things about the bath, the toilet and especially the frosted-glass shaving shelf. It's not like it's our choice of bathroom. It was my choice of frosted shelf, but it was only a stopgap until we could get the

89

whole room done. And, you know, we've been busy having a baby.

'They have to talk it up,' says Isabel. 'Everything on television is exaggerated.'

'Yes, but it's *our* bathroom. We don't need the whole world being told we had a horrible bathroom. And I don't like the way Geoff thinks he's better than everyone else, just because he has bad taste in home interiors.'

'You said last week you couldn't give a monkey's about the show because no one watches daytime television, anyway.'

Why do women have the facility to file things away like this when I can't remember what I've said from one argument to the next? It's like making a goldfish argue with a barrister. It's unfair.

'I know what they're going to do. They're going to make us out to be losers.'

'Stop being such a grouch. This is exciting for Alex. It's just what he needs. He's had a difficult year, what with all the stalking and the coming out. He's finally doing what he loves with someone he loves and we're getting a bathroom out of it. All they're asking in return is that they go for something truly original and that we exaggerate how much we like it at the end.'

'I'm sorry? What do you mean 'original'? I thought we were having a simple, stylish, timeless design.'

'Well, the programme format's come on a bit since then. There has to be an element of surprise. We're in the first show so we're the, er, guinea pigs.'

I told you nothing good would come of this.

Saturday 16 March

What started out as a typically extravagant baby present has degenerated into a massive pain in the neck. Isabel and I were forced to show Alex and Geoff round the house on camera, pretending we didn't know them, pretending we were really struggling without a proper bathroom. Isabel really hammed up her bathroom misery — it sounded like she lived in an unplumbed Calcutta slum. This gave Alex and Geoff licence to make cruel jokes about how they bet she wished she'd married someone who was practical around the house. Alex called her 'babes' a lot. So did Geoff. I really object to Geoff calling Isabel 'babes' on camera. He hardly knows her. It's overfamiliar. And even though I might not be able to put a bathroom in, I have other practical skills.

OTHER PRACTICAL SKILLS

1. I can make a paper aeroplane that only three other people know how to make.

2. I can skateboard.

3. I can yo-yo.

4. I can make a vein in my hand do the cancan.

5. I can eat a whole loaf of Marmite toast in one sitting.

Later, when we have been asked to make ourselves scarce so that Geoff, Alex and the team can get started, I read out my list of skills to Isabel. She points out that everything on the list dates from my childhood. When I look despondent, she tells me I don't need a list, I'm very good at other things, and she gives me a hug.

I don't need her pity. Well, okay, I do a bit.

Sunday 17 March

Another day wandering aimlessly around parks with a sling containing a baby while Alex ruins our bathroom.

Monday 18 March

Spend the day trying to find out how one goes about learning a manly martial art — and which one would be most suitable for a time-poor father of one. Karate is obviously out. I don't have months to paint a fence. Ju-jutsu is too hardcore. Maybe kick boxing. Turns out there's a class on Monday lunchtimes at the gym with the stupid name (Avocado) and they have one place left. On the website, there is a video of a man high-kicking another man before flattening him with a quick, brutal one-two. I'm not interested in violence, but Alex and Geoff might stop taking the piss if they know I can render both of them unconscious with one roundhouse.

Tuesday 19 March

That's four days we haven't been able to use our bathroom, and there's only so much washing one can do in a downstairs toilet. You would think they would be out by now, but apparently they've had a few technical setbacks. At least the bath is out of the living room so I can return to the luxury of sleeping on a sofa bed. Amazing how similar being a new dad is to being in the doghouse.

Thursday 21 March

'William. Isabel. Close your eyes. Walk forward three spaces. Now. Tell me. What was the problem with your old bathroom?' Alex is doing the full Laurence Llewelyn-Bloody-Bowen as the camera rolls.

[Nothing, I think. Relatively speaking, it was fine before you got involved.]

'It was cramped. It was stressful. Just the atmosphere made our new baby cry,' says Isabel untruthfully. Or half truthfully — everything made our new baby cry.

'And what did you want from your new bathroom?'

[A bath in a room. That's all.]

'We wanted light and space and a sense of happiness. Anything would be better than what we had, really. Somewhere to start the day positively would be enough for our new family.' She is completely made for daytime television; I am so disappointed in her.

'Well, William, Isabel. I am pleased to say that Geoff and Alex have . . . come to the rescue,' says Geoff. 'When I count to three, open your eyes. One, two, th — '

'Fucking hell.'

'Cut,' says the director. 'Let's take it again from the top.'

The stupid pink egg bath is in the middle of the bathroom, which is now also shaped like a giant egg, thanks to a rounding off of all the edges. It looks a bit like a hospital MRI scanner with a bath in the middle. When you press a button, water shoots out of hundreds of holes in the ceiling and floor. Water and bubbles.

The sink is behind a recess at the back of the room and Geoff has had his way with the lighting. A dial turns the LED lights from red ('Sexy,' says Isabel televisually) to green ('Soothing,' she purrs). If you clap your hands, whale-mating music comes on and I am immediately transported back to Isabel's labour.

Every inch of the room is stencilled with cartoon bonsais.

The taps don't even look like taps. They look like dildos. You have to squeeze them to turn them on.

It is the most ridiculous bathroom I have ever seen in my entire life. When I say this, the director says 'Cut' again, and we all have an enormous row. Then Isabel tells me I've woken Jacob so can I go and change him. I ask whether I should change him in the baby room or in the MRI scanner.

Alex calls me 'babes' in an attempt to calm me

down. I tell him I'm not his babe. Geoff tells me I'm homophobic. I tell Geoff that I am Geoffophobic and then wish I was better at comebacks and storm out.

An hour later, they have all left. Isabel comes into the front room where I am still explaining to Jacob that his mother is mad, her friends are evil and that he must understand, when he's older, that Daddy never wanted an egg-shaped bathroom with dildos for taps.

'Let's just wait until we've got used to it, darling. If we still don't like it then, Alex has promised he'll come and sort it out.'

Friday 22 March

Bath time is ruined. And bath time was the only time, apart from train time, when I could truly relax. This evening, I sat uncomfortably in an egg surrounded by a larger egg. I had the lighting in red mode because the green made me feel sick. The whale music was playing because neither Isabel nor I have managed to turn it off since Alex and Geoff left. 'Two claps for on, one clap for off,' they had said, but one clap only makes the whale mating louder. I closed my eyes and tried to blot it all out, and suddenly I realised why I felt so uncomfortable. This wasn't a bathroom. It was a womb. Not even three months on from near-disaster in Isabel's womb department, and Alex and his beardy boyfriend have constructed an ovarian monstrosity. And I am lying right in the middle of it.

Saturday 23 March

Isabel says I am being ridiculous. She says I am sleep-deprived. I need to calm down and think rationally. If I think our bathroom has become a giant uterus, then it's me that has issues, not the bathroom. I am about to tell her she is absolutely right, I do have issues and the bathroom isn't helping, but my mum arrives. She has been talking to Isabel's mum. She is delighted to hear that Jacob is such an easy child. Isabel starts pouting.

I put the kettle on.

Mum takes Jacob. Jacob immediately stops grouching and smiles. Seriously, is it us? Are we creating a horrendous atmosphere within which no child can prosper? Or has Jacob simply got a very dry sense of humour? Does he behave angelically when any grandparents are around simply to create the illusion that Mummy and Daddy are making a hash of things for his own amusement?

'It's me. I must be a terrible mother,' says Isabel the minute Mum leaves and Jacob starts grouching again. 'I must be projecting tension or lack of confidence or something.'

'You're not a terrible mother. You're an amazing mother. He just likes the super-attention he gets from the grandparents. They probably give him chocolate when we're not looking.'

'Well, it's annoying.'

'I know. Give him here. I'll have a chat with him about this, man to man.'

Monday 25 March

Johnson is equally suspicious of the idea of washing in a giant uterus. He thinks it sounds oedipal. This is even more disgusting than it being simply a reminder of the trauma of childbirth.

The work experience who is no longer behaving like a work experience, even though she only has a six-month contract that could be cancelled at any minute, has offered to put the best bits of *Alex & Geoff to the Rescue* on YouTube so none of us miss it. I say it's fine, Isabel will record it. She says it's really no problem.

I send Andy a nice truce of an e-mail asking how his trip to Sudan went. He e-mails back saying it went fine but he can't believe I snubbed Saskia on Facebook. I point out that I didn't. He says I did: remaining noncommittal about someone's offer of Facebook friendship is the same as refusing it. I tell him he's being oversensitive. He doesn't reply, thus proving my point.

Anastasia tells me I am to move desks to make room for the still-technically-a-work-experience girl.

At least I have the kick boxing. They have turned my house into female reproductive organs, they have humiliated me at work, they have betrayed me and they have whittled away at the very last vestiges of my self-respect, but they will be sorry. They will be sorry when I return and avenge myself with my kung fu fighting skills

97

like Jean-Claude Van Damme, back for one last high-octane adventure, back to settle scores once and for all.

Except obviously that's not quite how it turns out. For a start, does it seem unreasonable to expect that there might be some men in a kick-boxing class? The promotional video had men fighting in it, but the class I showed up for consisted of me and nine women in Lycra. I had clearly signed up for some horribly girly lunchtime aerobic work-out nightmare. There would be gym balls and skipping ropes and Travolta music and spinning and stepping and one-two-three-four, two-two-three-four, all together now . . .

I was wrong. It was worse than that. I had stepped into some kind of feminist boot camp. The instructor was called Ingrid. She had a six-pack, no breasts and a chiselled jaw Jean-Claude Van Damme would die for. She smiled frighteningly, broke several small bones in my hand by way of greeting and paired me with a woman who looked immediately familiar.

'Hi, I'm William. Do we know — '

'I don't think so. I'm Brenda,' she said dismissively. She was five feet tall if I'm being generous. It would be like fighting a child.

We began with a warm-up that consisted of skipping and twirling and generally behaving like we were in the Spice Girls. Then Brenda beat me up.

At home that night, lying in my giant uterus, I was amazed I didn't have more bruises.

98

Everything hurt. Isabel pretended to feel sorry for me, but I could tell she thought I was exaggerating. It is hard to believe that someone so small could pack such a punch. Or kick. Or punch-punch-kick-swivel-roundhouse-punch-and-dismount. But what she lost in stature she gained in what I'm guessing is an inner power developed to combat a society that routinely underestimates dwarves. And people called Brenda.

Tuesday 26 March

Still no bruises. She must have hit me in places that don't bruise.

Wednesday 27 March

I knew that I knew Brenda. She's the nail-filing, teeth-flossing ginger space-stealer on the train. I just hadn't recognised her in Lycra. She was there this morning, all snug in the seat she'd already bagsied further down the line from me. Her bag was on the seat next to her, warding people away. Normally, I'd make a point of getting her to move it, but this morning, I decided to go for another carriage.

Not because I was scared of her or anything. I just didn't want to have to say, 'Hello, what a coincidence,' particularly to a violent midget. And besides, maybe I was exaggerating. Maybe Brenda didn't kick the shit out of me. She

99

was only three feet tall, after all. And she was a girl. I'd have bruises if it hurt as much as I thought it did. It's probably that I'm just not used to getting hit. And I was quite good at the warm-up. I should persist with the whole thing. Just because it's all women, not counting Ingrid, doesn't mean it's not good for me.

Thursday 28 March

I was brushing my teeth this morning at the plinth/basin/Oscar podium Alex calls our basin when Isabel ran in and said, 'Quick, Jacob's still asleep. Let's have a cuddle.' That bloody euphemism again. So I said, 'I can't, I'm late for work.' This wasn't true — and I think Isabel knew it. She said, 'Fine, I'll have a shower instead, then. You listen for Jacob.' And then she put the rainforest shower thing on and I got soaked because Alex and Geoff thought a wet room would be appropriate for a young family. Then I left the house and got to work half an hour early because it now appears I'd rather be at work than having a 'cuddle' with my wife.

Anastasia arrived minutes later and said, 'Early for once.' And I felt pleased. Then I felt suicidal. I am now keen to impress the girl who used to be the work experience but is now the Editor so that she doesn't give the work experience who is still the work experience my job. This is ridiculous.

Friday 29 March

Thank God it's the weekend.

Saturday 30 March

Oh God, it's the weekend.

Sunday 31 March

It's okay. Everything is okay. We have had sex. We have had post-operative sex. I blocked. I blocked all the voices in my head saying I shouldn't be having my wicked way with the mother of our child. I avoided the breasts altogether in case she said something about them being painful or full or something.

And we did it. We had sex. I mean it was quick, but it had to be. I couldn't risk her saying anything like, 'Gently' or 'Careful, it's hurting' or 'My God, the scar has torn open. Call an ambulance.' But it doesn't matter — we are back.

'Is everything all right, darling?'

'Yes, darling.'

'It's just that you seemed distracted.'

'Nope, I was only worried Jacob might wake up.'

'But you were humming the theme tune to the *Antiques Roadshow*.'

'Was I?'

'Yes. It was quite odd.'

'Sorry.' But we have had sex and that is the

main thing. To celebrate, I make a cooked breakfast. Then Isabel says she's going to pop round to her mother's for coffee, do I want to come? I say, 'No, I'm going to have a uterus, sorry, bath.' Clearly, I feel able to joke about reproductive organs again. Hurrah.

This is how I remember what happens next.

I walk into the cocoon and massage the dildo taps.

The phone rings. It is Isabel. She has forgotten her breast pads and she's starting to leak. Could I run up the road with them? I suggest she uses kitchen towel. She suggests I hurry up.

I put on some clothes and run up the road with them.

I run back.

I make myself some mid-morning child-and-wife-free coffee and watch some mid-morning child-and-wife-free television. Rick Stein makes a rather fabulous-looking fish chowder and I think how wonderful it would be to surprise Isabel by making a fabulous-looking fish chowder. We can have it for dinner and then it will last through the week. Delicious and efficient — Isabel's favourite combination.

I pop to the shops to buy the fish chowder ingredients.

Isabel calls again. Her dad is doing a roast. She's staying. They'd like me to come over, too. This isn't quite what I had in mind, but her dad does do a nice roast. So I drive back to the house to drop off the ingredients, only to realise I left with such culinary enthusiasm that I've locked myself out.

I call Isabel. It's okay. She has her set of keys. I should come straight over.

I go straight over. The fish is still in the boot of the car, but it doesn't matter. It's a crisp spring day. It will keep.

We have lunch.

Isabel's dad is keen for me to sample a claret that he opened especially.

I sample the claret.

We get ready to leave, but Jacob needs a change, a feed, a change, a feed and a wind.

Finally, we leave.

We drive home and I notice water trickling down our path.

Isabel passes me her set of keys.

With difficulty, I open the door and a great surge of water rushes over my feet. Panicking, I step into the hall and notice that the ceiling in the living room is bowing dreadfully. I step back out and there is an almighty crash.

I step back in again and notice that the egg-shaped bath is back in our living room. All I can hear is water and whale music. Then the electrics short and the whale mating stops.

I had left the stupid dildo taps on all day.

I had destroyed our beautiful home.

'Let's go back to Grandma's house, Jacob, while Daddy sorts out this little mess,' says Isabel in her calm-sounding voice that isn't calm at all.

APRIL

'Henry James once defined life as that pre-dicament which precedes death, and certainly nobody owes you a debt of honour or gratitude for getting him into that predicament. But a child does owe his father a debt, if Dad, having gotten him into this peck of trouble, takes off his coat and buckles down to the job of showing his son how best to crash through it.'
CLARENCE BUDINGTON KELLAND

Monday 1 April

The chief fire officer told me that he had never seen so much damage caused by one tap. Normally, the bath overflows and people notice. It was unfortunate that I'd decided to go out for several hours, he said helpfully. And it was unfortunate that they were power taps. It was also unfortunate that the wet room drained the wrong way for the overflowing bath, other-wise everything would have been fine. Likewise, if the bath's own overflow pipe had worked. Likewise, if the egg hadn't held quite so much water. As it was, though, the house was now structurally unsafe.

Most of the first floor had fallen on to the ground floor because of the sheer weight of water that had built up and then raced out of the stupid-shaped bathroom. The electrics were ruined. The gas was ruined. The stairs had caved in and, what with several supporting beams torn down, there was a strong possibility that the roof would cave in as well.

We spent the night at Isabel's parents'. I didn't sleep a wink. In the morning, I returned to the scene of my inordinate stupidity to collect more things. Fortunately, the water had only reached the level of the bottom drawer of the chest of drawers in the bedroom before the ceiling collapsed. Only my clothes were ruined.

No one, not even Isabel's father, not even Anastasia, has called me an idiot yet. In fact, Anastasia has given me as much time off as I need to sort things out. This may be a while if my first conversation with the insurance company is anything to go by.

'Yes, hello. Good morning. I'd like to report a flood.'

'Your name please . . . and postcode . . . and house number . . . and policy number. Oh right, sir. Now, are you at the property right now, Mr Walker? Right, and is this claim for buildings or contents? Both? Oh, right, let me just check . . . no, I'm afraid you are not covered for flood damage, Mr Walker. It specifically states in

105

section 37.22 that — '

I explain that by flood, I mean accidental damage caused by leaving the bath on.

'Leaving the bath on?'

'Yes, leaving the bath on.'

'On what?'

'The taps. Leaving the taps on. I left the taps in the bath on.'

'And now you say you're homeless?'

'Yes.'

Skip forward twenty minutes while I go over and over my own stupidity.

'And you say the first floor has fallen through to the ground floor?'

'Yes. What happens now?'

'Is the house inhabitable, sir?'

'No. As I mentioned, the first floor has fallen through.'

'So the bedrooms are unsafe?'

'The bedrooms are now on the ground floor.'

'And you can't sleep in them?'

Skip forward another twenty minutes to the point where, with some difficulty, it transpires that I am entitled to £50 a night for emergency accommodation for up to four weeks IF we provide receipts and a claim form and the insurance certificate and a completed Rubik's Cube and a full explanation of exactly why E equals MC squared. After that, the insurance company will pay for alternative accommodation IF necessary IF the insurance assessor concludes that the property is still uninhabitable, IF we have broken none of the clauses on modification when we installed the new bathroom, IF we pay a £500 excess, IF the moon is in its fourth quarter and it's a Tuesday and a grasshopper crosses our path twice before sundown.

The assessor will arrive to do his assessing between 8 a.m. and 4 p.m. tomorrow.

'Could you be any more specific?'

'I'm afraid not.'

'I have a homeless wife and a homeless baby and all you can do is give me a time frame that would embarrass an IKEA delivery man?'

'I'm afraid so.'

'Is this conversation being recorded for legal reasons?'

'Yes, sir.'

'Right. Well, if it wasn't I would call you a dickhead. Since it is, I shall simply call you an imbecile.'

'Mr Walker, I am only doing my job. You were the one who left the taps on.'

At least I have a good excuse not to get kick-boxed to within an inch of my life by a female midget. Ingrid says I'm not entitled to a refund, but she can provide me with a receipt. And she hopes I won't chicken out next week. She clearly thinks I've made up the whole flood to get out of the kick boxing. Which I would have done if I'd thought of it.

Tuesday 2 April

Alex has offered to redecorate the bathroom and promises not to bring a television crew with him this time. Frankly, it's all his fault. I would have heard our old taps running and been reminded that I'd left the bath running. The new dildo taps were silent. That was the problem. That and the fact that the overflow pipe didn't work. And that Alex was involved at all. I don't care how gay he thinks he is; he continues to be responsible for making my married life a disaster.

Except Isabel, through this entire nightmare, has been incredibly circumspect and forgiving. We can argue for days about Marmite toast and whose turn it is to change a nappy and whether it's harder pretending to work at the office than being at home with the baby, but when the chips are really down, she is the rock of this family. She has gone into emergency mode. She has us all up in the spare room at her parents' and is behaving a bit like Sigourney Weaver in *Alien 3*. If, on top of everything else, we had to deal with killer aliens, it wouldn't be a problem.

On the less helpful side, her dad is now saying I'm an idiot. Albeit in a nice way.

'I knew someone once who left the taps on. Friend of my father's. Had his legs blown off in the war. Poor chap never recovered. Still, he was nearly ninety when he died. Brave chap. Very brave chap. But just before he died, he left the bath on. Shouldn't have really been still running his own bath at that age. Not without any legs. And senile dementia. And sciatica. And pancreatic cancer. Poor chap. Anyway, yes, so he left the bath on.'

'What happened?'

'Oh, he remembered after half an hour. No real harm done. Except he died a week later. I

108

think it was the fright of almost letting the bath overflow that killed him. Couldn't handle being so useless.'

The insurance assessor is only slightly more intelligent and helpful than the insurance phone person. He makes several remarks about the whole leaving-the-tap-on thing, asks several questions that insinuate I did it on purpose ('Have you made any late payments on your credit cards recently, Mr Walker?' No. 'What about less recently, then?'). We now have to wait for him to make a full report and get some builders to come and quote for repairs. It may take two or three weeks, what with it being spring.

'Why?' I ask. 'Do a lot of people flood their houses in spring?'

'Hahahaha. Good one, sir. No. You're pretty much the only one who's done that this year. Everyone else prefers to do home *improvements*. Like birds building a nest. It's a spring thing. So the building trade is busy. You see?'

Wednesday 3 April

Back to work. Anastasia's concern turned out to be momentary. Johnson tells me I'm an idiot. E-mail from Andy saying if there's anything he can do, I must shout.

'I could do with a pint, actually,' I reply eventually, because even though he is going out with the Destroyer of Relationships, he is my best friend and I am in need of an emergency pint.

'Afraid I can't. I've got to go to Stockholm tomorrow for a couple of weeks. Then Saskia and I are driving back down through Germany. Won't be home until mid-May.'

'So anything you can do to help provided it's doable from frigging Sweden? Cheers very much.'

Friday 5 April

Isabel is still the rock of the family, but only just. Her mother is wearing her down. I get home from work and everyone is rolling their eyes.

'Hi, darlink. Your wife thinks her mother doesn't know anything about raising children.' Eye roll.

'Hi, darling. She's been telling me that I should establish a routine.' Eye roll.

'It will make all your lives easier, don't you think, William?' Eye roll.

'Three-month-old babies are too young to have a routine forced on them.' Eye roll. I'm starting to wonder which one of them will be the first to sprain an eye. Or if that's even possible.

'Well, we managed it with you and you turned out all right,' continues her mother.

'Yes, now I've recovered from the deep psychological trauma of being abandoned in my cot like a Romanian orphan,' says Isabel, folding her arms.

'Bit of tough love never killed anyone,' says her father, always the master at timing an entrance. I haven't even put my bag down and said hello and all three of them are eye-rolling at me.

'Evening, everyone. Jacob all right?'
'Yes.'
'Yes.'
'Playing up a bit.'

Saturday 6 April

More of the same, but I'm not at work to avoid it.

Sunday 7 April

More of the same combined with the horror of my middle-of-the-night pee coinciding with Isabel's dad's middle-of-the-night pee and release of wind. And he is naked. And I am wearing Isabel's nightdress because I was cold and no one has got round to dealing with my flood-damaged wardrobe. We both give each other funny looks, then the next morning pretend nothing has happened.

Monday 8 April

Thank God for work. Sort of. I am tempted to dodge kick boxing again on the grounds of my continuing domestic crisis, but if I don't go now, I'll never go. And Ingrid forced me to pay for all ten classes upfront. I'm guessing she'd have a high drop-out rate if she didn't.

'Hi, Brenda. I knew I knew you. You get the same train as me.'

'Right. You're the one who always tuts at everyone.'

'Right. You're the one who always tries to take up two seats.'

'You should get on earlier if you want a seat.'

'What? Like further down the line?'

'That's what I do.'

'But I don't live further down the line.'

I've realised that Brenda is irritating not just because she's very smug for a short person but also because she speaks entirely through her nose. This makes her sound alarmingly like Miss Porritt, my vindictive geography teacher who would bore the class to sleep with long nasal monologues on oxbow lakes and then punish us for not paying attention.

After the Spice Girls routine, we begin with a warm-up. A few gentle hits, says Ingrid. So I give Brenda a couple of nudges, nothing more, and she punches me really hard, straight in the face, when I wasn't ready. Bloody hell. I know what's happening here. I'm taking the frustration of a woman who refuses to accept she is clinically short. She won't go to short-people bars and nightclubs to meet other short people. She tries to make her way in the normal-heighted world, finds nothing but prejudice, rejection and cans of beans that are out of reach. She has only two choices: retrain as a vindictive geography teacher or get paired off with a tall person in kick-boxing class and then cheat.

Well, I won't let her win. I shall take the punches and I'll give them back, even though it feels weird to hit a woman. Even though she moves too bloody quickly to hit properly.

'Sorry about the eye,' she sneers at the end of the class. 'Don't know my own strength.'

'No need to apologise,' I say. 'It looks worse than it is.'

This is the opposite of the truth. Isabel says she can hardly see a mark, but I feel like I've been hit by a bus, whatever that feels like.

Tuesday 9 April

Hurts more now. Pretty sure my nose is broken, but the internet reveals it might not be. If it were, it would feel crunchy and my eyes would be bruised, apparently. But we all know how wildly inaccurate the internet is.

Maybe it's a little bit broken or maybe part of it has splintered off and is now gouging a hole in my frontal lobe. That would teach Isabel to tease me. And Johnson, who has helpfully e-mailed me a picture of Johnny Owen, a skinny, jug-eared boxer from Merthyr Tydfil who was known as the Bionic Bantum and died after a knockout in Los Angeles in 1980. 'That's you, that is,' read the accompanying note. 'Except, of course, Johnny wasn't fighting a girl.'

Wednesday 10 April

Still no word from the insurance company about the builders' quote.

One of my virtual Facebook friends is full of

sympathy. Not for my sore nose. For the flood. Her husband once left the freezer door open. Nearly lost a steak box, she explains. I'm going to block her.

Saskia, whom I have now accepted as a Facebook friend even though she is a real-life nightmare, is ranting on about how sexy Stockholm is but breaks away long enough to say she hopes I'm okay. I don't want her to hope I'm okay.

The work experience, who is now not a work experience, wants me to be her Facebook friend even though I hate her. No wonder she has nine thousand other Facebook buddies if she's that indiscriminate.

I accept. One can't be too dismissive of the youth of today.

'OMG. You really do only have twenty-one friends,' she posts on my Facebook wall, whatever that is. 'Sweet.'

Bloody youth of today.

Thursday 11 April

Nose not broken and pain going away. No one realises how serious that was. I notice from previous updates on the workie's Facebook account that she thinks I am well old and well uptight. I tell her, face to face — not virtually, since we work in the same office — that I am not uptight. She says she was only kidding and that I should lighten up. I say, 'Are you serious?' and she says, 'What?' because she's not paying attention, she's texting. I say, 'Can't you stop texting for a second while I talk to you?' And she says, 'I'm not texting. I'm IMing.'

Isabel is uninterested in the frustrations of work. She wants me to get the insurance people to fix the bathroom NOW. I phone, press 4, then 2, then 7, then give my details, my mother's maiden name and accept that the call might be being recorded for training purposes, before establishing that there's nothing that can be done because builders don't work during the Easter holidays.

Sunday 14 April

Easter. Isabel, Jacob, me. Spring flowers in the park. Lambs bleating playfully. The distant prospect of summer. Our first summer with a baby. We will lie in meadows while our child learns to crawl a lot earlier than you would expect a child to learn to crawl. We will eat fruit and chat like we used to in the old days. And return each night to the tent we will no doubt be living in because the bastard builders won't have got round to patching up our house and Isabel won't be able to live in the same house as her parents any more.

Monday 15 April

Thank God for bank holidays. No girly kick boxing. No violent midgets. Only a father-in-law explaining to Jacob, our not-even-four-month-old, that he is too old to be crying so much. Far too old. And Isabel saying are we doing anything for her birthday and that she's only asking because her pre-baby friends, the ones still in London, still going out to parties, still without a care in the world, want to treat her to a night out. And me saying, 'Yes, we're definitely doing something.' And her saying, 'Really, that's exciting. Is it okay if I go out the following Saturday, then? I won't go for long and I'm sure Jacob can manage one evening without me.' And me, still panicking about what I'm going to do for her birthday, saying, 'Sure, of course.'

Wednesday 17 April

'Darling, it's fine. No one will see it. It's daytime television,' says Isabel like she's been practising what to say all day.

Didn't I say, right from the start, that this whole idea of getting Alex to do our bathroom was a bad, bad idea? Didn't I say that? Yes, I did. So not only do we end up with a bathroom that is completely inappropriate for our lovely house, not only is it a bathroom shaped like a uterus, which makes my brave attempt to recover from the psychological damage of witnessing childbirth far harder, not only does this, in turn, mean that the only time Isabel and I have had proper sex in the last nearly four months, I do it humming the theme tune to the *Antiques*

116

Roadshow, not only does the bathroom end up destroying the whole house but — and I think this is quite a large but — I also get humiliated on national television by the bastard.

'You saw it,' I reply, furious. 'You saw it and recorded it and now I've seen it. Your mum has seen it. Your dad has seen it.'

'The baby-group mums have seen it. They thought it was good.'

'What? How did the baby group see it?'

'Well, I might have mentioned — '

'Oh, thanks a million.'

'It's not that bad. I thought it was quite funny.'

It wasn't funny. The programme-makers have gone beyond their remit as makers of a yet another annoying daytime DIY show. They have attempted to make it comical. They have given me a superhero name, 'Captain Impractical'. They keep playing a little jingle every time I'm mentioned. There's Isabel explaining how she's wanted the bathroom decorated for years (exaggeration), but how I'm not very focused (more exaggeration) when it comes to house stuff. She then recounts a shelving saga very hyperbolically. And a run-in with an IKEA cupboard. And a fence. All the time, Alex and Geoff are hamming up the horror. And it is all interspersed with clips of me sitting on the sofa doing nothing. Then reading the paper. Then sleeping.

'They're just having some fun to make it more interesting,' says Isabel.

'At my expense. Where's the bit at the end where I said this is the most ridiculous bathroom I have ever seen?'

That's what bugs me the most. The nation needs to know that Alex and Geoff are rubbish. That, only a few months ago, Alex wasn't an interior designer at all. That he wasn't even gay. All they've shown is the third take, with Isabel banging on enthusiastically about how wonderful the bathroom is. She even cries a bit, as requested by the producer, when Alex tells her it's the sort of bathroom a young, beautiful family should have. And instead of me telling Alex and Geoff they've ruined our house, which they had, it shows me appearing to smile approvingly, even though I'm in a different room and not smiling about the bathroom at all.

'Hmm, yes, funny they decided not to go with the ranting, swearing disgruntled husband for their first show. Now, stop being silly, darling. It's all over now. It's not a big deal.'

Except that it isn't quite over.

It finishes with some more of the Captain Impractical jingle. Then Alex and Geoff promising to come to the rescue of all the poor women married to DIY slobs. And then a slow-motion clip of me sitting down on the sofa again, over which the narrator explains that, a few days after they left, I destroyed the bathroom by leaving the tap on.

'Captain Impractical strikes again, ladies and gentlemen. If you see this man, do not approach him. He is dangerous.'

'It's really not a big deal,' reiterates Isabel.

Thursday 18 April

It *is* a big deal.

I arrive late at work due to the late running of an earlier train (I mean, do the bloody railway people not understand that blaming the late running of a train on the late running of an earlier train is not a sufficient explanation?) and already there's a hammer on my desk with a note reading, 'Lesson one: this is a hammer'. Everyone is pretending to work, but sniggering. They've seen it. They've seen the daytime DIY programme Isabel said no one watches. How is that possible?

I have the no-longer-a-workie to thank. She's posted an even more cruelly edited version of *Alex & Geoff to the Rescue* on YouTube. Everyone at work has seen it. So have 6,427 other people, some of them in Brazil. People in Brazil are writing 'What a loser' in the comments box below the video.

Emergency lunchtime drinking session with Johnson, my only friend in the world. At least he's real, not like all the no-longer-a-workie's Facebook friends. And he only spends the first half of the lunch hour laughing his head off. Even though we are back in the office by 2.10 p.m., Anastasia has the temerity to reprimand us for treating work like one big social event. She then gets the Managing Editor to send round an e-mail stating that long boozy lunches are not conducive to efficient magazine production and will, henceforth, be banned.

She then leaves the office because she's having

a (boozy) dinner with George Clooney. In Italy.

I phone Isabel and tell her I'm going to have a quick drink with Johnson. Johnson's a good friend. He understands.

'I mean, it's completely ridiculous. Alex is still ruining my life.'

'A leopard can't change its spots.'

'I mean, how is it that I'm the one appearing useless and unreasonable when Alex is the one that put dildos on our bath instead of taps?'

'It's just not fair.'

'It's not.'

'I mean, it could happen to anyone.'

'What could?'

'Leaving a tap on and destroying your house. I mean, you know, we live in a hectic, perplexing world. Things are complicated. How are we supposed to keep tabs on things like taps?'

Now I'm not talking to Johnson, either.

Friday 19 April

Horrible, horrible, horrible start to the day. Got back late enough to be in the doghouse, mainly because I'd promised I would be back soon enough to distract Isabel's mum from offering any more parenting advice.

'You said you were only going for one for the road,' said Isabel, in the sort of furious whisper you do when you're rowing at your parents' house.

'I needed a drink.'

'Well, I needed a bloody drink, too.' The last

time she swore at me, she was six centimetres dilated.

'Look, I had a bad day.'

'We've all had a bad day.'

'Yes, but you haven't become a YouTube hit, have you?'

'Oh God, will you just get over yourself. This family needs you to grow up.'

I am well and truly in the doghouse. In pre-parent days this would have meant sleeping on the sofa, but at Isabel's parents' house, we have to confine our marital disputes to the one spare bedroom all three of us are attempting to occupy. So I am forced to sleep on the floor. As it happens, this is where I've been sleeping anyway because Isabel and Jacob sleep in the tiny double bed — all huddled up and cosy. I sleep on a lilo. So perhaps the best thing that could be said of last night is that there was no difference in sleeping arrangements despite the doghousing.

On the less positive side, Jacob woke up at 4.30 a.m., precisely three hours after I finally got to sleep because I felt so pathetic about having a family but not growing up. He didn't cry or scream or do a terrifyingly realistic impression of a baby choking to death like usual. He just lay there gurgling in a way that was almost but not quite possible to ignore.

'He needs a change. You deal with him, I'm still asleep,' said Isabel from under a pillow. So I got up, took him downstairs, changed his nappy, tried and failed four times to do up all the buttons on his babygro in the correct order and then sang him 'The Owl and the Pussycat'.

He smiled the whole way through, so I started singing it again. More smiling. Then I got to the end and he stopped smiling and started crying. So I started again. And I decided I wouldn't stop until he'd had enough. Because I might be a crap husband and a useless DIY man and a laughing stock, but I can make my son happy.

And then it was 7 a.m. and time to start a whole new day. I am never going to drink four pints again.

'Hello, this is William Walker. The one with the bath in his living room. Look, it's been three weeks since — '

'Claim number, please, sir?'

'467XP4 – 76565.V3423.128765.98AAF.'

'I'm sorry. Was that a hyphen or a dash?'

'What?'

'After the first six digits?'

'Do you not think it might be sensible to have shorter claim numbers?'

'I'm sorry, sir?'

'I mean, I've called every day this week and each time I call I have to read out this whole number. With all these letters and you lot — '

'Was it an 'F' at the end or an 'S', sir?'

'I mean, you'd have to have several trillion claims on the go to warrant such a long — '

'Yes, sir, well we are quite busy at the moment. Now, your surname?'

'Walker. Like I said.'

'And can you spell that, sir?'

They reckon the builders will come on

Monday. Almost certainly. Which means I have achieved something. On four hours of broken sleep, I have achieved something with my terrible Friday. Anastasia has been to Italy and achieved an exclusive interview and photoshoot with George Clooney. In the same time, I have been to the pub, drunk four whole pints, got through another night as a parent and got an almost definite time frame off the insurance company. There is no question who deserves the greater credit.

(Me.)

Saturday 20 April

Five days until Isabel's birthday, and it's a big one. I never really got her anything very special for the whole giving-birth thing, a fact which looks all the bleaker when you consider that Caroline's husband managed to attend the birth without fainting *and* to hand her some 'beautiful, absolutely beautiful' diamond earrings before she had even regained feeling in her legs.

The problem is that I've already left it too late to order anything on Amazon. And Amazon isn't really going to cut it, anyway. And earrings just seem like copying now. And Isabel has told me not to be extravagant because we're a one-income family now — and a homeless one at that. The time for extravagant gestures has passed.

Of course I can disregard the non-extravagant thing. I know she's lying because women always

123

lie when they're talking about birthday presents. 'Don't spend anything on me. We haven't got the money' means 'I will be very upset if you think you can get away with an M&S silk scarf'. I know this because, two years ago, I tried to get away with an M&S silk scarf. It's the thought that counts and apparently I hadn't. And last year, due to circumstances beyond my control, namely Isabel (temporarily) leaving me for a life of dry-stone-wall-repairing in the Welsh hills, I forgot altogether.

So this year, it has to be special.

And I have only an hour to sneak out on the pretence of going to the house to check that nothing else has fallen down. Except I don't have an hour because when I get into the car, I have to get out again because it smells of dead bodies, whatever they smell of.

'Our car smells disgusting. Come and have a smell.'

She has a smell. 'Blimey.'

'Did it smell like this the last time you used it?' I ask.

'I haven't used it since the flood. The car seat fits better in Mum's car.'

'Maybe a bird has died in the engine?'

There is no bird in the engine, but there is a plastic bag underneath my coat in the boot. Inside the plastic bag are the ingredients of the fish chowder I was going to make back when everything in my life was going relatively well. The juice from the rotten fish has leaked through the carpet and into the spare-wheel compartment. There is dead fish juice everywhere.

'I can't believe you didn't use the car.'

'I can't believe you didn't unload the car.'

'I can't believe you didn't tell me you were using your mother's car.'

'I can't believe you've destroyed the car as well as the house.'

So I spend the hour getting the car emergency-valeted instead of buying Isabel her really important don't-spend-a-lot-but-do-really-thank-you-for-having-my-baby-plus-thirtieth-birthday present.

Sunday 21 April

The car now smells of wet dogs and dead bodies. Unable to use it. Not allowed to borrow mother-in-law's car. Walk to the local shopping parade, which offers a selection of kitchen tiles, investment opportunities in Cyprus, local lamb and second-hand items from which all proceeds go to the World Wildlife Fund. What with all we're doing for barn owls and bumblebees, we can leave it to other people to worry about the pandas. I also think I'll have to leave the present-buying until tomorrow, which is fine. As long as I keep calm and don't panic-purchase like it's Christmas Eve, I'll be fine.

Monday 22 April

Kick-boxing Ingrid explains that we have to work twice as hard today because we had last week off. Brenda takes this as an opportunity to start hitting me in the face again. So when Ingrid

125

isn't looking, I punch Brenda in the stomach. Except, because she's so short, I accidentally hit her in the breasts. She falls to the floor squeaking, 'He hit me in the breasts. He hit me in the breasts,' and all the other women stop, fold their arms and nod approvingly while Ingrid reprimands me.

As soon as everyone has returned to their girly hitting, Brenda roundhouses me in the privates as hard as her little legs will allow. Which is quite hard. I fall to the floor shouting, 'She kicked me in the balls! She kicked me in the balls!' No one stops.

I am in too much pain to go shopping for Isabel's birthday present. Besides, she doesn't deserve one because she is a woman and all women are horrible.

'I can't believe you punched a woman in the breasts,' is all Isabel can say by way of support. 'Do you have any idea how painful that is?'

'Not as painful as being kicked in the balls,' I reply, wearily. 'And I was trying to hit her in the stomach.'

'Maybe you should give up kick boxing. I'm not sure it's bringing out the best in you.'

'I can't. I've paid for the whole course. I won't let them win. Did the builders call?'

'No.'

Tuesday 23 April

Car now smells of dead dogs and wet fish. Before I can phone the valet company to ask them how long it normally takes for the smell to go away, the builder calls. Says he's round the house. Any chance I can come over and let him in?

'But I've got to go to work. I thought you were going to call to make an appointment.'

'Yeah, sorry. I didn't think I'd make it today but I had a window.'

'You were supposed to come three weeks ago.'

'Yep, and you weren't s'posed to leave the tap on, Captain Impractical.'

'You saw the show?'

''Course. Made a bit of a job of your bath-room, didn't they? Even before you ruined it.'

'Yes, well — '

'Look, mate, can you come round or not?'

'Yes.'

There is so much tutting and muttering and teeth-sucking as he picks his way through the wreckage of our former house that I'm hardly surprised when he says, 'Four months.'

Isabel, on the other hand, does not have the benefit of the tutting to pre-warn her. 'How long till we can move back in?' she asks before I have even stepped through the door.

'Four — '

'Four weeks?! Oh my God.' Jacob, until then calmly having breakfast on Isabel's breast, is so surprised that he wheels his head around to see what's going on. Isabel's nipple stretches with him before pinging back like nipple-shaped calamari. 'Ow,' she says.

And then I say, 'No, four months.' And she says 'ow' again.

Anastasia, who has given herself twenty pages for the George Clooney feature, even though it is, as usual, about Italian lakes, Darfur and taking on the military-industrial complex, is unhappy that I'm forty-five minutes late. I tell her that's her problem. She says, 'We'll see about that.' I say, 'Ohhh, scary,' and she storms off. I still can't get used to the fact that she is the Editor. My boss. And that she can see about things if she wants to.

Wednesday 24 April

Late again because Isabel and I were arguing about where we should rent with the pittance the insurance company will give us for 'emergency shelter'. If we stay where we are, we can only afford a tiny bungalow and I hate bungalows. Isabel is all for moving half an hour further out of London to some remote village where we'd get a whole family house for our money. I think we should temporarily cut our losses and move back to London. The only thing we agree on is that we can't possibly spend the next four months at Isabel's parents' house.

'You can come and stay in our house,' says my mum, thoughtfully. 'Your father can give you his room. He can sleep on the sofa. It will be just like the old days.'

So now I have to find a new place to live, almost certainly a new fish-free car and, by tomorrow morning, a birthday-cum-birth present for Isabel. And it's now 6 p.m. and the posh little jewellery shops have shut and I'm already down to department stores, super-markets and petrol stations. If I lose department stores, I am in real trouble.

So I'm in Liberty, where handbags cost £600 and the clothes are all far too weird and fashiony and machine unwashable and not at all designed for people who might have babies throwing up on them every five minutes. And also all cost £600. And why is the temperature in here so high? It's spring now. Can't they adjust the thermostat so you don't have to sweat while you panic-shop? And I'm getting texts from Isabel asking how late I'm going to be because her mother is teaching her how to dress Jacob properly because apparently she's been doing it all wrong and if I don't get home soon there will be blood.

And now it's half six. I have an incredibly boring floral birthday book.

So now it's 6.50 p.m. In ten minutes, it's supermarkets and petrol stations. I need to make a decision. Do I stay in Liberty or make a break for John Lewis?

John Lewis. Not as posh. Potential for good thoughtful present. Some cutlery or something.

And now I'm running.

And getting snagged in a Japanese guided tour.

And knocking over the entire *Evening Standard* kiosk.

And apologising.

And helping the woman at the kiosk back up again.

And crossing between two buses. Then getting trapped on an island in the middle of the street.

Finally, I'm there. And the security guard says, 'No.' I am finished.

For a long time, I sit on a bench, head in hands, miserable. I've done it again. I've screwed up her birthday present. And this time, it's her thirtieth. The woman has chosen not only to spend the rest of her life with me but also to have a child with me. A beautiful child. And she is a perfect, dedicated mother, raising our perfect though high-maintenance baby with patience and devotion.

How do I repay her? I destroy the house. I destroy the car. I force us to move around the country like refugees. And, to cap it all, I get her a present from the late-night Tesco Metro.

This is not good enough.

It won't do.

I won't let this happen.

And then I have an idea. All I need is a notebook, preferably not too big, ideally with nice thick paper. Like Jason Bourne, I leap into action. The WHSmith at the station will still be open. It will sell notebooks. If I jump on that bus, it will take me to the station. And there's no way the CIA will be able to follow me. Sort of thing.

The plan goes perfectly. Notebook acquired, I sit down on the train and begin writing. This is the hard part. I get home. I apologise for being late. I then wait impatiently for everyone to go to bed before I creep downstairs and start writing again. It takes all night, during which time I can't help thinking that a pair of diamond ear-rings would have been much easier. But, anyway . . .

Thursday 25 April

7 a.m. A lie-in (thank God, given that I only got to sleep at five). Birthday breakfast. A very frumpy nightdress from her mother. A book on Japanese art from her father. And from me, a notebook explaining why I am the luckiest man alive to have Isabel. And a note to meet me at 6 p.m. at our house. Yes, the wrecked one. Her parents will look after Jacob.

I get into terrible trouble leaving work early. I would have been in a lot more trouble had Anastasia noticed that I'd spent all day on the phone to estate agents. Too bad. My marriage and my family are more important than work.

When Isabel walks in, I've laid out a picnic rug in the flood-ravaged dining room. If it wasn't for the strong smell of damp, the candles would have given the place an almost romantic feel. I haven't even started opening the champagne and she's already hugging me.

'That was the most beautiful present I've ever had. I mean, it was quite long, and rambling in parts. But I haven't had a proper love letter for ages.'

'Well, I meant it, darling.'

And we kiss. And then I ask her what other proper love letters she's had.

'Don't spoil it.'

'No, you're right. Anyway, what I also want to

131

say is sorry. Sorry for doing this to our house. But I think this might make things a little easier while we wait for it to get fixed.' And with a flourish, I hand her the photograph of our new (temporary) home.

I had decided to take matters into my own hands. I had rented a cottage in a village even further down the railway line from metropolitan civilisation. There would be green fields and stables and orchards and crappy little village stores that don't sell Marmite because it's too modern. And we would live the rural life people always talk about but never go for. And Isabel, a country girl at heart, would be happy. And so would I.

'Blimey,' says Isabel. 'It looks great. When did you go and see it?'

'I haven't yet. But the estate agent assures me it's fine. And another couple were interested. And it's the only house in a ten-mile radius available for short-term rental and — '

Isabel's mobile rings. It's her mum; she thinks Jacob's teething. So we scoff the beautiful picnic I had bought at great expense from a can-they-really-charge-£8-for-a-smoked-salmon-sandwich-and-keep-a-straight-face deli and rush back.

Saturday 27 April

The euphoria of my sensitive, loving, atypical approach to Isabel's birthday has continued, unabated, into the weekend. Neither the news that Alex got her a diamond bracelet (shouldn't he be getting one for Geoff these days?) nor the revelation that 110,000 people have now viewed a super-slow-motion YouTube spin-off clip of me as Captain Impractical can dampen my spirits.

We go to see the rental house and it is lovely. Yes, there is a mobile-phone mast at the end of the very small garden, which nobody saw fit to mention. Yes, that quiet country lane is actually a racetrack. And yes, it's not half an hour from our old house — it's more like forty-five minutes. But it's only temporary. And it's a house. And the bathroom is already on the ground floor, so the amount of damage I can do by leaving the (non-dildo) taps on is limited.

Sunday 28 April

Not even the pain in my neck caused by lugging all our junk over to the rented house can dent my happiness. This is the first breakfast we have had as a family unit without in-laws for a month. So what if the dishwasher doesn't work? So what if the bed in the spare room is springy? It's better than the floor. And so what if the local pub seemed quite unfriendly when we went in for a celebratory new-house drink? They'll get to know us.

Monday 29 April

So what if it now takes nearly an hour and a half to get to work? My family is happy. Isabel has already made her first friend. Another mother with a baby the same age as Jacob. They're going to have coffee on Wednesday. And she may even be invited into the woman's baby group. As long as she's happy, I'm happy.

So what if kick-boxing Brenda called me a loser under her breath when Ingrid wasn't looking?

'What did you say?'

'Nothing, fat boy. Let's box. Or are you frightened?'

And she did a quick one-two to my midriff before I had even put my mouth guard in.

Ingrid barked at us to pick up the pace. 'Nice and easy, Brenda. Remember, this isn't *Rocky IV*. And William isn't Ivan Drogo. Hahahaha.' Maybe it was because I had an extra spring in my step. Maybe I'd had enough of all this chippiness. Whatever it was, something snapped. And for once, it wasn't my nose.

The swing I took was perhaps a little too hard, perhaps a little too high and perhaps a little too soon after Ingrid blew her whistle. I caught Brenda square on the nose and she went down. There was no referee counting to ten. Just Ingrid asking for everyone to give Brenda space. And for someone to call a doctor.

I don't think I'll be going to kick boxing again for a while.

And I don't think I'll mention this to Isabel.

Tuesday 30 April

Still, no point crying over spilled midgets. The builders have started work already. We're going

134

to look at a new car at the weekend. Anastasia is out of the office on a long weekend. And it is our second wedding anniversary. Not only have I managed to hold down a marriage for two whole years, but I remembered that I have.

Breakfast in bed for my wife of two years. With freshly plucked spring flowers and a croissant and everything. Not a fresh croissant, obviously — everything in this village is six months past its sell-by date because, even though it's only an hour and a bit from London, it pretends it's as remote as Svalbard. Isabel likes this. I find it wilfully backward, but it won't annoy me. Not today, not when everything is going right for once.

Except it isn't. When we pop back to the village pub for a seriously-how-many-Brownie-points-does-one-married-man-need drink, I notice the one person in the world I wouldn't want to see in my new village pub on my wedding anniversary. Apart from Alex. Or Saskia. Or Anastasia. Or anyone who works for the insurance company.

There in the corner, nursing a white-wine spritzer and a very shiny black eye, her ginger, spiky hair tied spikily back, her nasal voice rising above the general murmur, her feet barely touching the ground despite the fact that the chairs in this pub are surprisingly low-slung, is Brenda.

Our eyes meet. She looks surprised, then furious, then away. I think about saying something to her. Something like, 'Blimey, this is an unpleasant coincidence' or 'I'm sorry I hit you, but we were at kick-boxing class' or 'Can I get you another ridiculous drink?' but I don't. I try to ignore her.

'What's up?' says Isabel as Brenda goes to the bar for another drink and a chat with the grumpy publican.

'Nothing,' I reply as the grumpy publican looks at me and then walks over.

'Are you sure?' asks Isabel just before the publican says, 'So you're the man who hit my wife?'

And I say, 'Well, hang on just — '

And he says, 'When she wasn't even looking?'

And I say, 'That's really, honestly not the way — '

And he says, 'Would you mind leaving? She can stay. So can the baby. But you're barred.'

Of all the villages in all of the just-about-commuter-belt, I had to pick the one in which Brenda's husband runs the pub.

MAY

'If nature had arranged that husbands and wives should have children alternatively, there would never be more than three in a family.'

LAURENCE HOUSMAN

Wednesday 1 May

REASONS TO BE HAPPY

1. I have proved myself to be a loving husband and father by rescuing my family from their homeless predicament while at the same time remembering a birthday and an anniversary in quick succession.

2. Jacob is definitely smiling now. When he's not crying or sleeping, he's smiling. And that's for at least a whole minute a day.

REASONS TO BE UNHAPPY

1. 1. The homeless predicament was largely of my making.

2. I have resettled us in a village inhabited by a midget who hates me.

3. Almost half a million people have watched the Captain Impractical YouTube video. I really don't see what's so funny. What has society come to when its main source of entertainment appears to be watching puerile internet video clips?

Isabel is having a good start to her month. Having accepted that I didn't just punch a midget for no reason, she has had her coffee morning with Annabel who, it emerges, is also a hippy who sleeps next to her baby (and is married to a man who, like me, gets to sleep on the floor). Not only that, she uses a sling. And she has never at any point owned a bloody Bugaboo. Normally, these mothers are kept locked up in Brighton but, somehow, Annabel has escaped.

Thursday 2 May

Having completely failed to ascertain that Brenda the kick-boxing midget lurks in my new village before moving to it, I now see her everywhere. I had to miss a train this morning because she was waiting on the platform. This meant I was even later than usual, which elicited yet another ticking off from Anastasia.

The other child at the office, the one who has a whole column of her own simply because she understands how to use Twitter and IM and Facebook, can hardly contain her pleasure at the sight of me being publicly told off like this. It is humiliating. I shouldn't even have to account for myself. I am a journalist. Journalists don't have to keep office hours. They work all the hours, then none of the hours, then some of the hours. They chase stories, follow leads, meet sources in underground car parks in Washington, DC.

'You work for *Life & Times* magazine,' says Johnson in the midget-free pub we escape to for lunch. 'Our last cover story was dinner with George Clooney, not Watergate II.'

'That's only because of Anastasia. We're still proper journalists.'

'No, we aren't. Now calm down and get me another pint.'

Saturday 4 May

I really thought I was ready for this. Isabel's friends had all insisted that she couldn't turn thirty without some sort of girly night out (why not?) and that I could look after Jacob for an evening. That was three weeks ago. Now is the Night She Leaves Us. At least she is going early, and she is driving, and she has promised she will arrive at the restaurant, eat and come straight back. Two and a half hours, tops.

6.25 p.m.: Isabel leaves.

6.25 p.m. and twelve seconds: Jacob starts screaming. I change him. Still screaming. I do bouncing. Still screaming. I take him for a walk around the block. Still screaming. I sit him down and attempt to reason with him. 'It's okay, Mummy has just popped out to see her friends,' I say as calmly as possible. 'Daddy is here and we're going to have a great evening and Mummy will be back before we know it.' Stopped screaming but looking deeply traumatised. It's not that he hasn't been left with me before. It's that he can sense that she's not in the next room.

6.52 p.m.: It feels like she's been gone for hours. It's only been twenty-seven minutes. Not even half an hour yet. He's not hungry. Isabel fed him to within an inch of his life before she left. But every time I put him down, he starts screaming again. He reminds me of the old portable television we had when we lived in London. The only way you could get reception was to stand on one leg, right arm outstretched, with one eye shut. Somehow, the TV knew if you were watching with both eyes and would immediately go grainy. Jacob is the same. If I rock him at precisely thirty-seven rocks per minute, he is happy. But only if we're in an entirely unilluminated room with track four of the Gorillaz' second album playing on loop with no more than two seconds of silence between each playing and only then if the rocking and the music are precisely off-beat and I am humming

140

the lowest note I can with my cheek pressed against his, not too firmly, but not too unfirmly either.

7.21 p.m.: He has gone to sleep. So have my arms and my spine, but I no longer have to rock. All I have to do is put him down on the sofa and the evening is all —

7.22 p.m.: Awake. Getting ready to scream again. Back to dark room, Gorillaz, rocking, humming.

7.31 p.m.: Gone again. Am not going to attempt sofa. That was churlish. Will just prop myself against the fireplace and watch television from there. I can have dinner later, or tomorrow. Only an hour and a half to go.

8.12 p.m.: Think the music from *The Bill* must have upset him. Or maybe he's hungry. He doesn't seem interested in the bottle. 'It's the same stuff that comes out of Mummy's booby, I promise,' I tell him, but this just makes him angry.

8.15 p.m.: Proper screaming again now. Not even the bouncing is working. We're both bored of that. Maybe I should try something different, but it's very, very hard to think straight, what with all the screaming.

8.18 p.m.: I phone Isabel. 'Hi, darling,' I say, as calmly as possible. 'Christ, is everything all right?' she replies because my 'Hi, darling' wasn't very calm at all and she can hear the screaming

141

in the background. 'Yes, fine, I just can't stop him screaming.'

'Have you tried the bottle?'

'Not interested.'

'What about getting him to sleep? Have you tried rocking him?'

'Please stop asking stupid questions.'

'Look, I'm only trying to help.'

'Well, it's not very helpful going out, is it?'

'Thanks, darling. My first evening out in four months and you have to — '

'Sorry, darling. I'm just stressed.'

'It's okay. You're doing fine. Does he need changing?'

'No, of course he . . . of course he does. Yup. Okay, fine. Sorry to disturb. Please don't be too late. I love you. Bye.'

By the time Isabel gets back, Jacob and I are both asleep. Neither of us has eaten. Neither of us is in our correct bedtime clothes. The house is a mess, toys — which he doesn't like, anyway — strewn everywhere. I must never, ever have an argument with Isabel about who works hardest again. Two hours with Jacob is like a month at the office.

She scoops us both up. Jacob smiles at her, as she says, 'My boobs are bursting,' and off they go to bed like it's the easiest thing in the world. I have a whisky, then another, then some Marmite toast, then another whisky and wake up four hours later in the cold light of a television that long ago stopped transmitting anything worth watching.

Sunday 5 May

The woman who runs the village shop, the one that pretends we're as remote as Svalbard even though we're only an hour or so from London, refused to accept my £2 coin as payment for my newspaper on the grounds that it was forged. She said she hadn't seen many £2 coins round here, but this one didn't have any date marks on it. I pointed out that they were around the edge, but she was unwilling to budge. I told her it was illegal to refuse perfectly legal money and she told me to adopt a less confrontational tone or she would bar me, like the pub had done. 'We don't allow violent types round here,' she said, haughtily. I was speechless and paperless all the way home.

Attempting to buy a car was no more successful, mainly because Isabel took a dislike to the salesman at the Skoda garage. I couldn't blame her. You would assume that people turning up to buy a Skoda Estate were likely to be family types, would you not? That they might have a baby in tow? That maybe halfway round the test drive the baby might need a feed? That this might require pulling over in a lay-by for a mere ten minutes or so? Hardly a lot to ask. But oh no, Mr Skoda had to insist that the test drive continue. And so Jacob started screaming. And so Isabel lost the bumper taking a roundabout a little too roundly. And so Mr Skoda shouted at her.

'We'll be taking our business elsewhere,' I said angrily.

'Good,' he replied. 'We don't like violent types around here.'

Before I could ask him what he had meant by that, Isabel had taken me to one side and pointed out that we really needed a car, given that the old one smelled of fish. So I had adjusted my negotiating position.

'No, actually, we'll take it as long as you fix the bumper.'

'No,' he countered.

'Okay, be reasonable.' Sometimes you have to play nice with these sharks.

'Why, will you punch me in the face if I'm not?' That's what he said. And even though the Skoda garage is twelve kilometres from our village, I realised in that second that Brenda's reach was further than one might reasonably expect from a midget.

We bought the Skoda without the bumper. On the way home, Isabel told me not to let Brenda get to me. I should rise above it.

I promised that I would.

Stupid midget.

Monday 6 May

No kick boxing because (a) it is a bank holiday and (b) I was asked not to attend kick boxing any more, anyway. This is fine. I shall invest my energies in other departments. We've had sex just once in nearly five months and that encounter is now referred to as the *Antiques Roadshow* night. It's not good enough. After a lovely afternoon

144

stroll through the countryside, which might have ended with a pint in the pub if I hadn't been banned, I make dinner while Isabel bathes Jacob.

I whisper a sweet nothing in Isabel's ear. Something along the lines of, 'Please can we have sex tonight?' And she whispers back, 'Fine, as long as you've stopped being weird about it.' This makes all the reasons I've been weird about it come flooding back. As does the gurgling noise of Jacob's bathwater vanishing down the plughole. Suddenly, I'm back in the operating theatre. It's hot, airless, too brightly lit. We're all dressed in blue and, from behind the matching blue curtain, all I can hear is a lot of sucking and slurping. Isabel's body moves in time to the noises. Then, there's one last slurp and the beautiful, piercing scream of our wonderful baby boy. Covered in blood.

'William? William? Can you hear me, William?'

'Sorry, darling. Lost my train of thought. What were you saying?'

'I said I'll get Jacob to sleep and meet you in the kitchen in ten minutes.'

'What?'

'Sex, William. Sex. If you want sex, you have to move it.'

I pull myself together and wait, naked, in the kitchen. Eventually, Isabel turns up and she is naked as well. She kisses me. It's like old times, except it's better because it's such a rare thing to have time to ourselves. We kiss more and it's still fine and actually incredibly exciting to be holding my naked wife again, and everything is going to be fine and then . . .

'Did you hear something?'

'No, it's fine. Don't worry.'

'I definitely heard something.'

Jacob has woken up. 'Wait here,' says Isabel, vanishing up the stairs. I have little else to do but stand there in the kitchen, naked and alone. For a while, I contemplate making a cup of tea but abandon it as being too ridiculously English: naked tea-making while awaiting the distant possibility of sex. I'm not ready for that.

After what seems like twenty-five minutes — because it is — Isabel comes back down in a nightdress. We have taken a step backward in our nakedness.

I kiss her.

She kisses me.

Things progress.

The phone rings.

'Leave it.'

'But it's late. Who could it be?'

'Leave it.'

The phone stops ringing.

We kiss again.

I tear off Isabel's nightdress skilfully (i.e. in a rampant enough way to suggest that we are still young, carefree and abandoned to passion but not in so rampant a way as to annoy Isabel by actually damaging an article of her clothing).

The phone rings again.

'Answer it,' I say, because all our family and friends know to call us after 8.30 p.m. only if someone has died or is dying or wants to die. I stand there, again naked, again alone, wondering why people insist on choosing these faux antique

146

kitchen cupboards while Isabel chats to her mum.

Eventually, the conversation ends.

'Was she dying?'

'No. But they're going on holiday. They wanted to say goodbye.'

'Do you want a cup of tea?'

'Yes.'

Mission unaccomplished.

Tuesday 7 May

Anastasia back from another long weekend (helping on an archaeological dig in north-east Colombia because, you know, one can't drop one's hobbies just because one has a demanding job) and has managed to find time to compile a new list of requirements (besides punctuality) for her team. She has now decided we must Twitter and blog and Facebook because we need to reach the next generation. We must work in close proximity with the internet department, because the internet is the future. Johnson reckons this is a way to weed out the old guard like us. I resent being called the 'old guard'. I'm thirty-one. That is not old.

'It is these days, mate.'

Wednesday 8 May

The girl who used to be a workie but is now the teacher's pet is hosting a lunchtime seminar entitled 'How to get a thousand followers on Twitter in one week'. I ask her how many real friends she has. She says she has hundreds. I ask her how many of them are real, real friends. She says hundreds. It's what comes from being a club fixer from the age of fourteen, she explains dismissively. You get to know the difference between real friendship and fake networking friendship. I say, since when has having real friends been the be-all and end-all and attempt to swagger back to my desk, but really I'm annoyed with myself: what is the point in trying to wind up these children we insist on hiring to run the magazine? Why can't I just be my own man?

Thursday 9 May

For the first time in my life, I remember that it's a bank holiday week and that therefore the bin collection would be a day late. Ha! No one else in the village appears to be as organised . . .

The bin men come anyway. They're obviously very well organised. Thanks, rest of village, for not telling me.

Friday 10 May

Today, I blogged. Next week, I may Twitter. How Anastasia thinks this will get more people to read our once-great magazine is beyond me.

Saturday 11 May

At a barbecue at Hippy Annabel's house with the rest of her baby group. This, I start by thinking, is the parenting dream. Late spring sunshine. Large garden. Babies on picnic rugs. Beer. Conversation. But then Teresa, one of the mums, starts explaining how routine is the only way to teach a child how to behave, right from day one. And Isabel can't bite her tongue long enough not to say, 'Yes, these horrible little babies. We mustn't let them get away with any of their nonsense, must we?'

From then on, the group divides into two: hardcore-routine mums on one side, hippies on the other. The dads are left in the no-man's-land, not wanting to get involved but at the same time not wanting to get into trouble with their wives later because of not getting involved.

Then it starts raining. And the babies become cranky. And everyone makes their excuses and leaves.

Sunday 12 May

My parents come over for lunch. The plan was to get Jacob to sleep by driving him around monotonously before they arrived. That way we would give the impression of calm and control. Didn't work. I was still driving around the village aimlessly half an hour after they rang the doorbell, Jacob babbling away happily in the back seat as if to say, 'How nice of Daddy to drive me

149

around the village like he's a chauffeur and I'm Lord Mountbatten. I had better not go to sleep and miss any of the tour.'

When I gave up and brought him home, he proceeded to scream until we treated him like a television aerial, me on one leg (because he cried if I used two), holding him at an angle that he found soporific but I found excruciating. Lunch happened in stages, some people doing the rocking and some people singing the 'The Owl and the Pussycat' in a French accent, because this is the latest thing we have become convinced sends Jacob to sleep.

'Difficult little bugger, isn't he?' said Dad. 'Is he sleeping through yet?'

'They do things differently these days, darling,' said Mum.

And I became more convinced than ever that Isabel was doing the right thing with our high-maintenance insomniac superchild.

Monday 13 May

There she is, on my train again. And in my carriage. Brenda. With her annoying hair in a tight bun, ready, I presume, for the kick-boxing class she got me thrown out of. It's almost like she knows. She knows that it's my train. She knows that I'll have to miss it, catch the next one and get in trouble with my nine-year-old boss who now appears to judge people solely on the basis of their punctuality or lack thereof.

Kick-boxing class, my only local pub, my

150

07.56 to London. Where will I be unable to go next, thanks to Brenda?

Tuesday 14 May

The answer is the village shop. Brenda must be behind this. I went in to complain about some bin liners I had bought.

'These bin liners . . . they tear when you try to open them.'

'Oh, it's you again.'

'Three quid you charge for these, which is approximately three times the price they are in the supermarket.'

'Well, we don't have the same buying power as those — '

'Look, I don't want a sob story about supporting your local shop. All I'm saying is that I *was* supporting my local shop when — '

'By buying one pack of bin bags? Probably because you'd forgotten to get some from the supermarket?'

'I *was* supporting my local shop, paying three times the going rate for these bin bags, and they don't work.'

'Right.'

'So I'd like a refund.'

'Would you?'

'Yes.'

'But you've used half of them.'

'I've used three of them. The other four broke. So if you think about it, I'm paying for a bin bag to put broken bin bags in. Now, can I have a refund?'

'No. And I'd like you to leave. If you don't, I'll call Bob and Brenda.'

'From the pub?'

'From the pub.'

Kick boxing. Pub. Train. Village shop.

Friday 17 May

Anastasia calls me into her office for a chat. The Managing Editor is also present. She would like to put it on record that this is my first official warning. Yes, for being late. Yes, my career has reached a new low where I am judged for being late. I ask for it to be put on record that I have better things to do than to worry about arriving within three minutes of nine o'clock. And besides, things are a bit chaotic at home at the moment.

The Managing Editor and Anastasia give each other knowing looks.

'Need we remind you that the last time you were given formal warnings, you attributed your erratic and at times violent behaviour to difficulties at home? And the Editor then was far more tolerant of that sort of nonsense than I will be.'

'This is all because of that cup of tea, isn't it?'

'Don't be childish.'

'Don't be adultish.'

'How, may I ask, have you reacted to my talk last Tuesday?'

I could have been honest at this point. She really does invite the honest response. But I

152

sense that this is precisely what she wants, so I bite my tongue.

'Last week, I blogged. And yesterday, I Twittered.'

'Tweeted.'

'Sorry?'

'Tweeted. You don't Twitter. You tweet.'

'Oh, for goodness' sake.'

'You need to get the language right if you're going to be a convincing member of the team that takes this magazine into the future.'

I wouldn't even be in here if it weren't for Brenda. Kick boxing. Pub. Train. Village shop. Possibly job.

To a pub I *am* allowed in with Johnson and Andy. It's just like old times, except that I have to be home by 9 p.m. and the girl Andy can't stop banging on about is still Saskia, the Destroyer of Relationships.

'I know you don't want to know, but Sweden was amazing. We could really be ourselves.' He had that starry look in his eyes. Johnson and I know that look well. The Andy Look. It's dangerous, but it normally vanishes after the first few days, right about the time when the plans to emigrate to Sydney, Somalia or, most recently, Switzerland hit obstacles like visas, money or a total language barrier. We have a few days of Andy moping about, occasionally trying to jump off things, and then he meets another girl in another city and we're all fine again. But he's been with Saskia for weeks now. And he still has The Look.

'On one beach, we went for a whole week without wearing clothes. It's only when you're naked that you realise how much we constrain ourselves as human beings. I mean, it wasn't even warm, but we soon got used to it. Just us. The beach. The forests. Our skin. The fresh Scandinavian air.'

I look to Johnson for some support.

'I know you've had your troubles with her, William,' shrugs Johnson. 'But she's pretty amazing. I mean, a whole week without clothes. Ali won't even let me in the bathroom when she's naked any more.'

'Can we stop talking about your nakedness and start talking about my job?'

'You need to get to work on time,' was as helpful as Andy could be.

Sunday 19 May

Out of the kindness of my heart, and because I was awake anyway, I take Jacob out for a walk around the village green so that Isabel can have a lie-in. Teresa-the-non-hippy-mum's husband, Pete, is already out there, strolling around.

'Morning,' I say.

'Morning,' he replies.

Turns out Pete takes their daughter out every Sunday morning from 8 till 10 a.m., weather-dependent. It's part of their routine. For a minute, while he's telling me this, I get the impression that he's trying to say something else. It's like he's mouthing, 'Help, we are being held

154

hostage by my mad wife. Call the police. Tell them she won't let us have dinner when we want it.' Then, as if he thinks he's given away too much, his expression changes. He has to get back or he'll be late for the second feed. We say goodbye, he scurries off and I'm left to contemplate whether I can face buying the newspaper from the village shop.

I can't.

Monday 20 May

Isabel wants to go on holiday. With a baby. Again. She appears to have forgotten the horror of Devon, as well as the fact that she believes the best way to raise children is to let them flourish at home rather than whisk them off to places only the parents could benefit from.

'Have you forgotten the horror of Devon?'

'Oh come on, it wasn't that bad.'

'I nearly went to prison. There was a hurricane. We went two days late. We left a day early. There was a barn owl. It was the worst five days of my life.'

'Well, let's go somewhere Mediterranean. The weather will be better and they're more child-friendly in Italy. We won't be treated like lepers. We may even be able to go to a restaurant with Jacob.'

The prospect of eating out was indeed a tempting one. We had done that only once this year and had spent the whole meal staring hysterically at the mobile phone. A proper Italian restaurant with wine and prosciutto and bread baskets and maybe some dipping oil would be just the ticket. And Isabel was right — the Italians love children. In *The Godfather*, when they weren't killing each other, wasn't it all about family? We would be welcomed with open arms. 'Ahh, *bambino*!' they would cry before giving us the best table in the house. The trouble is, we had to actually get to Italy first.

'I'm not driving all the way to Italy.'

'No, we'll fly.'

At this, I nearly swallowed my tongue in astonishment. 'What, in a plane, with two hundred other people, all tutting?'

'Look, it's only a couple of hours. Jacob will be fine. I need a holiday. You need a holiday. It will do us the world of good.'

Wednesday 22 May

She's booked it. Barely a second after I managed to convince Anastasia that I was due a whole fortnight off. A small villa in the hills above Lucca, leaving barely two weeks in which to train Jacob not to scream. I insist on British Airways flights, because the one thing I know intuitively is that Ryanair is no place for a new family.

Both Annabel and Teresa think it's a brilliant idea, which must be the first time they've ever agreed on anything.

Both their husbands think it's a terrible idea, because the one thing you can say about all new dads is that they quickly develop a very effective survival instinct. It's as effective as a baby's gag reflex. And it's universal.

THINGS NEW DADS INSTINCTIVELY LEARN WITHIN WEEKS OF CHILDBIRTH

1. Know your limits. Yes, you can change nappies. No, you can't put on babygros.

2. Working late is sometimes preferable to going home for bath time.

3. Sex is less important than sleep.

4. Never fly anywhere if your children are under the age of five, not even if your exhausted wife says she really, really needs a holiday.

'It will be fine, darling,' she says. Which is what she said about the home birth.

Saturday 25 May

We're okay. Isabel and I are okay. In the sex department. We have successfully copulated. Jacob fell asleep on the way back from lunch and a post-holiday slide show at Isabel's parents. Frankly, who could blame him? We left him in the car with the windows half down because we have now been parents long enough to know that sometimes treating children like dogs is the only way.

I did not feel the need to hum the *Antiques*

Roadshow theme tune. And I only had to run out to the car naked twice when Isabel mistook first a seagull and second a slight breeze for the screaming of an almost five-month-old.

Nobody saw.

Mission accomplished.

Monday 27 May

Actually caught myself whistling on the way to work. Tweeting, you might call it, but in the good old-fashioned way.

Wednesday 29 May

Tweeting well and truly over for three reasons.

1. Jacob has got yet another cold. The only way he can sleep is vertically. This involves much standing around in the middle of the night.

2. Was asked by a rival magazine if I could be interviewed about what it feels like to be the subject of a one-million-plus YouTube video hit. I declined. Journalists must never become the story.

3. Geoff, who has come over for dinner with Alex and been rude about our rented house even though it's his fault we're in it, thinks I should be grateful for becoming a YouTube sensation. He would kill for that kind of

158

publicity. Have to restrain myself from grabbing the steak knife and stabbing him a hundred times. And how come we're having steak? And how come Jacob has gone to sleep early when they're here? Treacherous child.

Thursday 30 May

He'd definitely started rolling, though. I left him on his front this morning while I nipped to the kitchen to make coffee. Came back and he was on his back, like butter wouldn't melt. It happened two days ago as well, but I hadn't been 100 per cent sure then, what with his cold and my sleep deprivation. This time, there was no denying it. My child, four months and twenty-nine days old, has mastered the art of rolling.

In comparison to the rest of the animal world, it's pathetic, I know. I'm pretty sure monkeys don't take this long. Even sheep are more advanced. But in comparison to Teresa's child, who has shown no signs of rolling whatsoever, Jacob is streets ahead.

'Children all learn at their own pace,' said Isabel by way of spoiling my good mood. 'It's not a competition.'

It is a competition.

Friday 31 May

He did it again. Always with me, first thing in the morning. But always when I'm out of the room.

It's like crop circles. All I need is visual confirmation before we can write to the Guinness World Record people with news that we have the most intelligent child on the planet. It will happen this weekend, I know it, I think to myself, setting off nice and early for work, old-fashioned tweeting again.

And, as if God knows this is not the sort of tweeting that is expected of me, he immediately begins to ruin my day.

1. First, the postman hands me a letter at the end of our drive with a tut, a clearly audible tut.

2. Second, I open the letter, which has no stamp on it, to find that it is an official correspondence from the parish council.

> 'Dear Mr Walker,' it begins officiously. 'It has been brought to our attention that you have been cavorting around your front garden not only naked, which would be disturbing enough, but also in a clearly 'excited' manner. While this sort of thing may be commonplace in your permanent place of residence, can we kindly request that you restrain yourself while staying in ours? If this sort of behaviour continues, we will refer the matter to the local constabulary.'

3. Thirdly, the letter's masthead lists Bob the publican as chairman, Brenda as treasurer,

the village shop con-artist as secretary and the bloody postman as the, well, postman.

4. Fourthly, I am so shocked by this letter, I have to show Isabel.

5. Fifthly, she thinks it is hilarious. It takes her so long to stop laughing, I miss the early train.

6. Sixthly, Brenda is on the not-early train and rather than confront her unprepared, I chicken out and get on another carriage, one which never has any spare seats.

7. Seventhly, the builder phones while I'm on the not-remotely-early train. I tell him I can't talk because I'm on the train. He says that's okay, he just wanted to warn me that August (despite still being three months away) is not looking feasible in terms of repairing the house.

8. Eighthly, another letter is waiting for me on my desk when I finally get to work. It is a written warning. Anastasia, the small-minded, little-pictured boss from hell will have me out within the month.

JUNE

'Men forget everything; women remember everything. That's why men need instant replays in sports.'

RITA RUDNER

Saturday 1 June

REASONS TO BE CHEERFUL

1. We're going on holiday next Saturday.

REASONS TO BE MISERABLE

1. Isabel will never be able to hear the phrase 'public display of affection' without giggling.

2. Job. House. Neighbours.

3. I think my hair's falling out.

4. We're going on holiday next Saturday.

Sunday 2 June

Refuse to leave house on account of cabal that runs village turning against me. Witness Brenda taking her whippet for a walk across the village green, watching it take an enormous dump right by the children's swings, looking around to ensure no one is looking and wandering off without clearing it up. And *I* get a letter for being naked.

Monday 3 June

Now have to hide when postman delivers. Thinking of reporting him to the Royal Mail. Sure you're not allowed to do non-postal deliveries at the same time as postal ones. Isabel insistent that I shouldn't take village politics so seriously. And we're only here for another three months, anyway. I haven't told her that the builder is pessimistic about that. Or that the reason the children's swings are covered in dog poo is because of the woman she's telling me not to get wound up about. No point in both of us having a terrible start to the week.

Wednesday 5 June

Saw Teresa's husband Pete looking haunted on the train home. We start chatting. I ask him if he knows Bob the publican. He doesn't, but

he was told by Teresa who was told by
the shopkeeper who was told by the barmaid
that he has a hell of a temper on him. Used
to be a policeman. Worked his way up
through the ranks. Knows how to get things
done. Not an easy person if things don't go
his way.

I'm actually glad we're going on holiday. We
can let this whole naked thing die down.

'Yes, we can let it droop,' says Isabel because
she still can't stop finding it hilarious.

Friday 7 June

All week I've been interneting. All week I've
tried to be punctual. All week I've tried to
stay positive. Then, just as I'm leaving, I
discover that the girl who was on work
experience and who now has an increasingly
popular techie column has written one about
a guy in the office with only twenty-six
Facebook friends.

How is it possible to be so undermined
by someone I care so little about with
something I so couldn't give a toss about? I
leave on a low note, get rained on all the way
home, tread in some yellow dog poo thirty
metres from my doorstep and get home to
find that Isabel hasn't started packing yet.
Stupidly, I say, 'Haven't you started packing
yet?'

THINGS YOU SHOULD NEVER SAY TO YOUR WIFE WHEN YOU GET BACK FROM WORK IF SHE'S BEEN LOOKING AFTER THE BABY ALL DAY

1. 'Haven't you started packing yet?'

2. 'Haven't you started dinner yet?'

3. 'Why is our child not in bed yet?'

4. 'Why is there toilet paper all over the living room?'

5. 'I've had a really bad day.'

It takes at least fifteen minutes for Isabel to explain, at extremely high pitch and volume, why she hasn't started packing yet, during which time I notice she is (a) covered in baby sick, (b) very, very tired and (c) at the end of her tether.

It takes another fifteen minutes for me to apologise enough for her to stop loading the dishwasher like she's chopping wood. And another fifteen minutes of foot-rubbing once Jacob has gone to sleep before she starts to talk to me again.

Note to self: a whole day of baby sick trumps five minutes of dog poo.

Saturday 8 June

Let us never discuss that flight again. Let us never mention the tears, the screaming, the sweat, the

165

red-faced man in front who put his seat back even though we're only flying to bloody Italy. Let us never discuss what happened with that nappy, that toilet and that queue of people. Let us banish for ever memories of the hire-car baby seat, of finding a way out of the airport without driving across actual fields, of the number of times we nearly died in head-on collisions that would definitely not have been our fault. I mean, why do Italians have to drive like that? But, no. Let us move on. We are here. We are in Tuscany. None of the locals are called Brenda. There's a bottle of rosé in the fridge. We have a terrace overlooking vineyards and the only sound you can hear is of a smug English family congratulating themselves on picking the perfect little villa.

Sunday 9 June

Breakfast on terrace. Conversation. Stroll. Lunch (ham, cheese, olives). Snooze. Stroll. Gin and tonic. Pasta. Wine. Bed at half nine.

Monday 10 June

Breakfast on terrace. Stroll. Conversation. Lunch (ham, cheese, sundried tomatoes). Stroll. Snooze. Gin and tonic. Pasta. Bed at half eight.

Tuesday 11 June

Breakfast on terrace. Snooze. Stroll. Snooze. Lunch (ham, cheese). Snooze. Pasta. Bed at half seven.

Wednesday 12 June

I think we could sleep all day today if we wanted. The three of us could lie under the thin sheets, sunlight sneaking in through the bedroom's open shutters to warm us, and nothing would stop our luxurious slumber. Except, perhaps, the thought of another perfect late breakfast on the terrace.

Thursday 13 June

These are the natural rhythms of a young family. Life without the intrusions of the office. The most complicated thing I have to do is get ham and mozzarella from the deli. Isabel nests with Jacob. I return from my low-stress adventure and we transport wine, wine glasses, plates and simple lunch ingredients out to the table. We then lounge and chat and drift in and out of consciousness. Jacob has never been so smiley. Isabel is not looking exhausted for the first time in a year. And this is the happiest I have ever been. If I am never this happy again, it won't matter.

Friday 14 June

Breakfast. Sleep. Etc.

Saturday 15 June

'Don't you think we should check out the local town or something?' says Isabel.

'No,' I say. But this is the beginning of the end of our paradise, I know it.

Sunday 16 June

'We could just drive there this morning. After breakfast.'

'No.'

'How about lunch out? If I have to slice another mozzarella ball, I think I'll go mad.'

And so we settle on a walk to the next hamlet for lunch. At the trattoria, we hand Jacob in at the entrance like he's a handbag and this is a trendy nightclub. He vanishes in a hail of kisses and hugs and 'Ahhh, *bambinos*', while we are treated to a nine-course feast. Paradise continues.

'You think we should check if he's okay?'

'No, he'll be fine. Leave him.' I love the fact that Isabel is one of those mothers who can let her child out of her sight for more than a second without becoming hysterical. While I've spent every minute of every day of this holiday trying to anticipate and prevent the horrible ways in

168

which our precious son might kill himself (knocking head on pointy villa step, grabbing and eating killer mountain mushroom, learning to walk three months ahead of schedule at the precise moment we leave him on the edge of the highest bit of terrace above the sharpest bit of rockery), she lets him be.

He re-emerges with our espressos, smothered in mama's pinkest lipstick and neither scalded nor sold into the white slave trade.

We walk back through the vineyards, mission accomplished, itchy feet itched. And then Isabel starts throwing up.

Monday 17 June

According to Isabel's mother, whom I phone in a panic, you can't pass food poisoning through a boob. Aren't women's bodies clever? This means that Jacob can still feed. The rest of the time, he is my problem. And suddenly our holiday changes from pure idyll to something even Sisyphus would have found unbearably repetitive. I push Jacob up the hill in the buggy. The buggy rolls down. I push it up again. As the sun comes up, this task becomes more and more onerous. The angle at which I push becomes flatter and flatter, the pace slower and slower.

Must. Keep. Going.

Must. Stay. Out. Of. House.

Must. Let. Isabel. Sleep.

169

Tuesday 18 June

While Isabel lies prone in bed, trying not to think about whether it was the wild boar pâté, the fungi pasta or the smoked salami, I continue full parenting duties. It is mundane, repetitive, tedious, dull, fruitless, and by lunchtime I catch myself marvelling at how anyone could do this full time. But after lunch, something changes. Jacob starts to smile at me more frequently. Almost as frequently as he smiles at Isabel.

I feed him some fruit purée. He smiles.

I tell him a story about a midget who lives in a pub. He laughs. Pretty much at the punch line, where the midget gets run over by a post van. Then we go for another Sisyphean stroll and he starts babbling. We stop on the top of the hill. I lift him out of the buggy and he says, 'Dada.' Clear as day. 'Dada.' Then he says, 'Dadadadadadadadadadadada.' Which is less impressive, but all the same I think we can safely say Jacob's first word was 'Daddy'. Ish.

Isabel is asleep and I don't dare wake her. I just sit on the terrace next to my favourite bug of a baby, no longer wondering how anyone could do this full time. Maybe when Isabel's maternity leave comes to an end, I can resign and become a stay-at-home dad. It can't be much worse than being a stay-in-Tuscany one.

Wednesday 19 June

Except, you know, how long does it take to recover from a little local food poisoning? Two hours, I slept. Two. Jacob wanted to play between the hours of two and four. Isabel needed her brow mopping between the hours of four and six. Jacob was up again at six and so on. It's good to be needed. It's even better to be useful. But, you know, I'm not Margaret bloody Thatcher. Anyone who can survive on less than seven hours' sleep a night is clearly not human.

Thursday 20 June

She's ready to eat again but doesn't want anything containing pasta, ham, pizza, tomatoes, basil, mozzarella or olives. I have to drive for miles and miles to find a shop that sells porridge and Nutella. By the time I get back, some months later, she is better. Thank the Lord.

Saturday 22 June

Isabel has sworn that she will handle any in-flight nappies on the return journey. Irritatingly, Jacob doesn't so much as wee. He is now an accomplished international traveller and we take great pleasure in tutting at the family in front of us whose unaccomplished baby screams all the way back to Britain. Tut tut.

Sunday 23 June

Massive post-holiday blues. Despite that first wonderful piece of Marmite toast, the familiar settle of the poorly sprung sofa, the middle-aged excitement of going through the post, there is no ignoring the fact that all is not well. We are back in the village that behaves like it's in deepest Devon when it's only an hour from London, and the moment I step out for a late-morning walk with Jacob, I feel its hostility. I get a shrug from the shopkeeper. I get blanked by the postman. Bob, who is wiping tables in the pub garden, looks furious. He hasn't even seen me so his ire must be directed at some other innocent soul. Or perhaps that's just his normal face. Such an unpleasant way to conduct yourself. And so unreasonable to ban me from the only pub in the village, particularly now the sunshine is out and I could do with a cheeky pre-lunch half.

Annoyed, I turn and head for home. As I do, I sense that Bob has stopped wiping the tables. I look back. His expression has changed from anger to malevolent pleasure. He is clearly delighted that he can subvert an Englishman's God-given right to drink beer in the sunshine.

'We're going to another pub in another village,' I tell Isabel the moment I get back home.

'But I have to put another wash on.'

'Please.'

'Okay.'

The policeman was standing by his car in the lay-by on the outskirts of our village as we

172

headed back home but the minute he saw our perfectly harmless, law-abiding Skoda, he gestured for me to pull over. For a minute, I thought he was the postman, but as he strolled over to my window, it became clear that he had a slightly bigger nose.

'Step out of the vehicle, sir.'

'Is there a prob — '

'Your driver's licence please, sir.'

'I know I wasn't speeding. My wife won't let — '

'I have reason to believe you are driving under the influence of drink or drugs.'

'Drugs? What are you talking — '

'I can smell alcohol on your breath.'

'I had half a pint.'

'Stella, was it, sir?'

'No, it was IPA.'

'Kindly breathe into this, sir.'

'I can't believe this. On what grounds did you pull me over? Were you waiting for me?'

'Are you refusing to take the test, sir? If you are, then we will have to go to the station.'

The result, of course, was negative.

'Are you, by any chance, related to a postman?' I asked, once the policeman had had a good snoop around the car and made a sarky comment about the fact that we had no bumper.

'None of your business. Now, on your way, sir. And watch that drink-driving. We don't want any accidents, do we? Not with a little baby in the back.'

Monday 24 June

None of this would matter if I had an excellent job to escape to, but I don't. It appears I no longer even have an excellent desk.

'Why are you sitting at my desk?' I say to the girl who used to be a work experience but got overpromoted by the girl who also used to be work experience who herself got overpromoted just because her dad knows Bill Clinton. 'I can't believe the workie is sitting at my desk.'

'I do have a name, you know. It's Evangeline and, as you know, I'm not a workie any more. Anastasia had another little desk reshuffle while you were away. You're over there. Hope that's okay.' She points to the deepest, darkest, most windowless corner of the office.

I won't let her win, even if she does have a name. With impressive self-control, I walk over to the deepest, darkest, most windowless corner of the office and start work. Or rather, I start blogging and tweeting and Facebooking, because apparently that is now what constitutes work.

'I don't know why I'm here any more,' I tell Johnson in the pub at lunch.

'You're like a mayfly. You have fulfilled your reproductive obligations. You have outlived your usefulness to your species. You now have no reason to exist. There is nothing but decline and death to look forward to unless you decide to reproduce again, but that's environmentally unfriendly so I doubt Isabel will go for that. Nope, that's the end for you, sonny. Just be glad you aren't a spider. Spiders have an even rougher

174

time than men. They have sex. They get eaten. If I were them, I'd refuse to have sex in the first place. Don't give away your one bargaining chip, spider. At the very least, make not being eaten a prerequisite of hanky-panky.'

'I meant about my job. *Our* jobs. Since when does everything have to be all internetish and cyberish and blogospherish?'

'I've got nearly seven hundred followers on Twitter.'

'You, too. They've got you, too.'

'You want to play *Who Wants to Be a Millionaire?*' asks Johnson. 'I almost won a pound while you were away.'

Tuesday 25 June

Johnson might be able to take all this lightly, but he's not thinking it through. This is Anastasia's revolution. She's sidelining all the people with sensible names and replacing us with Evangelines. All I have done is turn up late a couple of times in the last few months. The rest of the time, I have been as cooperative and productive as possible. And how am I rewarded? With a removal of window perks. Just in time for summer.

Wednesday 26 June

Evangeline is basking in the sun she gets from *my* window. But I have had this morning's last laugh. I have written a blog, which is to say I have typed something and it has gone on the internet. And people are reading it. It is the ninth most popular post on the *Life & Times* website. And I've been ever so slightly clever: my first blog is about how much better life was before the internet. I'll go along with the Anastasia revolution, but I'll do it in a way that shows how ridiculous it is.

Thursday 27 June

My blog is the sixth most popular post on our website. I am the future. I am technoman. I write a second blog about how virtual popularity is inversely proportional to real popularity and immediately get comments about how much people agree. Anyone can do this whole internet lark, but how many can do it ironically?

Evangeline looks a bit hot and bothered in the suntrap that is my desk. She has competition.

Anastasia looks miffed when she walks out of the office. The old dog has learned to blog — and our readers seem to be liking it. Ha ha ha!

Friday 28 June

I get to work and Evangeline has brought in three new workies called Octavia, Cordellia and Maybelline. And because there are no spare desks, they are all sitting right next to my desk typing things into their iPhones. I don't see why I must have these children tapping away next to me, but Evangeline says she needs the space to test a new virtual computer. The next thing I know, she is dressed in a silver cat suit and is doing what looks like Tai Chi. So are the three workies. And they're all floating around my desk, laughing and moving holograms around. Then I look at my hands and they're made entirely of wires and microchips. Then I wake up in bed at home, face down with my arms crossed.

As I wait for the feeling to come back into my arms, I notice that it is 9.30 a.m. and I am still in bed. Well not bed-bed. Camp-bed-bed. Now I remember the last thing that happened before the aliens attacked . . . Jacob was crying and Isabel ordered me into the spare room. 'There's no point both of us being awake and you have to work in the morning,' she had said. Half asleep, I had dragged myself to the spare room, got comfortable in the camp bed, thought to myself that I absolutely mustn't fall asleep before setting the alarm, then fell asleep without setting the alarm.

Nine minutes after I have regained feeling in my arms, I am at the station, unbreakfasted, unshaven, untoileted, mildly hysterical.

Thirty-nine minutes after that, I am still at the station because apparently there's hardly any need for off-peak trains from this stupid village.

Some time after eleven, I get to the office and I've decided, in anticipation of yet another unbearable reprimand from Anastasia, to say a truck crashed through our living room because the one thing I've learned about lying is that the more ridiculous it sounds, the less likely anyone is to question it.

There are no Maybellines or Cordellias. There is an Evangeline, and she smirks as I walk past. I brace myself for Anastasia, but she's not there. What I find instead is an internal memo tucked into the keyboard on my crappy, unnaturally lit desk. I have spent all week being positive and upbeat and not complaining and going along with the revolution, and the very first time something, through no fault of my own, goes wrong, I get another bloody memo. She doesn't even wait to find out what's wrong first. I mean, a truck could have crashed through our living room.

I power up my computer and try to take a deep breath. I will open the memo once I have had a coffee.

I get up to get a coffee and notice, only then, that someone has taken my chair, the special blue one that has been ergonomically examined by HR to ensure that I don't turn into a hunchback before I'm forty. In its place is a red one that doesn't look very ergonomic at all. I look over at smirking Evangeline and there it is — my chair.

'That's my chair.'

'Oh, yes. Well. They said I could try it since you weren't in. See if I want one like it.'

'It took me three years to get that chair.'

'It *is* very comfortable. Much better than those old red ones. You can have it back once the HR woman's been up to assess me.'

Enough is enough. There comes a point where you have to stand up for yourself. If Anastasia wants me out, it's going to be on my terms. And my terms are that I'm the one who writes the letters around here. I chuck her memo to one side, type a furious letter of furious resignation, march into her office and leave it on her keyboard.

Calmly, I gather my things and walk out. Johnson is trying to say something to me, but it's too late. I'm not listening. I am free. I am Braveheart. No, too much. I am Jerry Maguire. No, I am Michael Douglas in *Falling Down*. Except that instead of going on a rampaging killing spree around Los Angeles, I go on a drinking binge around London. Except that it's more of a drink than a drinking binge because I get halfway through the first pint and suddenly come to my senses.

What have you done, you idiot? You have a family. You have a family living in temporary accommodation. You can't just resign. What will you do now? But I had to resign. I was being pushed out. Isabel will understand.

No, she won't. Of course she won't. She'll think you're just throwing a tantrum because someone else has a column and you don't.

Why would she think that?

Because it's true. You've chucked in your job because you're jealous. And that makes you an idiot.

Shit.

Maybe it's not too late. Maybe Anastasia hasn't seen the letter. Frantically, I dial Johnson's number.

'William, what the hell — '

'Is she back?'

'Who?'

'Who do you bloody think . . . Anastasia, of course.'

'Yes.'

'Has she seen the letter?'

'Of course she has. She's already had Human Resources clear your desk.'

I wander the streets for what seems like hours. I feel sick. I feel dizzy. I keep trying to gather my thoughts but I don't know where to start. What have I done? What was I thinking? How am I going to tell Isabel? With nothing resolved, I get my normal train home and walk through the door like normal. And she says, 'You're back. We've missed you. How was your day, darling?'

This would have been the right time to tell her what happened, but they both look so pleased to see me, so delighted that the bread-winning hero has returned, that I say, 'Fine,' instead.

Idiot.

Saturday 29 June

Tell her. Tell her. Tell her. Tell her.
   Idiot. Idiot. Idiot.

Sunday 30 June

I mean, what are you going to do? Are you going to live a double life? Are you going to dress for work each morning, leave the house, get the train

180

and sit in a coffee shop all day? She'll notice. Women always notice, not least when there's no money in the joint bank account any more. And anyway, you have to tell her. This isn't one of those weird marriages where nobody ever tells anybody anything.

Tell her, tell her, tell her.

Here goes.

'What?! Please tell me you're joking . . . '

Why did you tell her? Idiot.

' . . . you can't just resign. We have a baby. You have responsibilities.'

She has an expression on her face that I haven't seen before — and I really thought that after two years of marriage and six months of motherhood, I'd seen all her expressions. It is 70 per cent incredulity, 20 per cent sadness, 10 per cent betrayal. I explain how there comes a point when a man can't take it any more. That I was being driven out of the job. That it was making me miserable. That I would rather be penniless and happy than rich and miserable. Which is precisely what Isabel always says.

'I don't want us to be rich, but we need to pay the mortgage on the house we can't live in. I mean, this is ridiculous. Could you not have waited a few more months? Could you not have taken it for a little bit longer? Could we not have at least discussed it before you did it?'

So I explain that it was only a matter of time before I was fired, anyway. She says nonsense. I take the letter from Anastasia out of my bag. Exhibit A.

As she opens it, I notice her hands are

shaking. I haven't seen her hands shake since she was standing in front of me at the altar. This is slightly different. I feel sick. Why have I done this to her? Why am I putting my family through this?

'Dear William,' she reads, her voice strained but measured. 'Despite recent problems, I just want to say that I am delighted that you have chosen to get behind the magazine's drive into online business. Your blog, though controversial, is exactly the sort of thing we need if we're going to move forward.

'It is crucial to our continued success in an increasingly competitive marketplace. I hope that we can now put our issues behind us and that you will continue to contribute so positively. I have completed the review of staff performances this year and I am pleased to say that there will be an across-the-board bonus of 3 per cent. Best wishes, Anastasia.'

Damn.

JULY

'People who say they sleep like a baby usually don't have one.'

LEO J. BURKE

Monday 1 July

Pinch, punch, first day of the month. Punch, smack, kick in teeth. I'm an idiot. After twenty minutes of honest reaction from my beloved wife involving the sort of swearing I really don't think a six-month-old should be subjected to, Isabel remembered that she was a romantic hippy at heart and told me everything would be all right (it won't), that we have enough money in her parents' emergency ISA account to last us (we don't, it would run out in three months and, anyway, I felt quite insulted that they set it up for her in the first place and swore to myself we would never need it), and that we could always move to a Welsh hovel (we couldn't, not after last year's misguided dry-stone-wall-building adventure in Llllanlleydolloo).

Then she went out for a very long walk with Jacob and hasn't said much since. This is even worse than when she was shouting. Now she's trying to put on a brave face to support her flaky husband but is so stressed that she has to go for long walks and can't really talk to me. I go to bed cursing myself, but I awake with new resolve: I shall find a new job within the week.

Isabel attempts a smile when I offer her a cheery-despite-the-situation morning's greeting. 'Seeing as you've elected to become a house husband,' she says, 'Jacob thought you might like to join him on his first swimming lesson.'

'But I'm off to get a job.'

'It's his first ever swimming lesson.'

'Okay.'

Just like kick boxing, I am the only man present at the water-babies' class, and this feels even weirder. Teresa has already cornered the instructor by the time we arrive, checking over what will and won't be achieved over the six-week course. Annabel is even later than we are.

The theory goes that you teach your children to swim while life as a submerged fetus is still fresh in their minds. The theory also goes that they will automatically hold their breath when underwater. So less than five minutes into the class, each mum takes it in turns to dunk her child. If you landed from another planet, you would assume this was some sort of ritualised torture because the babies don't appear to be following the theory. They come up spluttering, a look of total astonishment on their faces, as if to say, 'How could you betray my trust like that?'

Isabel asks the instructor if it's right that Jacob should be coughing and spluttering like a drowning baby. The instructor says it's perfectly normal. Uncertain, Isabel passes Jacob to me. When I dunk him, it's worse. He takes ages to recover. Teresa is dunking twice as often as everyone else, increasingly frustrated that her child refuses to hold her breath. One of the older babies is laughing so much with relief at having survived the first dip that he completely fails to prepare for the next one and comes up crying.

I can't believe this is the sort of thing mums get up to when dads are working. They are water-boarding their children. I look down at my poor defenceless little cherub and he looks up at me with the same mournful look. We have a sudden and profound understanding of our respective predicaments. We are both drowning at the hands of a cruel and insensitive world. All we want is to be left to prosper at our own pace. Is that too much to ask?

'And one, two, three, under!' cries the instructor, a big-armed woman with waterproof lipstick and a swimming costume that's gone bobbly. She looks a bit like the postman, too, but I'm not going to ask. I know what I have to do.

'Come on, Isabel, we're leaving,' I whisper because even if I am Michael Douglas in *Falling Down*, the woman with the waterproof lipstick scares me.

'I was about to say the same thing,' she replies, and in spite of everything that's happened in the last few days, we are united again. I make some pathetic excuse about feeling seasick and we leave. Teresa looks smug as we do. Her baby has won, even if it is turning blue.

Wednesday 3 July

After I have spent two whole days trying to find a job without luck, Isabel suggests I have a meeting with Anastasia and explain that it was all one big misunderstanding. We have an argument about whether or not male pride can be directly attributed to all the suffering of humanity through the ages. I win. She says this proves her point and storms off to yet another coffee morning with the baby group.

I give up looking for a job and watch adverts for baths with doors in them.

Then I have a cheeky daytime beer.

Then I watch some more adverts.

Then I have another beer because the fruitless search for employment in difficult economic times can make a man self-destructive.

Then I have another beer.

Then Isabel comes home and is furious that I have achieved nothing domestic.

'I have been looking for a job,' I reply impertinently.

'In the bottom of a beer can?' she replies, and suddenly we're making our own version of *EastEnders*.

Thursday 4 July

Independence Day for America — and for me. Let us not forget that I have escaped the chattels of labour. For the moment, at least, I can do what I want. As long as what I want to do is help with the washing (does this babygro really need

186

washing? He's only been wearing it for two hours and it's not *that* damp), the ironing (are we still bothering to iron the muslins?) and the rocking to sleep (could we not just leave him to cry himself to sleep? He's six months old, for goodness' sake).

Friday 5 July

'Hello, can I speak to Anastasia, please? . . . It's William . . . Walker . . . William Walker. The bloke who used to sit in the seat two along from the one you're sitting in now, you silly bint . . . No, I was only joking. No, look, sorry, can I — Hello? Hello?'

Saturday 6 July

'No, Dad. William wasn't enjoying his job . . . yes, it was a good job, but there was a personality clash . . . no, she was . . . no, she didn't . . . yes, we'll be fine . . . two months . . . no, he's got several options.'
    I feel sick. I feel useless. I feel tired.
    'You can't go to sleep now. We have to go to Teresa's barbecue.'
    This doesn't help. Pete, the haunted husband, is already being physically abused by the time we arrive. 'I . . . told . . . you . . . we'd . . . need . . . more . . . Pimms,' Teresa shout-whispers at him, prodding her nasty finger further and further into his chest. The whole family is

dressed in matching outfits and, from the extent of the spread, they must have been up all night making intricate finger foods. There are platters of canapés that would embarrass an African dictator. There are champagne glasses so pretentiously tall, it is virtually impossible not to knock one over. And there's no room for sausages on the barbecue: it's all crayfish and asparagus and lightly grilled new potatoes.

'This must be what it's like to have lunch with a premiership footballer,' whispers Annabel's husband. I laugh, but not too much because Teresa is looking over at us from behind a fruit pyramid. You would think she'd be in her element, but beneath a very thin veneer of calm, she is obviously stressed. Her right eye is twitching alarmingly.

'Great party, Pete. Amazing food. You haven't got any beer, have you?' asks Annabel's husband.

'Not allowed,' replies Pete nervously. 'She says beer wouldn't go with the lobster. Sorry. How's work?'

When it gets to my turn to answer that question, I find myself stuck for words. The two of them are waiting for a bland Saturday afternoon response and I could give it to them, but then I'd be lying. I could be honest but that might spoil the lobster more than a rogue beer and then Teresa might stab me to death with a barbecue prong. No, it would be best to grumble a bit about the commute, whisper conspiratorially about how at least it was easier than being at home with the baby and then move on to another equally inane topic like nappies.

'I've resigned.'

188

I said it a bit louder than I'd planned. And a bit more defensively. Pretty much everyone at the barbecue stopped their conversations and turned to stare.

'I've resigned,' I repeat, but more to myself this time. And all I can hear now is the babbling of unattended babies, the burning of unattended lobster tails and the smash of crystal on patio one second after Teresa drops her champagne glass in horror.

I should have run off with a secretary. Much more socially acceptable.

Monday 8 July

After another fruitless day scouring newspapers for non-shitty jobs, I behave yet more irresponsibly by going all the way to London to drink beer with Johnson and Andy. I had started negotiating for the trip on the basis that two coffee mornings equals one beer night but that got me nowhere, so I did some begging. I don't know why I bothered, given Andy's choice of conversational opener.

'Is it possible to have too much sex?'

'Oh God, Andy. I don't want to know about you and bloody Saskia. I'm unemployed in the middle of a recession and my family needs feeding. I'm having a life crisis here.'

'I'm having a life crisis, too, okay? I think I might have a condition. Some sort of sex addiction.'

'It happens,' says Johnson with a weary sigh. 'Medically speaking, there is no risk. Psychologically, it can be a problem.'

189

'I know. You have all the sex you could ever possibly wish for. Then it just starts to become something you can't function without. Then, before you know it, you're constructing your whole day around it. And it's no longer fun or exciting. It's just sex.'

'Give it another few weeks. It will wear off,' says Johnson.

'That's what I'm worried about,' says Andy.

'Look, can we stop talking about all the sex? I am having almost no sex *and* I've lost my job.'

'You resigned,' corrects Johnson.

'Thank you, yes. I resigned.'

'I think you did the right thing,' says Andy. 'Too often, we continue in jobs we hate for money we don't need. Saskia always says — '

'I'm sorry. Can we leave Saskia out of this for one minute? And I didn't do it because I was making some proletarian stand against the industrial-military complex.'

'Why did you do it?'

'I don't bloody know.'

'You did the right thing,' Johnson says into his pint. 'The magazine is going to pieces. It was the right time to leave.'

Tuesday 9 July

Johnson calls to tell me that his original advice was wrong.

'What, I didn't do the right thing?'

'No, you can develop medical problems if you have too much sex. Women are fine with too much sex, but according to the internet, it's different for men. If the penis tissue doesn't rest up and receive new oxygen, the erection can swell beyond safe limits. It can lead to pain and/or numbness.' He's worried that Saskia is some sort of black widow. First, she tried to destroy my marriage with her sexual prowess. Now, she's trying to kill Andy with the one weapon she really knows how to use.

'Don't you think you should do some actual work rather than fantasising about Saskia?'

'No, it's fine. Anastasia's out today. She's preparing for some sort of award thing we've been nominated for.'

'I thought you said the magazine was going to pieces.'

'Well, er, yes. You know, what do these award ceremonies really tell you?'

'Bye, Johnson.'

Wednesday 10 July

Isabel and Jacob are at the Wednesday baby-group coffee morning. This is distinct from the Tuesday afternoon one, the Friday morning one and the alternating Thursday lunchtime one. It gives me three clear hours to concentrate on job-hunting. After twenty minutes, I have determined that there are no jobs in my sector. I decide to treat this whole minor blip in my career as an opportunity. Maybe I should change careers altogether.

After a further twenty minutes browsing the wrong bits of the job section (could I be a car-damage appraiser or a lead functional consultant or a senior obsolescence engineer?), I give up altogether and watch some more adverts for walk-in baths. Then I make some toast. Then I update my Facebook status: William is looking for a job: (

Isabel still won't be back for two hours, so I decide to get some fresh air. I walk past the pub. I walk past the village shop. I go home again. Still more than an hour. I check Facebook. Predictably, the girl I played clarinet with when I was fourteen has responded. Is she somehow permanently plugged into her computer? She tells me she makes good money selling aloe-vera products from home. I type, 'I don't want to sell bloody aloe bloody vera,' but I delete it before I click 'send'. No point in taking it out on an ex-clarinettist.

I'm watching a repeat of *Who Wants to Be a Millionaire?* when Isabel returns. 'How are you, darling?' she asks.

'Fine, I'm trying to work out if it's even more pointless watching a repeat of *Who Wants to Be a Millionaire?* than it is watching the original. It shouldn't be — it's the same level of suspense, the same stake, the same questions. It's not as if I've seen it. Or if I have, I can't remember it. To all intents and purposes, it is completely new to me, so it should feel the same. But I'm sitting here thinking that this bloke, this idiot who is struggling to guess whether a cantaloupe is a type of elephant or a fruit, already knows how things went for him. He may be driving round Stoke in a Ferrari. Or maybe he's in Benidorm in some horrible condominium because I can't see

192

him making it past £5,000 and that's probably enough for a deposit, don't you think? Or maybe he's sitting on his sofa right now, watching this as well. Kicking himself that he said elephant, thinking that if he'd said fruit, he might be in Benidorm right now.'

After a long, bemused pause, Isabel says, 'Can you bring Jacob in from the car? He needs a nappy change.' I walk out to the car and, even though I'm fully clothed, an old lady walking along the pavement noticeably quickens her pace when she sees me.

I walk back in and I was right, he said 'elephant'.

Thursday 11 July

Lathered up for a shave and then realised there was no point. And besides, blades are expensive. And besides, what's the point in anything?

Again, I gravitate towards the television. *Neighbours*. *Loose Women*. Alex and Geoff ruining someone else's house. I should write an exposè. The truth behind A and G: how the camera always lies on makeover shows.

Friday 12 July

This has officially been the longest week of my life. The most exciting thing that happened today is that the revolutionary aloe-vera anti-wrinkle cream I ordered from Louise arrived with a smirk from the postman (is he opening my post?).

Sunday 14 July

I'm out with Jacob, giving Isabel a lie-in. My world has shrunk to the size of a village, a village in which I am not welcome. And there's Pete with a pram, his eyes deeper set, his feet shuffling like a man resigned to a lifetime of misery and toil. Teresa must have been extra cruel to him last night.

'Hi, Pete.'

'Hi, William. How's the job-hunting?'

'Terrible.'

'I meant to say, my sister-in-law is doing extraordinarily well with some aloe-vera thing. Can find out the details if you want?'

'She didn't used to play the clarinet, did she?'

'I don't think so.'

Jesus.

Monday 15 July

Two weeks. Two weeks unemployed.

Tuesday 16 July

Two weeks and a day.

Wednesday 17 July

Two weeks, two days.

'Can I speak to Anastasia? It's William Walker. I used to work there . . . Hi, Anastasia. Look, I'm sorry about all this silliness. You see, I got the wrong end of the . . . oh, right. Right . . . no . . . no . . . okay. Sure . . . yes. Okay . . . okay . . . okay . . . thanks. Bye.'

Anastasia's not hiring at the moment. Needs to cut the headcount by 20 per cent. The recession, you see. Good thing I left because she was going to have to get rid of Princess Evangeline. Last in, first out and all that. Would have been a shame, wouldn't it, since she has her whole career ahead of her? But if I fancied writing an article about what it's like to be unemployed in a recession, that would be great.

Thursday 18 July

Freelance article for *Life & Times*. 'I love being unemployed.' By William Walker

> ~~People assume that anyone resigning from a perfectly good job in the midst of a recession is mad. Well, mad they may be, but is madness such a bad thing? Or is madness actually a sign that you're still alive?~~

> ~~People assume that anyone resigning from a perfectly good job in the midst of a recession is mad. Well, they're wrong. If everyone resigned in a recession, the world would be a better place.~~

195

People assume that anyone resigning from a perfectly good job in the midst of a recession is mad. Well, they can fuck off.

Friday 19 July

The aloe-vera anti-wrinkle cream appears to be having a miraculous effect. Or maybe it's because I'm not working. In only a few days, my face is recovering from the hard toil of office work. I look younger, fitter, happier. If I continue to loaf around the house eating fruit (not out of choice, of course, Isabel orders an organic fruit box every week and if Jacob and I don't eat our own body weight in knobbly apples and under-ripe pears, we are severely chastised), I could live for ever. I could be one of those little wrinkly 127-year-olds they find in the remote foothills of Azerbaijan who, when asked the secret of their world-record longevity, say stuff like, 'I always smoke at least nine cigars a day, but I've never liked butter' or 'I always walk to the pomegranate tree and walk back again with four pomegranates, which I then eat simultaneously.' And sales of cigars or pomegranates go through the roof.

Except when they interview me, I will say, 'Being unemployed and eating fruit against my will.' And I might add, 'Standing on my head for forty minutes each morning,' for fun.

Saturday 20 July

With Isabel out spending money on things we don't need, like magazines and branded biscuits and non-home-brewed alcohol and organic goat's milk, Jacob and I set up a self-efficiency spreadsheet because it's more fun than trying to write an article about how great unemployment isn't.

We are both keen to cut down on excess spending in an attempt not only to take the pressure off my job hunt but also to reduce the need for me to be a wage slave until my late seventies. Perhaps, if we could reduce our costs sufficiently, I could work from home. I could find the male equivalent of aloe-vera selling, supplement it with a poorly paid but enjoyable writing income and spend enough time in the garden to produce sufficient food to cut Isabel's eye-watering Waitrose bill.

'We need to cut our costs, darling.' In hindsight, given that this is my fault, I could probably have introduced the concept more gently.

'Right,' she says confrontationally, dumping all the bags on the floor. But it's important, so I continue.

'Currently, we spend £127 a week on food. With a bit of planning, we can reduce this to £18.'

'Right.' I'm not going to let her resistance to change put me off.

'Because our current accommodation is only temporary, I intend to grow all our salads in portable pots.'

'Okay.' It's understandable, I suppose, that she isn't immediately on board. People are so indoctrinated into the system, trapped in the matrix that requires us to work like slaves to buy things we don't need to keep the capitalist wheels turning, they simply can't see it.

'We could also buy an Eglu.'

'A *what*?'

'Jacob and I have been doing some research on the internet. For a reasonable outlay of £388 including delivery, a man will come to our house, install a very cool-looking chicken coop, install two chickens and explain how we clip their wings. We'll get about six eggs per chicken per week, as long as we don't spook them. That's six hundred a year and they live for four to five years. Given that organic eggs in Waitrose cost £1.50 for six, that's £150 of eggs every year. We'll have made back the cost in . . . less than three years.'

'What about the cost of the organic feed?'

Obstacles. Just putting up obstacles. So predictable.

'Well, that won't be that much if we buy it in bulk and, anyway, I shall be baking our own bread and only having cold baths from now on.'

'Good.'

'What?'

'Good.'

'Right.'

Sunday 21 July

What I've done here is fallen into Isabel's trap. She's lulled me into a hippy existence. It's an

198

ingenious trap because she's still pretending to be lukewarm about it. And so I have to persist in claiming it's the future. Still, my life has new purpose. The chickens arrive on Wednesday. I've bought pots and planted endive, red lettuce and dwarf peas. Have also secured four semi-mature aubergine plants. I don't like aubergine, but it's the most expensive vegetable in Waitrose.

Cold bath really enjoyable, mainly because Isabel was watching and expecting me to add some hot and I didn't. Instead, I took the opportunity to explain that not only am I saving money on electricity, but that as someone who now takes cold baths, I will generally on average enjoy better health than someone who doesn't.

She says she's delighted. She's always said hot baths are bad for me.

Annoying.

Monday 22 July

Yes! Have lined up interview at main rival to *Life & Times*. Because, obviously, one must balance determination to escape a life as hamster on military-industrial complex's wheel with need to have money. Though not money for eggs or aubergines.

Secret hot bath to celebrate.

Then rattle off article for Anastasia.

Provisional title: 'Why work isn't the be-all and end-all'.

Provisional subtitle: 'William Walker celebrates the frugal but happy life of the freed wage slave'.

Ha!

Tuesday 23 July

Cold bath because it's pathetic being one of those people who starts something and doesn't follow it through. Not as enjoyable as the first one.

Anastasia likes the article. She's glad I'm happy now that I'm out of *Life & Times*. I'm glad I've given the impression that I'm happy.

Wednesday 24 July

Eglu has arrived. Eglu courier assures us that wing-clipping doesn't hurt our two chickens at all. It's just like clipping toes or hooves, only it's with the wings instead. Not remotely convinced but, you know, if we're prepared to eat chicken, we should be prepared to chop wings off.

'I'm not doing it,' says Isabel.

'I'm not doing it, either,' I reply.

'Well, you're the one who bought the things.'

'They're not *things*. They're chickens. And I thought you always said you wished you'd fallen in love with someone practical, like a farmer.'

'Yes, because a farmer would be able to clip the wings of a chicken. And he wouldn't order a chicken coop over the internet for £388, either.'

'I thought you thought this was a good idea.'

'Look, darling, I love you. I know you're having a hard time at the moment. And I'll do whatever it takes to help you get through it. I'll even stand there while you pretend to enjoy cold baths. But I never said I thought spending £388 on two chickens was a good idea.'

She thinks I'm having a midlife crisis. Rest of day's concentration ruined. I have reached the stage when my wife thinks I'm cracking up. I'm sure that's not supposed to happen yet. When she leaves for yet another coffee afternoon, I decide to drink beer and watch *Countdown*. Will have job within the week. May as well enjoy not having job while still can.

And another beer.

And another.

Drunk before 6 p.m. Isabel will be back in a few minutes. Four cans looks bad. Hide cans in outside bin and brush teeth. Pathetic.

Thursday 25 July

WHAT ARE THE FIRST SIGNS OF ALCOHOLISM?

'Here is a self-test to help you review the role alcohol plays in your life,' it says when I type 'What are the first signs of alcoholism?' into Google.

201

Question 1. Do you ever drink heavily when you are disappointed, under pressure or have had a quarrel with someone?

Yes.

Question 2. Can you handle more alcohol now than when you first started to drink?

Of course. I threw up all over a girl's impossible-to-unhook bra the first time I drank. Because it was Malibu, neat, and I was fourteen.

Question 3. When drinking with other people, do you try to have a few extra drinks the others won't notice?

I have occasionally had an extra swig at the fridge.

Question 4. Do you sometimes feel a little guilty about your drinking?

No, not sometimes. Always.

Question 5. Are you in more of a hurry to get your first drink of the day than you used to be?

Look, are we not being a little alarmist about this? I mean, it's just one afternoon of secret drinking.

Question 6. Has a family member or close friend ever expressed concern or complained about your drinking?

No, because they don't know. Daytime drinking is my terrible secret.

Question 7. Do you try to avoid family or close friends while you are drinking?

Can we stop now?

Question 8. Are you having more financial, work, school and/or family problems as a result of your drinking?

Ha! No! It's the other way around. You lose, stupid internet test. You lose.

Have early drink to celebrate fact that I don't have a drink problem.

And a hot bath.

Friday 26 July

Cold bath.

Chickens yet to lay. It will take four weeks, apparently, but the brown one looks all set. Isabel is already coming round to the whole idea. Wants to call them Thelma and Louise, but I am refusing because this is a self-sufficiency exercise. If we name them, they'll be like pets and then I'll get weirded out about eating their eggs.

The post-lunch drive to get Jacob to sleep lasts longer than expected. He is clearly wising up to the strategy. I can see him steeling himself to stay awake, no matter how ultra-soporifically I drive.

There will come a point when I fall asleep before he does and wake up in a ditch with Jacob still awake and grinning.

ULTRA-SOPORIFIC DRIVING: ESSENTIAL TIPS YOU WON'T FIND IN THE HIGHWAY CODE

1. The engine must be kept at precisely 3,400 revs or 46 miles per hour in fifth gear. Under no circumstances should this change if your child is about to nod off. The child will detect the change, and it will not nod off for another half-hour — if maintaining this speed requires driving straight across mini roundabouts, or indeed not-so-mini roundabouts, so be it.

2. Talk in low, muted tones over the low, muted engine. If your wife is in the car, she mustn't talk at all. She must only listen while maintaining a neutral expression. If you are on your own, a rhythmic murmur will suffice. Like you're participating in the early stages of a ritual sacrifice at the end of an Indiana Jones movie.

3. If it is a bright day, you should drive only on shaded roads in a direction that doesn't cast sunlight directly into the back seat of the car. Sunshades are not the answer. Your child will sense that you want it to go to sleep and resist for longer.

4. If at all possible, minor potholes and bumps should be incorporated, though anything more than a gentle jolt will have the opposite of the desired effect. Cats' eyes are perfect.

5. In extreme circumstances, driving on the thick white line delineating the fast lane of a motorway and the central reservation can provide fast-track sleepiness. It should be noted that wives generally oppose this method.

By the time Jacob finally passes out, I am almost back at the house that I destroyed. There hasn't been a peep from the builders for weeks, which, if I were a glass-half-full person, I'd attribute to the fact that they were so busy putting in the new ceilings and floors that they'd not had a chance to update me. No harm in paying a surprise visit, though.

This is why it's pointless being a glass-half-full person. The house looks worse than when I destroyed it. Everything has been torn out, but nothing has been put back again. The garden is lost to weeds. The windows are filthy. I must not let Isabel see it like this. She's happy enough in our unfriendly village. She has the divided baby group to keep her together. And as long as these builders get on with it, the malicious Brenda will be out of our lives for good within weeks.

'Yes, it's William Walker. I'm calling about our house. It seems to have been abandoned by you. I'm standing outside now, and you're not here. None of you. Could you call me back urgently?'

I am thinking of becoming a glass-entirely-empty person.

Saturday 27 July

Cold bath.

No eggs.

No call back from builders. Nothing to do but address Anastasia's issues with my brutally dishonest article about the joys of unemployment. It needs more emotional honesty, she says. She's twelve. What does she know about emotion?

Monday 29 July

Called builders five times before one of them answered, irritably, almost as if he's been trying to ignore the previous calls.

'Sorry, mate. Got your message. We're trying to keep the project moving, but we've been tied up on something else, which has overrun.'

'But you were doing my house. How come you're on something else?'

'Well, it's filming, isn't it, mate? It's unpredictable.'

'What do you mean, filming?'

'We're doing some of the Alex and Geoff shows. Didn't I say?'

Tuesday 30 July

'Hi, William, come in, come in. Take a seat. Coffee?'

This is more like it. A proper editor. Old. Like fifty-five. Huge office. Drinks cabinet.

'I'd love a coffee,' I reply, attempting to project a calm, sophisticated persona, like I always have coffee, which I do and it's not something unusual, which it isn't, it's only coffee, so I should probably stop thinking about it and sound a little more normal, rather than overly self-confident with all this I'd-love-some-coffee nonsense. Jesus.

'So what happened, William? Fell out with Anastasia? I hear she's running a tight ship over at *Life & Times*.'

'No, no, no, no, no, nothing like that. Well, yes. A little.' Now I'm sounding hesitant and defensive. Straight from the I'd-love-some-coffee swagger to this. He must think I'm some sort of schizophrenic. All outgoing with the hot beverages, but evasive with the previous employment question.

'Let's just say Anastasia and I disagreed about the course the magazine was taking.' Better, much better. Maybe a bit much, though.

'Right,' he says, nodding at the PA who has just brought in our espressos. 'In what way?'

Couldn't we leave it at that? It sounded sort of impressive. I've got a whole list of brilliant ideas for his company. Let's get to the positives.

'It was a technology thing. Internet. Twitter. Blogging. You know, 'the future'.'

207

'You had a problem with that?' Oh, Christ. What sort of idiot-hole are you digging for yourself? Have a sip of coffee. Calm down. Take a deep breath. No, not when you're still sipping the coffee. Now you've slurped. You've slurped your posh espresso in this big swanky office like you've never had espresso before. You've slurped it, it's gone down the wrong way and you're choking. You've never choked on an espresso before. Just calm down. Calm down and lie. Your family is depending on you.

'No, no, not at all. I was all for it. I thought that if we were going to move into the next generation of publishing and stay ahead of the competition and, umm, you know, interface with our readers on many platforms, then we needed to be up on the latest technology. Like, umm, blogs. Anastasia, perhaps too young to have learned that you need to keep up with the pace, didn't see it that way.'

The editor looked inscrutable. Typical editor. Poker face at all times. But I had the feeling that I'd nailed it. I took a more successful sip of espresso, crossed my arms and then, remembering it was defensive body language, uncrossed them. Finally, he spoke.

'I think it's all bollocks. Twitter. Facebook. The trouble with all you hacks is that you can't write a good old-fashioned story any more. You're all too busy marrying imaginary girlfriends in SecondLife. Now, look, I've got a meeting. I've got your CV here. We'll let you know.'

He must have pressed a red button hidden under his desk because the second he'd finished speaking, the PA came in, no longer all smiles and espressos. Before I could backtrack, I was following the PA out. The interview was over. I was not beginning an illustrious new career in the beautiful offices of *Life & Times*' arch rival. It could have been worse. The button could have opened a trap door into a shark-infested swimming pool.

'Oh, Janet,' he called as I was just about gone. Maybe he'd had second thoughts. Maybe he was going to give me another shot. 'Janet, get hold of Anastasia at *L & T*. Fix lunch. She sounds like she's worth meeting after all.'

Wednesday 31 July

Two letters. One confirming I had not got the job, which is fine, absolutely fine, don't want the stupid job, anyway. One from the village elders, delivered by the colluding postman, which is absolutely *not* fine. There have been reports, it suggests melodramatically, that we have changed use of land within the village perimeters. Agricultural pursuits are not permitted under clause 14.2 of the village charter. Given that they have received no response to their last letter (dated Monday 27 May, regarding indecent exposure on front drive), they can only assume this is yet another attempt to disrupt the calm progress of village life.

'Now they're going after Thelma and Louise,' I shout up to Isabel.

'What?' she shouts down.

'They're trying to take away our chickens,' I clarify.

'What?' she shouts down again.

'This has gone far enough,' I shout up, louder. 'I'm going to stop them, once and for all.'

'What, darling? I can't hear you. I'm in the bathroom.'

This is pointless, I think to myself. Why am I shouting upstairs at a wife in a bathroom when I should be resolving this with action? I am sick of being a talker. It's time I became a doer. I storm out the front door and on to the street. I should really have a baseball bat or, since I'm English, a cricket bat or a squash racquet or, yes, a croquet mallet, because not only is Bob an ex-copper but, if this turns nasty, I have no way of knowing how far Brenda advanced in the kick-boxing classes she got me thrown out of.

Too late now. I'm halfway across the village green. I can feel the curtains twitching, but I'm not going to stop.

I reach the pub and, I'll be honest, my resolve is weakening ever so slightly. This is just an overreaction to the terrible interview, says one voice, psychoanalytically. No, it's not, says another. You're fighting against a corrupt and bullying parish council. There are principles at stake here. But he might hurt you, insists the first voice. Well, maybe just have a stern word with him, then, says the second.

Ignoring both voices, I knock on the pub door as unpleasantly as possible. It's only 9 a.m. The pub won't be open for hours. Maybe they're not awake yet. I knock again. Still nothing. Then I hear a noise round the back.

As I put my head around the wall of the pub garden, I see two things: Bob's whippet and Bob standing over it, clutching a full-size croquet mallet, of the sort I wished I'd brought with me.

Bob has an almost serene look on his face, although an angry sweat glistens on his brow in the morning light. His voice never changes pitch as he calmly explains to the dog that he has chewed his newspaper for the last time.

I don't have time to shout, 'Stop.' I don't have time to do anything. Before the whippet knows what hit him, Bob has swung the mallet down hard on the hapless creature. A gruesome yelp, a canine crunch and then silence.

Then Bob swings the mallet down again and only as a fine mist of whippet blood sprays across his shirt does his expression change to one of fury. 'That's my favourite shirt,' he screams before striking again and again, shouting terrible profanities at the increasingly flattened dog. Deciding now might not be the best time to have it out, I retreat back across the village green. I notice my hands are shaking as I quickly close the door behind me.

AUGUST

'My father had a profound influence on me, he was a lunatic.'

SPIKE MILLIGAN

Thursday 1 August

I phoned 999 and they said it wasn't an emergency if the dog was already dead. So I phoned the 0845 non-emergency local number and got through to an answering machine. I didn't leave a message because I didn't want them to know who had witnessed the murder. I called again later and got through to a man who sounded like Bob but couldn't have been because Bob was retired. I explained what had happened.

'What, Bob from the pub?'

'Yes, Bob from the pub.'

'He doesn't play croquet.'

'Look, I saw it with my own eyes.'

'Your name, sir?'

'I no give name. I wish remain anonymous,' I said, in a suddenly Spanish accent.

'This isn't some practical joke, is it, sir? Because that's a very serious allegation.'

'Go see for yourself.'

'Can't today, sir. We're flat out. We'll take a look first thing tomorrow.'

'But he got rid of body by then, *que*?'

'Are you a resident of the village, sir? Your voice sounds fam — '

I hung up. And ever since then, right through the night, apart from a couple of hours when I nodded off, I've been looking out through the curtains, across the green, waiting for the police to turn up. Isabel is in a state of shock. She thought the whippet was quite well behaved, relatively speaking. She seems to be missing the point. Bob, the husband of the evil kick-boxing midget, brutally bludgeoned his own pet to death. Think what he might do to me.

'Are you absolutely sure he killed it?' she asks pointlessly.

By lunchtime, just as I'm starting to get sofa sores, a police van arrives. A policeman who looks like Bob gets out, adjusts his cap, looks over to our house and strolls up to the pub. Bob answers and, from a distance, it looks like they're having a jolly good laugh. Then Bob retreats inside and, moments later, returns, followed closely by a whippet. The policeman returns to his van, waves back to Bob and the whippet, then leaves.

After that, I sit in the garden for a long time, watching Thelma and Louise pace up and down their Eglu. I saw the mallet. I saw the whippet blood. I definitely did.

Saturday 3 August

In the furnace heat of the first August weekend, the village green is crying out to be covered by a picnic rug, but it's too soon after the whippet slaying to venture out. I can almost hear the clink of Pimms jug on Pimms glasses in the pub garden. But I know what happened on Wednesday. I saw it. I'm sure I did. I mean, how mad do you have to be to imagine a whippet being pulverised by a croquet mallet? So I stay indoors, sweating, wishing it was winter, until Isabel says, 'Enough,' and we make a sudden break for the fields and woodland beyond the reach of the dog-murdering cabal.

'Maybe it wasn't a proper croquet mallet?' Isabel offers after a contemplative silence.

'Or maybe I just made the whole thing up?' I reply furiously.

I spend the afternoon consoling myself in the placid company of Thelma and Louise. I find myself admiring the simplicity of their existence, even though they've now eaten so much organic feed without laying an egg that I'm beginning to doubt the economic model.

Monday 5 August

Woke early after a vivid nightmare about being forced to eat whippet-and-kidney pie at Bob's pub. Decided the coast was clear enough for a walk with Jacob. Brenda had obviously decided the same about a walk with the replacement whippet.

Me on one side of the green. Her on the other. And she just stopped and stared. I stared back, partly because even if her husband is a psychopath, I still refuse to be stared at without any retaliation, partly because I'm curious to know whether she can look me in the eye knowing that the whippet she's dragging around is not the original whippet but a replica, and that she is therefore an accessory to dogslaughter.

She can. There is no trace of associated guilt. She just stares impassively until I continue on my way.

'Can I speak to Anastasia?'

'I'm afraid she's at lunch. I can ask her to call you back, but — '

'Don't bother.'

Tuesday 6 August

I think I'm over the whippet tragedy. I wake up feeling resolved to defend our two lovely chickens from a similar fate. 'Here is your response,' I say to the postman, handing him a letter. 'Give this to your leaders.'

He nods because, as enemies, we are beginning to understand each other. Then he hands me an invitation to take out a new credit card because he is still the postman.

Dear Village Cabal,

I find your persecution of my family both distasteful and small-minded, and all because of the unfortunate but entirely unmalicious incident at Avocado some months ago for which I have long since apologised. You will be delighted to know that we can't wait to leave your village and get back to civilisation. In the meantime, please be assured that two chickens in a hutch do not constitute a farm. Thelma and Louise stay. Any further harassment shall be reported to the police and county council.

Yours faithfully,
William Walker

Wednesday 7 August

The heat is unbearable. Five weeks without a proper job is unbearable. The cracks are beginning to show, even with the miracle aloe vera anti-wrinkle cream.

Thelma, Louise and Jacob all seem to be taking the heat particularly badly. No one in this family sleeps any more. Having assumed, initially and quite selfishly, that global warming might not be so bad for those of us who would find ourselves living in a climate suitable for the production of fine sparkling wines, I am now considering climbing a power station to protest against fossil-fuel consumption.

Had another cold bath. Watered rapidly growing seedlings with siphoned bathwater.

Thursday 8 August

This morning, while Isabel is at the shops, I have two options: I can sit through *Alex & Geoff to the Rescue*, which is currently the only thing that stops Jacob crying, presumably because a seven-month-old finds their stupid overexcited voices entertaining, or I can stick Jacob in front of the television on his own and continue the job hunt.

Ten minutes into Alex enthusing about a faux-marble fireplace that will never, ever suit the small cottage the *To the Rescue* team are in the midst of destroying, I can take no more. I prop Jacob up on some pillows and sneak off to the computer. Action is called for.

It is while considering life as a hospital caterer that I notice a little advert flashing away in the corner of the screen. I click on it, a box pops up, some soothing music starts playing, and a nice-sounding American woman starts speaking out of the computer. 'Today I'm going to tell you how you can begin making over $100,000 CASH as soon as this year! All from the comfort of *your home.*'

I wasn't born yesterday, I think. And as if she can read my thoughts, the nice-sounding American woman says, 'I'm sure you're probably accustomed to hearing a bunch of GIANT numbers when it comes to making money online, but the truth is, I can show you how to make anywhere from a *realistic* $50 to $675 a day online.'

That does seem realistic, but before I can

investigate further, Jacob starts crying from the next room. *Alex & Geoff* has finished. The child is inconsolable.

Friday 9 August

Postcard from Andy. He's in the Caribbean. Hadn't even mentioned he was going. We have friendship-by-postcard now. He's with Saskia. The weather's beautiful . . . not humid like England. Oh, I'm so pleased for him. He's even more worried about all the sex now that he's in the Caribbean, which I think is an embarrassing thing to put on a postcard. Isabel tuts when she reads it and mutters something that sounds like 'slag' under her breath. I change the subject by mentioning that one can make a realistic $50 to $675 a day online.

Isabel is halfway through telling me that any website promising vast home-based earnings in return for the initial outlay of only a few dollars is clearly a scam, and I am halfway to agreeing with her, when the phone rings.

'Hi, Alex. You want to speak to Isabel? Isabel, it's Alex. He obviously wants to talk to you.'

Isabel takes the phone and, from the tone of her voice, I can only assume Alex has been stricken with some incurable flesh-eating super-bug and has decided to utter his last words to his beloved Isabel before succumbing to a horrible lingering, flaky death. Unfortunately, it's not that, but it's still the best news I've had for weeks.

Alex & Geoff to the Rescue has been canned. It never lived up to its hilarious opening episode. I don't know how my traitorous son will cope but I am delighted.

'Is it okay if I'm out tomorrow evening? Alex and Geoff want us to help them drown their sorrows. We can't both go.'

'What, so I have to stay here and look after Jacob?' I ask. 'I mean, I would but I've got to look after Thelma and Louise. We live two hundred yards from a man who kills animals with mallets.' I get another don't-be-unreasonable look, which is ridiculous because why should Thelma and Louise be the ones to suffer because Alex and Geoff's show was rubbish? I didn't even want to name them. I wanted them to be working animals, not pets. But it's too late now. They're part of the family. Alex isn't.

On the other hand, an evening failing to convince Jacob that I can be an able parent in Isabel's absence is a small price to pay for blessedly Alex-free television.

Saturday 10 August

I don't believe it. He's gone to sleep. There I was, ready for an evening of hysteria, interminable loops of the block and a few desperate prayers for forgiveness from any gods willing to listen, and he's nodded off. Scoffed a whole jar of disgusting broccoli pasta, laughed his head off while I did my rain dance, cried when I stopped, laughed when I started again, cried when I kept going, then fell asleep when I stopped. Suddenly, I have an evening. No need to spend the next four hours doing the rain dance or anything.

It is while taking another brief, noncommittal look at the how-to-make-millions-without-leaving-your-village website that I notice another ad for a poker site. Now, I am well aware that gambling is an addictive, dangerous and, in cyberspace, largely unregulated way to lose money. However, this particular virtual casino will match my £50 with one of their £50s. So I could play £50, then quit. I might not be up, but I wouldn't be down.

Within minutes, I am playing poker with people I can only assume are bored American housewives.

By 8.30 p.m., I'm on £180. Somewhere in the Midwest, a housewife is going to have some explaining to do when her hubbie gets the credit-card bill. By half nine, I'm on £390. By the time Isabel walks in, I'm on £850.

'What are you doing, darling?'

'Nothing. Just checking e-mails. Good evening?'

'Well, sort of. Geoff didn't come. They're having a fight about the television show. So it was the two of us, but the restaurant was nice.'

'Is he still definitely gay?'

'Very funny.'

Sunday 11 August

Managed to sneak in another couple of hours in the middle of the night, but it didn't go so well. Dropped £200. Mustn't get cocky. Must keep

220

calm. Keep doing what I did. Found an article by a professional online gambler. He makes £20,000 a month. If I could manage a fifth of that, all our worries would be over. Not that this is anything more than a bit of a flutter. You have to be very careful with this whole internet gambling thing. It's a mug's game. So I shall proceed with caution and only tell Isabel about our new source of income when I'm a real pro.

Monday 12 August

On the plus side, I'm up £200 again. On the minus side, it took all night and I was discovered by Isabel. On the plus side, I managed to flick to e-mail and profess insomnia in the nick of time. 'Darling,' she said, 'everything will be all right soon enough. Try not to worry so much.' On the minus side, I'm feeling guilty because I should have told her. The longer I don't tell her, the longer I'm living a lie. On the plus side, she would have killed me if I'd confessed, regardless of the fact that I'm up. Much better if she continues to feel sorry for me while I amass a fortune.

Also on the other plus side, the builders are now back to our house following the demise of *Alex & Geoff*. On the other minus side: 'Mid-September, mate, like we said in the first place.'

'You said four months on April 22. That's August 22, not September.'

'Right, well, you know, things slip. Bit like your ceiling. Ha ha ha. No, sorry, mate. We'll do our best, but I'd say mid-September all done, hand on heart, is a good bet. We weren't expecting to have to replace the ground floor as well, were we?'

Tuesday 13 August

An egg. Louise, or possibly Thelma, has laid her first egg. Am quite emotional. More emotional than you'd expect with an egg. Must be lack of sleep due to new nocturnal career as a professional gambler (£926, thank you very much). The egg unites the family. Isabel is delighted. Jacob is nonchalant.

'Can we eat it?' I ask Isabel.

'Don't see why not.'

'Well, it's the first one. It might be like the first, you know, nappy.'

'Don't be ridiculous. It's an egg.'

'It might be all treacly inside.'

'Poached or boiled?'

'I can't eat it now. It doesn't seem right.'

Wednesday 14 August

Two interviews today for jobs on magazines about, respectively, kit cars and babies. A stopgap, really. I failed to convince the first that I have a sufficient background in engineering (I thought they were joking when they asked, then pretended I'd enjoyed physics at school, but by then it was too late) and managed to appal the editor of the second with a joke about Medised, which she would have got if she had children, but she didn't, she just had a sanctimonious attitude to parenting.

Very depressed until I get home to find Jacob sitting.

'He's sitting,' I say to Isabel, who is reading a magazine she no doubt bought from the village shop, even though I've asked her to boycott it, but I'm overlooking that because . . . 'Look, he's sitting!'

She glances over, all matter-of-fact. 'Yes, he is. He's been doing it all morning.'

'Well, that's good, isn't it? Just over seven months. Is that good? I mean, how does it compare?'

'What do you mean?' She knows what I mean.

'How does it compare to the other babies in the group?'

'He's the first,' she sighs. 'But he is a month older than the others.' Why does she have to spoil it? Why does she have to qualify Jacob's epic achievements?

'Well, are the others showing the slightest sign of sitting up? Or are they all just lying around?'

'Babies learn at their own pace. It's not a race.' Here we go again. I'll have to resort to the internet for proper answers.

And now I'm depressed again. Once I've ignored all the hippy websites urging me not to set a timetable for my child, I find one that says seven months is perfectly normal for sitting up. 'Right on schedule,' it says. So he's only normal . . . although I still think he's on a fairly hyperbolic developmental curve. He'll be walking in no time. Then we'll see if he's normal.

I console myself with a quick flutter. So close to being up £1,000, but then Isabel walks in and I obviously look suspicious.

'What are you doing?'

'Checking e-mail.'

'Again?'

'This job's not going to find itself.'

Isabel narrows her eyes and walks out. When I return to the casino screen, I have lost a hand. Back to £910, and my wife thinks I have an internet-porn addiction.

Thursday 15 August

Louise has laid another egg, but Thelma seems to be struggling. She has had a large red egg hanging out for the last hour. After a long and deeply unpleasant discussion about whether a first egg could be red (given that we didn't see Louise's first one come out and maybe there's some sort of hymen-like membrane), we resolve to wait.

An hour later, I am on the Eglu chat forum. Nothing about red eggs, but a rather harrowing discussion about chicken prolapse. A chicken called Fenn has a bleeding vent, which the other chickens have been pecking.

'Might be worth bathing her vent with warm salt water to clean it up,' says another Eglu user.

224

'If it's a prolapse, it can be pushed back in very gently with a bit of Vaseline or K-Y Jelly.'

Oh, Christ.

In no mood for village silliness, I stride across the green to the village shop. 'Some Vaseline or K-Y Jelly, please. And before you ask, it's not for anything depraved. It's for Thelma. She's a chicken. Okay?'

I get halfway back across the green and turn around.

'Because she has a prolapse. Not because I want to have sex with her. So don't send me another letter. Okay?'

'I've got the Vaseline, darling.'

'Okay, here are some gloves.'

'I'm not doing it. This is definitely a woman's thing.'

'You *are* doing it. She's your chicken.'

I can't talk about what happened next. Suffice to say that the red egg went back in — and then came back out again. Then again. Then again. If the prolapse keeps coming out again, take the chicken to the vet, says the forum. I call the vet and their offices are closed for the day, even though it's only 4 p.m. Thelma will have to make it through the night. I offer to stay up and keep an eye on her.

By 4 a.m. I have lost £700, mainly to American housewives who seem to be a lot better at online gambling than they were last week. Either that, or the strain of Thelma's illness and the knowledge that I can't even get a job on a kit-car magazine are beginning to take their toll.

I am still on £210, though. Or £160, if you deduct the £50 I put in myself. I should just call it quits now. We need the money.

Friday 16 August

Two more eggs from Louise, who appears to have no tact given that her sister has an enormous red lump hanging out of her bum. Isabel agrees to cancel her ninth coffee morning of the week so we can all go to the vet.

The vet looks like Bob.

'It's a prolapse,' he says coldly. To him, Thelma is just a chicken.

'I know. Is there anything you can do?'

'Not really. If it hasn't gone back in by now, it requires quite a complicated operation.'

'How much will that cost?'

'Hard to say. Anything up to £910.' The exact amount of money I had won gambling, up until 3 a.m. last night. If I hadn't been such a chump, I could have paid. I could have told Isabel about the winnings, and she may have been delighted and she may have let me spend the money on saving Thelma. But now, Thelma must die.

'How much is it to put her down?'

'Ninety, plus VAT.'

'That's okay, thank you. We'll take her home,' says Isabel. 'We can do it ourselves.'

And now, because of me, Thelma must die at the hands of amateurs.

Saturday 17 August

Still can't believe Isabel did it. Stamping on a broom held across the neck of poor Thelma. Could she not have dreamed up a less barbaric method? No, apparently it is quick and painless. She saw it on a BBC 4 documentary and if we weren't prepared to deal with the realities of poultry farming, then we shouldn't keep chickens or eat chicken or anything, she said. Fine, I said, but was she absolutely sure the whole minute Thelma spent running around in ever-decreasing circles, her neck lolling, a look of surprise on her little chicken face, before collapsing and breathing her last, was absolutely painless, because it wasn't particularly quick?

'Yes,' said Isabel and we haven't spoken about it since.

Sunday 18 August

Brenda out walking the replaced whippet. Me out walking Jacob to give Isabel her weekly lie-in. Neither of us in the mood to take diverting action, so we have no option but to walk past one another.

And she smirks. She bloody smirks.

'What are you smirking at?' I ask, and she says, 'Oh, nothing,' still smirking, and, even though we haven't spoken directly for months, I remember immediately how much I dislike her.

'No pointless, picky, small-minded little letters from your little gang of jumped-up councillors

227

for a while,' I say, which wipes the smirk off her face.

'Sorry to hear about your chicken,' she says, which wipes the smirk off mine.

'No such thing as vet-patient confidentiality in this place, then?'

'Bob's cousin likes to keep us abreast of developments in the area.'

'Is that a chicken joke?' I say, but she looks blank.

'Will you be staying in our village for much longer?' she asks. 'Only, you said in your letter that you were leaving soon.'

'We'll leave when we're good and ready, thank you.'

'Well, let's hope the other chicken doesn't have any . . . accidents . . . in the meantime.'

'What do you mean by that?'

'Chickens are vermin. They shouldn't be in people's gardens. They attract rats.'

'You touch that chicken, and there will be hell to pay.'

'What, you'll punch me in the face again? When I'm not looking? You wouldn't stand a chance. Don't forget, *I* finished the kick-boxing course.'

And with that, she storms off. Which takes ages because she has such tiny legs.

★ ★ ★

To cool off, I gamble. By the time Isabel wakes up, I have only £1. So I'm down £49. And a chicken. I fake a headache to get out of going to

228

lunch at her parents' house and, by the time she gets back, it's more like minus £150. Or £200, if I'm being honest.

Monday 19 August

My birthday. Thirty-two years old. Unemployed. Unemployable. Spending money we don't have on a gambling addiction rather than on a beautiful son and a terminally ill chicken. This is the worst day of my life.

And it soon gets worse. Mum phones to wish me happy birthday, tells me in excruciating detail, like she always does, how my birth was horrendous ('This time thirty-two years ago, I was in a coma brought on by the size of your head') and then tells me a friend of hers is doing very well selling aloe-vera products door to door. She can find out the details if I like.

Isabel has listened to my stern warnings about not buying me anything extravagant for my birthday because we don't have the money, and I don't want anything, anyway. So she got me some marmalade and a very large mug.

Even though this is a good thing, I can't help but look disappointed.

'You told me not to spend any money,' she says anxiously.

'Yes, but you didn't have to take that quite so literally,' I reply, spreading the birthday marmalade on toast.

'But I thought you'd be pleased. Living sustainably. Self-sufficient. Escaping the tyranny

229

of the industrial-military complex. Yadayadayada.'

'How would you feel if I got you a jar of marmalade for your birthday?' I ask, knowing full well that no man has ever got away with birthday marmalade.

'I would be upset because I would have known you were really buying it for yourself. But if you'd bought me jam, I would have been delighted.'

This is not true, but I am not in the mood to argue. I need to win back that money. And, no, I don't want to have a birthday picnic.

Tuesday 20 August

I'm £250 down. I have spent the night of my birthday losing more money. Briefly, it was only £150, but I panicked and now it's £250. I must just cut my losses and stop. I must cancel my account, cut up all my credit cards or take up some other, less destructive addiction, like injecting heroin. Or I must calm down, convince myself that although I'm down now, I could be up to where I was last week in a matter of hours. And then I'll stop.

Wednesday 21 August

I am £780 down and I haven't slept for days. The double life is becoming unsustainable. I told Isabel that *Life & Times* had asked me to do another piece, which is why I am spending so much time at the computer. But Isabel keeps wanting to read it. And I keep saying it's not ready. So in order to keep this whole nightmare secret, I have to win back the money I've lost *and* write an article that *Life & Times* doesn't want. Because I can't tell her now. This all started because I have to support my wife and child, who depend on me to be responsible and breadwinning. And it's turned out to have quite the opposite effect — who would have bloody guessed? I have to make it better. And I have to do it without anyone ever finding out.

Thursday 22 August

£1,200. Shouldn't there be some sort of limit in place? Shouldn't the credit-card company step in and tell my relatives that I am spiralling hopelessly out of control? Shouldn't my luck change at some point?

Friday 23 August

£1,900. I don't care any more. My life is over. I have to tell Isabel. Secrecy is all fine if you have some hope of fixing things, but I don't. Honesty is now the least bad option, but she will have to leave me. And I won't accept that because I will have become a hopeless, desperate alcoholic online gambler. I will turn up in the middle of the night outside her house and cry like a big girl. She will have no option but to take a court order out against me. I will be banned from seeing Jacob and will have to dress up in Bananaman costumes and climb cranes in protest. Jacob will grow up without a father figure. He will have no competitive instinct. He won't learn to walk until he's four. He will throw like a girl.

'Hello, this is *Cat World*.'

'Hi, it's William . . . William Walker. I used to work there. Here. Yes. Could I speak to Janice? I'm just wondering if there are any jobs available at the moment . . . yes . . . Janice . . . Hi, how are ya? How are the cats? Yes, I know . . . ahhh, he's such a little tinker . . . really. They're so clever, aren't they? Sometimes you think they understand everything you say . . . Now, look, I'm just wondering if there's any chance you have any jobs going at . . . what? Really. No, no, that's fine . . . Yes, I can. Yes. Okay. No. See you Tuesday.'

Old job back. A stopgap. But I can't have the 'Good enough to eat?' column any more. Janice is now doing that herself.

Saturday 24 August

Isabel can't understand why I'm going back to *Cat World* because (a) I hated it and (b) I don't need it because I seem to be working so hard on articles for *Life & Times*. I spend the whole day not going into the same room as the computer. Then I become concerned that Saturday might be the day that the non-professionals play. So I have a quick go . . . ten minutes at the most

232

. . . and four hours later, I've missed another of Jacob's bedtimes on the pretence of work. And lost another £100.

Monday 26 August

It was our turn to host the baby-group barbecue on an all-important bank holiday Monday and apparently what happened was all my fault. In my defence, I was stressed because I was burning everything and we were only doing sausages, anyway, not lobster and lamb racks and champagne fountains like at Teresa's, and I was exhausted and it was really, really, really humid. And Teresa said something like, 'Oh, Jacob's sitting at last. We've been sitting for two weeks now, haven't we, coochikins, and we're only six months old. Don't they grow up fast.'

And I said something like, 'I've got a good idea, Teresa. Let's have a standing race. See which child can manage first. I'll put my child in leg splints. You can construct some sort of puppet harness for yours.'

And Annabel sniggered. And even Pete, Teresa's haunted, harried husband, smirked.

And Teresa said, 'Piss off, Annabel. And piss off, William.'

And then burst into tears because apparently she is a lot more fragile than she lets on.

And now the baby group has properly split in two. Isabel is angry with me because, while it's fine for me to make enemies all round the village, she and Jacob spend 24/7 here and would prefer to have friends. This is a problem because I was going to tell her about the whole gambling thing tonight and now I have to continue living a lie a bit longer.

And I've lost another £250.

Tuesday 27 August

Nothing has changed at *Cat World*. It still smells of cats. The people who work there still love cats. They are still totally opposed to dogs.

£2,312 down.

Wednesday 28 August

I have to sit there while Janice eats cat food for the 'Good enough to eat?' column. It was my column and it was supposed to be a joke. But whereas I used to have a tiny, tiny bit, then wash my mouth out, then make up the stuff about it having gooseberry overtones with an aftertaste of rabbit lips, she eats the whole tin instead of lunch. And her column is all deadly serious, with nutritional paragraphs and chat about the quality of the meat used.

£2,619.

Thursday 29 August

Today, I interviewed a woman who breeds very rare chinchilla Persians about how to keep a cat's coat shiny. To think, I once (nearly) interviewed Hillary Clinton.

£3,221.

Friday 30 August

Some readers brought in their cats today, and nobody did any work because they were all so excited about the cats. Someone emptied old cat litter into the bin near my desk. This is not a humane or hygienic place to work. And I keep gambling away more than I make.

£3,412.

Saturday 31 August

Ahh, the weekend. No cats. No cat interviews. Just me, my wife, my wonderful son and Louise, our highly efficient egg-layer.

Except Isabel makes me go over to Teresa's house to apologise. And rather than accept my apology graciously, Teresa says, 'Oh, that? I was only joking. I'm not bothered at all. Thanks for the sausage rolls.'

And then, when I get home, Isabel is as white as a sheet.

'Has something happened to Jacob?' I shout before realising that she has opened the credit-card bill. And seen the total. Oh, Christ.

'Fourteen hundred pounds?!' she exclaims before I can start explaining. And I don't reply because I'm thinking, Thank God, she's only seen the transactions up until last week. She'd be furious if she knew how it has snowballed since then. But I really should reply because . . .

'On LiveBetPoker? Are you insane? Is it not enough that you've just swanned out of your job and made us homeless? Now, you're gambling all our money away. Not even *our* money . . . my *parents'* money? Who have I married? What have I done?'

'I'm sorry, darling.' I can't believe it says LiveBetPoker on the credit-card statement. About a hundred times. Couldn't they pick something less damaging, like RedHotHouse-wives?

'Is this what you've been doing every night? When you said you were working? You've been gambling?'

'Well, yes, but — '

'But, why? Are you mad? Why would you do that? Why?'

And now she's crying. And now she's leaving. She's packing bags and ordering me to put the Bugaboo in the car and telling me I'm an idiot and not listening to my explanations, which are pathetic anyway, and she's telling me she's going to stay with her parents — again — and that I'd better sort myself out before she comes back or it's over, and as the door slams and the car screeches away, I can't help being a tiny bit impressed, amid all the self-loathing and worry and desperation, that Isabel has managed to get out of the house with a baby packed for an overnight stay in less than ten minutes.

But that doesn't change the fact that I am the

world's worst husband and father.

All I have left is Louise, a bloody chicken.

And now I don't even have her. Because as I traipse back through the house to open the fridge and begin to drown my stupidity, I notice a ginger tom in the garden. Around his mouth are feathers. Around the garden are bits of Louise. We must have missed the terrible and, by the looks of things, prolonged attack because of all the shouting and crying indoors.

The cat has killed the only thing in the world that still loved me.

I become enraged. I rush outside, grabbing the bread knife and a pestle. The cat makes a dash down the side of the house and runs straight out on to the village green. I chase it, mad with fury, as it races towards . . . the pub.

The pub door opens and there's Brenda calling out, 'Here, Smudgie, here, girl,' and she sees her cat and she sees me twenty yards behind. And she runs forward.

The chicken killer scurries inside. Between me and vengeance now stands a ginger midget in a Crouching Tiger pose. I have a pestle and a bread knife. For a moment, I can't decide which one to use first.

SEPTEMBER

'Govern a family as you would cook a small fish — very gently.'

CHINESE PROVERB

Sunday 1 September

THINGS TO BE PLEASED ABOUT

1. I have a job.

2. I have a wife.

3. I have a child who is on stage-3 baby food despite only being on stage-2 age.

THINGS NOT TO BE PLEASED ABOUT

1. My job is at *Cat World* and I hate cats.

2. My wife has abandoned me because she's found out about my gambling debts.

Or one-third of my gambling debts.

3. She has taken our extremely advanced child with her.

4. I have lost my last chicken.

5. I have been told by a policeman who is almost certainly related to the man whose cat killed my last chicken that if there's any more trouble, I will be arrested for threatening behaviour and disturbing the peace.

I hadn't even battered Brenda or Smudgie to death. All I had done was to point at her and then at her cat, which by now was staring at me cockily from behind a twee hydrangea. I had then done a sort-of-Crouching-Tiger pose myself, which was strange and confused everyone, not least the cat. I had then reverted to a shaken fist and a 'Your cat killed my chicken.'

'Really?' had been Brenda's response. That and a callous smirk. So I raised the pestle. Of course I was never going to bludgeon anyone with it. I might, possibly, have entertained the idea for a split second because it really would have been enormous fun, but then I lowered the weapon, smirked back and retreated.

The policeman turned up about six minutes later and asked for my side of the story. At the end of my entirely reasonable presentation of the facts, he said, 'Cats don't attack chickens.'

I protested because I had seen it with my own

eyes. He said that I might be the sort of person to attack innocent, defenceless small women, but I wasn't about to intimidate him.

I explained that Brenda was by no means defenceless.

He said, 'Oh, so you did attack her, then?'

I said, 'No.'

He said, 'Not this time.'

And, not for the first time, I wished that I'd never gone to that stupid girly kick-boxing class. Because there's no equality, not in this day and age.

The rest of the day was spent clearing up the remains of Louise (she had obviously fought tooth and claw to the very end, even though hens don't have teeth and her claws look like they came off pretty early in the proceedings). I debated whether it would be more respectful to eat what was left of her than to bury her, before burying her and getting drunk.

Now it is Sunday. While happy families are playing on the village green, I am sitting in my pants, drinking.

I call Isabel and at least she answers. She's very upset. Not about the chicken. Louise clearly meant nothing to her. She's upset about me. She doesn't think she knows me any more. She wants a couple more days with her parents and then she'll call. And now she has to go. The roast has just come out of the oven.

Her parents shouldn't be cooking the roast. *I* should. A nice shoulder of lamb or a chicken.

Oh, Louise. You poor thing.

Monday 2 September

I miss Louise. I miss Isabel. And I miss Jacob. His little smile. His near-crawling. His perfect pronunciation of his first and only word: 'Daddy'.

★ ★ ★

I arrive at work to an e-mail from Isabel. She starts by saying that she loves me, which is always bad. Then she says she knows I've been through a lot. So I skim through the bit about how it's been a tough year, what with the bathroom and the job and blah blah blah to the bad bit.

She has had enough.

She doesn't want a drinking, gambling person who eats cat food for a living as a role model for Jacob (I haven't mentioned that I am no longer allowed to be the guy who eats the cat food). She then gives me an ultimatum. If I don't sort myself out, she's leaving for good. I have one week.

Then Janice walks into the office clutching a smug-looking cat and I realise that in the wake of Louise's death, my hatred of cats is becoming obsessive.

The morning is unbearable: an article on why you should never trim whiskers followed by a roundup of cat toys. All to the rasping, hacking purr of Janice's cat. ('I'm so sorry, everyone, he just gave me such a mournful look when I was about to leave the house, I simply couldn't leave

241

him at home all day. Not while Dennis is in Birmingham.')

I have a pint at lunch. On my own. Then another.

I manage another two hours in the office before pretending to receive a call from Isabel to say that Jacob is ill and asking Janice if I can leave early. The realisation that I am now so pathetic that I pretend my son is ill to get out of work causes me to buy two gin and tonics on the train home rather than the usual one. I get home, have two beers and watch a rerun of *Alex & Geoff*.

It's at this point that the door opens. It's Isabel. She's come back to get some more things. (I knew her record departure had been too good to be true.) I am not in the office and I am drunk. It's not even 4 p.m. She takes one look at me, says, 'A week,' quite threateningly, and leaves.

I consider going for a walk to get some fresh air and then remember that I live in the village from hell. So I have another beer.

Tuesday 3 September

The only way I can survive the whole day at work, with its over-whelming aroma of pilchards and fur balls, is the promise of the emergency pub meeting I have called with Andy and Johnson. Andy is looking tanned, even though he got back from his Caribbean shagfest about nineteen years ago. He explains that he and

Saskia had just chilled on their private little beach all day, every day, rubbing oil on to each other. It was perfect. He is even getting used to the sheer amount of sex he has to have. He thinks it was just a question of building up the stamina and strengthening his lower back muscles.

Johnson says he hasn't had sex for a month, and even that was hate sex.

This seems like a good time to change the subject.

'So, I've lost almost £4,000 at internet poker,' I announce.

'Bloody hell,' says Andy, torn away from his fond memories of Caribbean rub-downs.

'Christ,' says Johnson, torn away from his fond memories of hate sex. 'Does Isabel know?'

'She found the credit-card bill for £1,400, went mad and moved back in with her parents. She says I have a week to clean up my act or she's leaving for good.'

'And she doesn't even know about the rest of it?' asks Andy, helpfully.

'She was pissed off enough about the £1,400. Another £2,600 might have made her leave for good. And now I can't exactly phone her up and say there's more.'

'You're an idiot,' they say in unison.

'I know,' I say, because I am. 'And I have no idea what to do.'

'You have to win back the money,' says Johnson, sage-like. 'And luckily for you, I have a foolproof system.'

'He's wrong, and your system isn't foolproof,' says Andy.

'Tell me about the system,' I say, sipping another pint.

Wednesday 4 September

The system worked right up until the point when it stopped working. I have now lost £6,759 across four credit cards, two of which Isabel doesn't even know about. I now have to hide four different credit-card bills. Why did I listen to Johnson? Why didn't I listen to Andy? Why can't I stop making this worse, accept that there is no magic solution and start behaving like a grown-up? Thank God Isabel isn't here. I have five days to sort this out.

Thursday 5 September

She's here. I'm home from work, all ready to sit down with a calculator and some figures, some horrible, horrible figures, and some pamphlets from some companies offering to consolidate my different debts into one easy-to-manage bigger debt, but instead, she's here.

And so is Jacob and he gives me an enormous smile.

'Aaaaaaaddaaaaaa!' he exclaims and starts almost crawling towards me.

'I couldn't take my parents for another minute,' says Isabel. 'Even my gambling, drinking idiot of a husband is preferable to Mum and Dad over any length of time. Do you know

244

they actually iron their newspapers now? I thought that was something that only happened in sit-coms.'

And I nearly tell her. I nearly tell her that the £1,400 is actually close to £7,000. But I don't. I can't.

Saturday 7 September

Johnson says his system is foolproof as long as you stick with it. So now I'm at £7,432 and I'm beginning to think I might tell Isabel and then try to convince her that the most sensible strategy is for me to stage my own canoe-related death, move to Venezuela and set up a new life. She could join me with Jacob a few months later. She wants him to be bilingual, anyway. I might be able to present it as an opportunity.

Sunday 8 September

Isabel is off with Teresa and Annabel on some ill-fated shopping expedition (how she can spend money at a time like this?). I am left at home alone with Jacob, who can now just about crawl. So rather than spending every millisecond trying to rock him to sleep, I now have to spend every millisecond making sure that he doesn't crawl off a staircase, sofa, bed or table. Of course all he wants to do is throw himself off something, so our aspirations for the morning are in direct opposition.

This is quite draining.

Isabel comes home three hours later, even though she swore she would only be two hours at most and finds a house that looks like it's been burgled. I explain that we have a self-destructive child. Because she's still angry with me for the mere £1,400 gambling loss she knows about, she says that I'm a pot calling the kettle black. And then explains how she's read a book called *Letting Go*, which is all about how children in Amazonian jungles never fall down stairs because they are allowed to learn about risk from a very early age. Their parents trust their survival instinct.

I point out that the infant mortality rate in South America is probably an awful lot higher than it is in the UK.

She points out that this isn't because the children are falling down stairs.

I point out that this is because they don't have stairs in the jungle.

She points out that I'm an idiot.

Given that I'm still well and truly in the doghouse, I point out that this is fair enough. And I don't even say anything when she opens up her shopping bags to reveal lots and lots of 9-12-month clothes for our child, even though three months is not a very big window and couldn't Jacob manage with only a couple of babygros while money is so tight?

We all go to sleep in the same bed for the first time in a long time. I wake up briefly and watch my family sleeping. The moon lights up their intertwined bodies and I feel overcome with emotion.

I am the luckiest person alive — and the stupidest. What have I been playing at? Why have I been taking these risks? This, right here, is what I should be concentrating on. My family. I have made this boy with this woman. If I can do that, then I can get us through these difficulties. I can stop mucking around and change things. I owe it to them.

Monday 9 September

No more drinking. No more gambling. No more whingeing about jobs or people or anything. I need to count life's blessings. I need to change.

'Andy, we're going to enter a triathlon.'

'Okay.'

'I'm starting training this morning.'

'Okay.'

And I'm off, running at lunch, leaving Janice and her cat to share their tin of tuna. Twenty minutes in, I'm not even that tired. Despite all the drinking and the late-night gambling, I have strength. I have endurance. There can be only one explanation for this: I have Daddy Power.

DADDY POWER

For more than eight months, I have been carrying a baby around. Sometimes, I have had to rock the baby at obtuse angles, angles that require shaman-like pain control. Over the eight months, the baby has grown heavier and

247

wrigglier. Back in January, my arms got tired a mere half-hour in, and that was when the load was only a couple of kilos. Now, I can go all day with more than double the weight. I could be an extra in the early part of a ninja movie when a monk makes his disciples hold bricks at arm's length in a thunderstorm or something.

I have also developed the mental strength required to get up and out of bed at any hour and be immediately alert. I have SAS levels of endurance. I can listen to the Gorillaz album *Kids with Guns* (still Jacob's current and only favourite) ninety-eight times back to back without crying once.

This is Daddy Power. Gritty strength, mental acuity, endurance. It is, of course, nothing compared to Mummy Power.

MUMMY POWER

All the above, but tripled and with a laser stare that can stop an eight-month-old (or, indeed, a thirty-two-year-old) in his tracks at thirty paces.

Tuesday 10 September

No gambling. No drinking. Another lunchtime run. I am now transferring my newly realised Daddy Power to work. Not once did I think about cats or Brenda despite writing a whole article about a new wave of super-deluxe cat beds and seeing bloody Brenda on the train. I

248

blocked. I parried. I stood firm. I am putting my life back into perspective. I am winning.

Wednesday 11 September

I have consolidated all my debts into one large, easily-hideable debt. The monthly interest is less hideable. I still need a plan.

'Still on for training this Saturday, Andy?'

'Yep.' Andy is a good friend, after all. 'How's the gambling?'

'Over. But I need to find £5,000 or Isabel will still kill me. All I've got at the moment is bloody aloe-vera pyramid-selling.'

'Aloe vera?'

' 'Fraid so.'

'I bloody love aloe vera. Saskia and I are really into it. It's all about the mannans and the anthraquinones and the lectins, isn't it?'

'Is it?'

'Yep, we use it all the time. For bathing and massaging. It's great for sore bits.'

'Oh, for Christ's sake.'

'Saskia spends a bloody fortune on it, though. You know where we can get it cheap?'

Thursday 12 September

I am now officially an aloe-vera salesperson. I have signed some forms and I have watched a video that says I could have a Ferrari by the end of the year if I create a pyramid of aloe-vera sellers beneath me. I don't want a Ferrari. I just want to be back on track. I shall sell my aloe vera and all will be well. Of course, technically, I am now more in debt after putting £400 on the debit card for the aloe-vera area sales manager. I also have a boss who isn't delighted that the store cupboard normally reserved for cat food samples is now full of aloe vera.

'It will only be for a few weeks, Janice.'

'Why can't you keep them at home?'

'Because Isabel can't find out.'

'What an exciting double life you lead.'

I go for yet another Ninja Daddy run.

Friday 13 September

It's Friday the 13th, and it was all going so well. The builders actually called me. We can move back next Wednesday, although the paint may still be wet.

Dennis is back from Birmingham, so the office of *Cat World* is catfree.

I took a whole minute off yesterday's run.

I sold £100 worth of aloe-vera products over the phone. Yes, it was to Andy, so I had to give him a discount and get over the idea that I was selling my best mate some gel to rub on my ex. But I was making money. Secretly. At this rate, I could be debt-free by . . . oh.

And then Andy phoned back to say he had to cancel tomorrow's triathlon practice because he was going to Paris with Saskia.

'But it's our first one.'

250

'I know. I'm sorry. But I was thinking, you know, we haven't been away since the Caribbean.'

'That was five weeks ago.'

'And, well, I might, you know, pop the question.'

And rather than being a best mate and saying, 'Wow, that's amazing, you two really deserve each other,' or some other nonsense, I said, 'Isn't this all a bit fast?' as if I were his dad.

And then I got home all ready to break the bad news to Isabel (about Andy, not the £8,000 debt that she only knows about one sixth of) and found Jacob teetering on the very top step of the staircase.

'Jacob!' I shouted. And he looked around in shock, and in so doing, lost his balance and fell. I was too far away to do anything except scream. Isabel appeared through the doorway at the bottom of the stairs and caught him on the second bounce.

For a good two seconds, there was silence.

This was when I thought, 'His neck has snapped. His skull has fractured. He is paralysed. He will never play rugby, not even for an average club side.'

Then he started screaming. He was alive. He was fine. He had a bruise and a bump, but he was fine. He wouldn't be screaming if he wasn't going to be all right. That's what the doctors always say, isn't it?

'What on earth was he doing at the top of the stairs?' I shouted above the screaming. This, of course, was not the time to be allocating blame, but I was too shocked not to be angry.

251

'I can't believe you did that!' said Isabel.

'Me?'

'You made him fall.'

'What?'

'I was there. I was watching him from the doorway. He was climbing the stairs perfectly well all by himself. And then you came in and shouted at him.'

'He was about to fall.'

'No, he wasn't. He's been up those stairs plenty of times. He's self-aware. He's learning the risks. And then you just bellow at him, and he falls.'

'That's ridiculous. He shouldn't be crawling up stairs. We need a stair guard.'

'We are *not* having a stair guard.'

'We are.'

'We. Are. Not. Now leave us alone.'

I'll tell her about Andy and Saskia and the debt another time.

Saturday 14 September

We have agreed to disagree about stairs. I have explained that dads spend every minute imagining the millions of ways in which our children can kill themselves with anything from a staircase to an egg whisk. She has explained that if we don't expose Jacob to risk, he can never learn to look after himself. She starts talking about children in jungles again and I set off on my solo triathlon-training programme.

I am a machine. Nothing can stop me. Not

252

even the knowledge that my wife is still content to experiment with her Mowgli theory of parenting while I am away.

SOME OF THE THINGS THAT COULD KILL JACOB AND HOW

1. Staircases. Falling down them, obviously. But also falling up them.

2. Egg whisks. Fingers get stuck in the whisk end. Jacob panics. Waves hands about. Gouges eye with non-whisk end. Infection spreads. Death.

3. Forks. As above, but without stuck fingers or panic.

4. Baby swings. Daddy pushes too hard. Neck snaps.

5. Bugaboos. Brake not working properly. Looking away for a second. Slight hill. Across road safely but quickly. Continues down pavement, through gate, tips into shallow pond. Can't undo the buckles quickly enough. Drowns.

6. Umbrellas. Obvious.

7. Dishwasher doors. Obvious.

8. Baths. Death traps.

9. Bouncer. We're not getting one. Teresa has one and it's a human catapult. The torque is too high. If anything were to snap, baby would be fired at high velocity into the door frame. Death.

Sunday 15 September

Neck has gone.

Must have slept funny.

'Maybe you were training too hard. Or worrying too much. Have some arnica and wear this neck brace. It will help.'

Jacob has a bruise on his temple, the poor sausage. His perfect body. Damaged. Neither Isabel nor I mention it.

Monday 16 September

Ninja self-control has taken a hit, thanks to the neck giving way. On the way to the station, Brenda smirks at the neck brace. I smirk at her ginger hair. I am not one hundred per cent sure she knows it was the red hair I was smirking at.

At work, I write something sarcastic about people who buy cat magazines in an article about, well, cats. Then forget to delete it. Janice asks if I have a problem with cats. I say I was only joking. I love cats.

Then Andy phones and declares an emergency pub meeting. He says he has news. I have declared the last six emergencies in a row, so this is something of a novelty. Nevertheless, I say I can't until tomorrow night, which is mean.

No one at work wants to buy any aloe vera, despite its many and varied health-giving properties. Sceptics.

Then Isabel phones to say that Alex is upset. Geoff has gone off to Morocco to design Sting's yoga tent without him after they had a fight about whether Danish white and ochre can be used on the same fireplace. He's going to stay with us for a few days. Is that okay?

There are a million reasons why that is not okay, not least because, on Wednesday, we're moving back to the house that Alex was primarily responsible for destroying. We don't need Alex hanging around while that's going on. Patiently, I explain this to Isabel and she says we aren't moving on Wednesday after all. We're moving at the weekend because we'll have more time then and she hates the smell of paint. And Alex is staying. And I have to be more charitable.

I say fine, but I'm afraid I have to go out with Andy tonight. He wants to talk. She says fine, so I phone Andy and say I can make the pub after all. And I'm sorry for being mean.

Andy has got engaged to Saskia. It was perfect. They were having dinner on some terrace on the Left Bank. There were candles. There was a bowl of *moules frites à deux*. They fed each other. They kissed with their aloe-soft lips. A jazz band struck up across the cobbled street, and Andy got down on one knee and proposed. Saskia burst into tears and accepted gladly. They looked up at the night sky, and he swears — he absolutely swears — that a shooting star shot across it. Then they got the bill and went back to their tiny, seedy hotel room and made passionate love all night. He spanked her. She spanked him. He tied her up. She tied him up. It was amazing.

'I'm going to be sick in my mouth, Andy,' I said supportively. 'But I'm delighted for you. Marriage is a wonderful thing. Don't listen to anything Johnson will tell you. And don't mess up like me, either. Ignore both of our approaches to the marital challenge, and you will be fine. Congratulations.'

'So will you be my best man?'

Oh God.

Best man at Saskia's wedding. Oh God, oh God, oh God.

'Of course I will. Now come here and give me a hug. And mind my sore neck.'

Tuesday 17 September

Over breakfast, Isabel seemed to receive the news of Andy's engagement to the Destroyer of Relationships quite well. But Alex, who was sitting in *my* seat eating *my* cereal out of *my* bowl, started sobbing. 'Everyone else always finds true love. I never will. I'll die sad and alone.'

'Tush, tush,' said Isabel, as if she was a folkloric Russian grandmother and Alex was a child who'd just had a nightmare about a wolf. 'You love Geoff and he loves you. You're perfect for each other. You're just having a little tiff.'

'I try to do everything he wants and it's never good enough. He's such a perfectionist.'

I may, at that point, have snorted but I think it was masked by the coffee machine. All the same, Isabel gave me the Mummy Power look before declaring that she was late for a coffee morning.

'Bit early for you lot, isn't it?' I said, concerned that I might be left in the house with a snivelling Alex.

'Well, Annabel and Teresa keep arguing about parenting methods. I thought they were going to kill each other in Bluewater the other week. Something to do with bibs. So I thought we'd meet earlier this week. They have higher blood sugar early in the morning. Do you want to come, Alex?'

'No, thanks,' he moped. 'I'll stay here, if it's all right with you, William?' And he looked at me weepily, so I had to say, 'Fine.' And the minute Isabel and Jacob pranced off to their social engagement, Alex turned to me and said, 'How can I make him love me?'

'I'm really not the right person to ask.'

'I mean, I do everything I can to show how much I love him, but it doesn't work. The harder I try, the worse it gets.'

'Yeah, you're trying too hard. It's obvious. Blokes hate that.'

'Well, what should I do, then? He has to know how I feel.'

Half an hour later, I left for work. In the space of those thirty minutes, I had become Alex's chief relationship adviser, his counsellor, his Zen Master of Love. He hugged me in gratitude. I hugged him back. And he wandered off into the garden repeating his new mantra: 'I shall be mean. I shall keep him keen. I will win his heart through ruthless aloofness.'

Wednesday 18 September

'What did you say to him?'
　'Nothing much.'
　'Well, thanks. He seems much happier today.'
　'I suppose.'
　'He said you'd really put things into perspective.'
　'Right.'
　And she gave me a kiss. A naughty kiss. A we-might-have-sex-when-you-get-home-from-work kiss. After days and weeks of tetchiness caused by my idiocy, one chat with Alex and she's being properly nice and doing proper naughty kissing. Except that Jacob was watching, so I cut it off early and ruined it. But you can't kiss naughtily in front of your children, can you? You'd traumatise them for life.
　'Does this mean he won't be staying tonight?'
　'He's staying until tomorrow, okay?'
　Sex is not possible.

Thursday 19 September

Ninja self-control is back. I am a triathloning, counselling, decisive and hard-working father of one crawling, sitting baby. Without even having

258

to set foot in a Gamblers Anonymous meeting, I have thus concluded that there is no system and that the way to pay off my £8,000 debt is not via the magic of a change of luck in online gambling. Consequently, I have closed my online poker account. Not only that, the cleaner at work bought a tub of aloe. Things are on the up. Except that I get home and Alex is still there . . .

'Why's he still here?' I shout-whisper to Isabel in the kitchen after dinner.

'Because he had another row with Geoff,' scream-hisses Isabel back.

'I thought everything was all right again?'

'Well, it obviously isn't, is it? What did you tell him?'

'I already told you. Nothing much. I just said that sometimes being an obsessive lovesick puppy isn't necessarily the way to a woman's or, in his case, man's heart.'

'Oh great, the William Walker approach to relationships.'

'Look — '

'Hi, Will,' mopes Alex by way of interruption.

'Hi, Alex. Sorry you had another row.'

'You two boys have a chat while I get Jacob to sleep,' says Isabel and scarpers with Jacob. And so it happens again. I have to listen to Alex moan on about his terrible relationship and how he loves Geoff but he's not sure Geoff loves him back. That he tried being less clingy on the phone today, but Geoff was still distant with him. When I point out that this might just be because Geoff's in Morocco — which *is* distant — he brightens up. Then he asks me what to do.

259

I point out that I am by no means an expert and then urge him in as diplomatic a way as possible to stop being a psycho.

'So I shouldn't call him?'

'Not every day.'

'And I shouldn't tell him I love him?'

'No. Not every time you talk to him. Treat 'em mean to keep 'em keen.'

'But I'm so miserable. I think I might die if I don't see him again soon.'

Jesus. 'Shall we watch some television? It might take your mind off things.'

'Okay, Will, thanks for the chat. You're so good at this stuff. I can see why Isabel stuck with you,' says Alex, sort of complimentarily, as we traipse through to the living room.

'*Chicago* or *Road Wars*?' I ask, charitably.

'*Chicago*.'

Annoying.

Isabel comes down. She hates *Chicago*, too. We sit there, three being a crowd. Then she says she's tired. And I say I'm tired. And Alex says he'll probably stay up a bit longer. So Isabel and I go upstairs together and, out of the blue, Isabel kisses me naughtily. And I kiss her. We're in the bathroom. We start undressing, but there's no lock on the door.

'Sssshhh, let's go into the bedroom,' says Isabel, even more naughtily.

'No, we'll wake Jacob,' I reply, unused to the naughtiness.

'No, we won't. He's out for the count.' She really is intent on being naughty.

It was three, maybe four seconds after we had

finished being naughty that Isabel gasped.

'Oh, shit!' were her exact words. My mind raced. Had I done something wrong? Was she having some sort of post-traumatic sex panic? Had she realised she hadn't wanted it? Had her neck gone? Or worse, had she suddenly realised Jacob had been wide-eyed throughout? Was he now traumatised for ever? What? What?

'What?'

'The baby monitor!'

'Oh, shit!' I said, jumping out of bed. 'The baby monitor.'

And there it was, on the bedside table, its little green light flashing away.

'Turn it off,' mimed Isabel. I turned it off and we listened. Five seconds later, we heard the beeping, the terrible beeping from the monitor's speaker. The monitor's speaker in the living room. Yes, it had happened. The audio track of our naughtiness had been played through a loudspeaker. And Alex had heard the whole thing.

Friday 20 September

Breakfast was embarrassing. Apparently, the reason he hadn't turned his bit of the monitor off was because he didn't know how. On-off buttons are so tricky. His solution to the problem had been to turn up *Chicago*. Hmmm. I decided I needed to get to work early.

'Can I just say, guys, that I am glad you two are my friends,' said Alex as I made for the door. 'And I'm glad you are still very much in love.'

No, you can't. You can't *just say that*.

In my haste to escape from the house, I nearly knocked over Brenda as she came tearing round the corner with the replacement whippet. Irritating that she was on my side of the green.

'I hear you're leaving tomorrow?' she squeaked.

'Certainly am.'

'Well, safe journey.'

'Thanks.'

'And sorry about the chicken.'

'Right, thanks.' Maybe she was being nice at last.

'Mind you, you have to admire Smudgie, don't you?'

'Who's Smudgie?'

'Our cat. It took Bob ages to train her to attack birds. Most cats don't have it in them. But she came through in the end, though, didn't she? You should do something on her in your little magazine.'

And off she jogged before I could react.

This is, indeed, my last day in the village. The village run by the midget bitch and the whippet killer. And it is only on my way to work that I remember I have the perfect leaving present for them. In the cupboard mostly full of my unsold aloe-vera products is a large bag of Lion Poo, sent in to the magazine by an enthusiastic marketing person who clearly hadn't understood that a magazine called *Cat World* might be pro-cat.

I take it home.

I bide my time as we say farewell to Annabel and Teresa.

I wait for darkness to fall.

I wait for the pub to shut.

I wait another hour.

And then another, just to be sure.

And then, dressed head to toe in black, I sneak across the green. Crouching by the fence, I open the bag and start flinging whole handfuls of the pellets into the pub garden. When I get back to the house, Isabel is changing Jacob in the bathroom, half asleep.

'What on earth are you doing still awake?' she asks.

'Nothing,' I reply.

Nothing, except at last exacting my revenge on Smudgie for the death of Louise.

Saturday 21 September

We're back at our house. Almost six months since the flood, and we're back. And everything is as it should be. Jacob is so delighted to be home that he immediately crawls up the stairs while neither of us is watching. But he doesn't fall.

He just sits at the top and says 'Dadda' proudly. This is definitely closer than 'Aaaaaad-dddaaaaaaaaa', which, until now, I have been convincing myself is 'Daddy'.

It takes all day to unpack our junk. I get my old drawer back. Jacob gets his old nine drawers back, even though one of his babygros is one-eighth the size of one of my babygros.

By 6 p.m., we are all exhausted. Jacob tucks

into his courgette-and-pasta bake, gumming the bits of courgette in the absence of teeth. I tuck into a G & T, gumming the lemon in the absence of courgette.

'I thought you were training,' says Isabel, as she walks into our newly restored living room. Oh God, I know I've been in the doghouse, but can't I have one G & T without being made to feel guilty?

'Yes, I am training,' I reply testily. 'But we've got our house back. I thought I might celebrate a little bit.'

'Me, too,' says Isabel, her angry-at-husband face breaking into a be-nice-to-husband smile as she taadaas a bottle of champagne and two glasses out from behind her back.

And then she makes a little speech about how she still loves me, even though I broke the house and became a gambling, drinking reprobate in the year — the very year — we start a family. And I start a little speech about how I completely don't deserve her, given everything she's listed, but I'm interrupted by the phone.

'Don't answer it,' I beg.

'I have to answer it.'

'Don't answer it.'

'I have to . . . Hi, Alex. Yes, I'll just get him.'

'I don't want to talk to him.'

'You have to talk to him.'

'I don't want to talk to him — Hi, Alex . . . No . . . not at all . . . yes . . . no . . . no. No, just because you didn't call, it doesn't mean he will call. You don't need to speak to him every day. Give him some space. We talked about this . . . No

. . . No . . . Look, it's fine. Just because he hasn't called, it doesn't mean he doesn't love you . . . But he's in Morocco . . . Yes, but mobile calls are expensive . . . No, don't call him. It's good to give each other a bit of space . . . No . . . Don't call him tomorrow, either . . . That's what he's expecting. You have to play a little harder to get, okay? Okay. Be strong. He might have won today's battle, but love is a war. Byeeee.'

'That's ridiculous advice,' says Isabel, who has been eavesdropping.

'No, it's not. He's being too clingy. Men hate that.'

'Yes, but the opposite isn't that appealing, either.'

'Yes, it is. You wait and see.' The Zen Master of Relationships strikes again.

Tuesday 24 September

In order for me to be best man, Andy wants me to become proper friends with Saskia. To bury the hatchet. I email Saskia.

'Hi, Saskia. I just wanted to say congratulations.'

'Thank you, darling. Are you jealous? You know you could have had me.'

'Umm.'

'Don't be a naughty boy, William. I meant marriage. You already had me the other way, didn't you?'

Oh God, this is going to be difficult.

'I was wondering if we might have a quick drink?'

'I'd love to. Usual place?'
'No. Let's make it a sandwich.'
'Ooooh.'
'A lunchtime sandwich.'
'Okay.'

Wednesday 25 September

Geoff still hasn't called. Alex must hold firm.

Thursday 26 September

I should really tell Isabel that I'm going to meet Saskia to bury the hatchet. But I don't because every way I rehearse saying it out loud it sounds like a euphemism. Even burying the hatchet sounds naughty when Saskia is involved.

Still not a peep from Geoff. He's good at this game.

Friday 27 September

Geoff called. Alex didn't answer, as I instructed. Geoff left a message asking Alex to call. Alex has called me to ask what to do. I said he should call but not yet. Maybe leave it a couple of days. And if he calls again during that time, leave it. Isabel says men have no idea about relationship politics and I should phone Alex back and tell him to call immediately. I don't.

Saturday 28 September

Geoff hasn't called again. This guy's playing hard ball.

Sunday 29 September

He has called. Again. And Alex left it, again, as instructed. Alex is miserable. 'I want him. I don't care what's happened in Marrakesh. I'll forgive anything. I want him back.'

'All right. Calm down. Call him tomorrow. He'll be eating out of your hand.'

Monday 30 September

I chose lunch as the most suitable time to meet Saskia. Whether it's more neutral than meeting for coffee is debatable, but it's a lot better than drinks or dinner — and she is about to marry my best mate, so it's not like anything bad is going to happen.

Except that she's managed to find the only low-slung smoochers' couch in the whole otherwise-entirely-unsexy sandwich bar, she's wearing a dress that wouldn't cover a budgie and, speaking of budgies, I can't help noticing — although I'm trying very, very hard not to — that she's had some sort of breast enhancement.

'Do you like them?' she says as I sit down next to her. Oh God, she saw me looking at her breasts. Why did I look at her breasts? These are the very breasts I should not be looking at. These are evil breasts. These breasts destroy lives.

'Like what?' I reply pathetically.

'The new boobs.' She heaves them forward, we both plunge into the middle of the sofa and I plunge into the middle of her cleavage. I'm like Tarzan when he falls in the quicksand. The more he struggles, the deeper he gets. 'You can have a squeeze if you want.'

'Umm.'

'It's okay. I only had the jab. It's the latest. Gives me an extra D for a couple of months. But don't worry, darling, it's still all real. See?'

'Umm.'

They are right there, right in my face — her relationship-destroying breasts — and I can't think of a thing to say. I try to look at the floor, but it is obscured by the breasts, so I look at the ceiling. A piece of crust goes down the wrong way and I start choking. Her murderous breasts are choking me.

'I'm delighted you are marrying Andy and I'm delighted I'm going to be best man,' I say after I've gulped at my water and pushed myself back on to my side of the sofa.

'That's sweet, sweetness. I'm delighted, too. He's amazing in bed, you know.'

Why does she talk like this? Why, over an egg-and-cress sandwich and inflated breasts, do I get to hear all about how she never thought a man could make love so sensitively, so beautifully, so expertly as Andy? She says it's almost like making love to a woman, a woman with a penis. And that's as close to perfection as you could ever wish for. So she, too, is delighted to be marrying Andy.

As I leave the sandwich bar, Isabel calls.

'Hi, darling,' I say in the voice I know I use when I'm trying not to sound guilty about something even though, on this occasion, I really don't have anything to sound guilty about.

'Hi,' she replies, immediately suspicious. 'Where are you?'

This is the moment in the conversation that calls for direct honesty. I need to tell Isabel that I met Saskia to congratulate her on her engagement, that it all went well and that I'm now heading back to the office. It's not difficult. It won't cause any problems. Isabel will be fine with that. The one thing I mustn't do is try to conceal my meeting with Saskia.

'Nowhere. Just walking. Going back to the office.'

It must have been the breasts. I must have felt an urge to conceal the lunch because Saskia hadn't been concealing her breasts. Or maybe I'm intent, subconsciously, on making my life so pointlessly impossible that I have to create these ridiculous situations.

'Okay, darling,' she replies, even more suspiciously — and who could blame her, you idiot? 'You need to call Alex. Geoff's split up with him.'

It turns out Geoff was in a car crash in Marrakesh. He wasn't hurt — just a few cuts and bruises — but he was shaken. He didn't leave a message because he didn't want to scare

Alex. But he has now ended it because Alex wasn't there for him when he most needed him. And it's my fault.

'This is fine,' I say to Alex when he's finally stopped ranting. 'He's simply adjusting to the new you . . . and that new you is what he wanted in the first place. It will be fine. You simply need to do the following . . . '

Text message from Saskia. 'There was nothing wrong with your penis, either. Thanks for the lunch.' Delete. I can never speak to Andy again without thinking of him as a woman with a penis, a penis that is as acceptable as my penis.

Then Isabel phones to ask why I didn't tell her I was having lunch with Saskia.

Then Andy phones to ask what I thought of Saskia's new breasts.

Then Saskia phones to say she phoned Isabel, given that we're all friends now, and didn't realise I hadn't mentioned our little sandwich à sandwich.

I tell Saskia she's a nightmare.

I tell Andy he's marrying a tart.

I go home and I'm halfway through telling a frosty Isabel that I'm an idiot when the doorbell rings. It's the policeman from the village in which we're lucky we no longer live.

'Evening, sir. Can we have a few minutes of your time? You're not under any formal caution.'

'Certainly, come in. It is bath time, but I'm sure I can spare a few minutes. What seems to be the problem this time, officer?'

'A cat has been murdered.'

'Sorry?'

'A cat has been murdered.'

'What cat?'

'Smudgie, the cat you have, in the past, threatened with violence, was found this morning by her owners. She experienced a long, slow, painful death.'

'Blimey. Is 'murder' technically the right word?'

'For the last ten days, she became increasingly deranged, unable to stay in her own garden. Something, we don't know what, was terrifying her. Her owners suspect poisoning. Then, it is our theory that the would-be killer grew tired of waiting for the poison to take full effect. Smudgie was found this morning, her skull crushed by what we assume was a heavy mallet-shaped object. Do you own a mallet, Mr Walker?'

'This is ridiculous.'

'Please just answer the question, sir. Let's try to keep things cooperative for now, if we don't mind?'

'I don't own a mallet. But I'm pretty sure they've got a croquet set at the pub.' The policeman ignores my insinuation. I'm tempted to say it was me who made the anonymous tip-off about the death of Brenda's whippet, but something tells me that won't help.

'You work for a cat magazine, sir?'

'Yes.'

'So you would have knowledge of how to poison a cat?'

'No, that's not something we've covered on the magazine. Our readers tend to prefer more positive features.'

'Please don't take that sarcastic tone with me,

sir. Where were you between the hours of six and eight this morning?'

'I was out cycling. I'm training for a triathlon.'

'Anyone else training with you?'

'No, my best friend is supposed to be, but he's too busy rubbing aloe vera all over his fiancée's new breasts.' The policeman doesn't laugh, so I continue. 'Look, do you really think I'd kill a cat?'

'There's not enough evidence to know who did it for sure. But there will be.'

'Isn't this a lot of fuss over a cat?'

'Sir, in my twenty-four years as a policeman, I have never seen such a brutal killing of an innocent and loved family pet. The man who did this needs to be stopped. Good evening, sir.'

As the door closes, Isabel is standing in the living room, arms folded. Jacob stops tearing the newspaper I had yet to read into a thousand tiny pieces and looks up intently.

'What did you do the night we left the village?' asks Isabel.

'I poured Lion Poo all over the pub garden.' There was no point in trying to make this sound any worse than it already was.

'What?' exclaims Isabel, astonished.

'Dadda!' exclaims Jacob, dismayed. My nine-month-old child can do dismayed. Teresa's child can do happy and sad. Mine can do dismayed, nonchalant and three different types of perturbed.

'It was to avenge the death of Louise. I was upset.'

'So, where were you this morning? Butchering

a cat?' This is Isabel again, not Jacob. He is now looking mortified, which is even more impressive than dismayed.

'Don't be ridiculous. I was cycling. But I know who killed Smudgie.'

As Isabel swept Jacob up to bed, I walked to the computer and started playing Minesweeper despondently. Only when I lost the first game did I notice the e-mail in my inbox. 'We haven't seen you for a while at Poker54321.com. Come back and have a flutter with this free £50 bet. For our most trusted customers only!'

OCTOBER

'Adam and Eve had many advantages, but the principal one was that they escaped teething.'

MARK TWAIN

Tuesday 1 October

Saskia isn't talking to me.

Andy is angry with me and hardly talking to me.

Isabel is only 96 per cent sure I didn't stave Smudgie's head in.

But . . . I deleted the e-mail. I am no longer a gambling addict. I still have £8,000 in secret debt, but it's no longer spiralling out of control.

And . . . Alex is talking to me.

'It worked. William, you are a master of love. You have saved us. Geoff does love me after all. He was just a bit hurt, you know, psychologically as well as physically. It's brilliant. Thank you.'

'This is fine, young Alex. You still have much

to learn, but if you keep to my simple Guide to Not Being a Bunny Boiler, you will prosper.'

GUIDE TO NOT BEING A BUNNY BOILER

1. Being totally in love is very unattractive. If this is unavoidable, hide it (though not in a creepy secret-dungeon kind of way).

2. Saying 'I love you' hourly is too much. So is more than once a day. Once a week is fine. Twice a month in the early stages of a relationship is ideal, moving to once a month, bi-monthly and, finally, on birthdays in the twilight years.

3. Equally, the more you phone, the lower the value of the currency of your phone calls. If you can't stop yourself, leave your phone at home or wear boxing gloves so you can't dial.

4. Presents should match the moment. Three hundred red roses for a second date? Too much. Six pink carnations for a second anniversary? Not enough. The balance is hard to gauge but either way, err on the side of caution until you are well and truly past the dating stage.

5. Your motto should be: Cool and Aloof. Only laugh at her, or indeed his, jokes if they are genuinely funny. Laughing at everything is

unattractive. Being early for dates is unattractive. Planning for the distant future is unattractive. You should be operating hand to mouth on dates for at least the first year. 'Sure, let's do it again next week. I'll see if I'm free. Oh no, it'll have to be the week after' and so forth.

6. If he doesn't call, he doesn't write, he doesn't text and he doesn't come round, he doesn't love you.

Wednesday 2 October

Isabel says she is now 100 per cent sure I didn't bludgeon the cat. (I decided to get quite shirty about her suggesting she wasn't 100 per cent sure, which was a gamble given all the other things I've been keeping from her, but it paid off. Sometimes you need to draw a line in the marital sand and, this time, she didn't cross it.) She thinks I should register a complaint with the police about the blatantly partisan behaviour of the village bobby. I point out that I did throw Lion Poo all over Brenda's garden, so it might be best to lie low and hope it all blows over.

Surprised at my self-control and calm deliberation, she agrees.

I'm also surprised, and to make things even better, I go for a swim. This is the new me. I am a swimming, cycling, running superdad. I live in a nice house with a lovely wife and a child who is wearing 12–18-month clothes despite being only nine months old. I am strong. I produce strong, healthy offspring. I have strong genes. No challenge is too great. Not the triathlon, even though it's less than two months away and it's called the Xtreme 3 and it will be November. Not the accusation of cat murder, even though I am partly implicated. And not the selling of aloe vera.

Well, maybe that. I have upset Saskia and Andy, my two most loyal customers. They have threatened to use another distributor. I shall have to find alternative sexoholic hippies. But still, I am strong. Nothing can stop me making this year, this first year of fatherhood, a success.

Thursday 3 October

Brenda and Bob are on *South-East Today* and *Meridian* local news. Brenda has puffy red eyes. Bob looks like granite. He isn't even pretending to be upset any more. They are appealing for witnesses to the brutal murder of a cat they treasured like a child. Even the earnest presenters are using the word 'murder'.

Cheered up by a nice text from Alex. He is sticking to the Ninja Code and Geoff is now the keen one.

Friday 4 October

Brenda is on the train that I catch in order to avoid bumping into Brenda. She sees me. I see her. Normally we ignore each other. Today, she marches over.

'I will make you pay,' she hisses and the whole carriage, except the guy who always falls asleep against the window and dribbles down his tie, jumps to attention. This is a posh train. People don't have arguments on it.

'Listen, Brenda. I didn't kill her.' Even the dribbling guy has been elbowed awake to watch the excitement.

'You did. You killed her. You drove her mad with poison and then you stamped on her. And now she's dead.' Brenda, the poor irritating woman, is now pointing her stubby little fingers into my chest. The dribbling guy assumes we're talking about a child, I'm sure of it. He has automatically leaped to the conclusion that I killed a child, perhaps the ginger woman's child, perhaps years ago, and that I got sent to prison but I'm now out on day release. He has plainly watched too much ITV drama. I need to clarify the situation before the audience starts heckling.

'It was only a cat.' There is a collective gasp.

'So you admit it.'

'No, of course not. I had nothing to do with it. And even if I did, which I don't, you killed Louise.'

Another gasp.

'It was only a chicken,' says Brenda to the rest of the carriage, not to me, and no one gasps. She turns back, her ginger pointy eyes burning gingerly up at me. 'You killed my cat — and I'm going to make you pay.'

And with that, she walks off into a different

carriage. 'It was only a cat,' I mutter. Because it was only a cat.

At *Cat World*, Janice asks if I saw the news story about the cat that was brutally murdered. I say I didn't, but would she like a peppermint. She loves peppermints. It's her catnip. I always have some to hand if I need to take her mind off something.

Saturday 5 October

Geoff and Alex have popped round for lunch and to play tonsil hockey with each other in front of my nine-month-old child. I don't know if this is acceptable or not. I worry, briefly, that I'm homophobic but then realise I'm not: any tonsil hockey in front of a nine-month-old is unacceptable. Isabel seems to think everything up to early-stage fore-play, including affectionate spanking, is acceptable. This is partly because she's read a book about how, in Germany and other northern European countries, they teach sex education to toddlers.

'It means they don't stigmatise sex. It's simply another part of human life. Perfectly natural. Nothing to be secretive or weird or ignorant about,' she says.

'To toddlers, though?'

'We're very happy to teach our kids about where meat comes from.'

'Sorry?'

'Sex is just another part of life. Why shouldn't

our children know about it? Isn't it better that they grow up with a matter-of-fact attitude to it rather than thinking it's something dirty and grubby? The Germans don't have that behind-the-bike-shed mentality. Nor do the Danish.'

I don't know where to begin. All I can think of is that the one time I went to Copenhagen, all the girls were beautiful and half of them were pregnant. And that whenever Johnson sends me a gratuitous hardcore porn picture — usually a fat woman in a Viking hat doing something unspeakable to a barnyard animal — it's German. And that I'd be very happy for Jacob to know absolutely nothing about any of this until long after his twenty-first birthday. And that teenage years are supposed to include a succession of embarrassing behind-bike-shed encounters, otherwise how else are English people supposed to develop their lovable sexual hang-ups?

And now Alex is licking a bit of mascarpone off Geoff's cheek, and Jacob is wide-eyed and Isabel is giving me a don't-be-weird-it's-fine look, so I abandon my pudding (I don't like mascarpone, anyway, I've said this a million times) and escape to do the washing up.

'Thanks,' whispers Alex conspiratorially, breaking my leave-me-alone-when-I'm-doing-the-washing-up rule. 'Thanks again.'

'It's fine.'

'But, my God, this treat 'em mean strategy of yours, it's driving him crazy.'

'I haven't noticed any particular meanness. All I saw was you licking mascarpone off him.'

'Oh no, don't you worry. That's all part of my

game. Later, I'm going to say I've got work to do — and I'm going to go back to my place. Alone. It will drive him wild.'

I have created a monster.

Sunday 6 October

Andy arrives for our first attempt at a mini-triathlon. He's still not really talking to me. At first, I assume this is because we are swimming and it's hard to talk underwater. Then I assume it's because we're cycling and you're supposed to pedal in each other's slipstreams. Then we're running and I think I'm going to puke, so I don't care if we're not talking. Except I do care. Andy never gets upset about anything.

'Look . . . I'm . . . sorry . . . I . . . called . . . her . . . a tart,' I say, using the energy I really could have used for not puking.

'I don't want to talk about it,' replies Andy, less breathlessly. He doesn't have Ninja Daddy Power, but then he doesn't have kids. So he still feels young and well-slept. And he's obviously fit from all his female-with-a-penis sex marathons.

'This . . . is . . . silly . . . I'm . . . pleased . . . for . . . you.'

'No, you're not.' Andy has stopped running, thank Christ. 'Ever since I got together with Saskia, you've been rude about her.'

'I've always been rude about her, ever since she went out of her way to ruin my marriage. Don't take it personally. You know what she tried to do to me.'

281

'Get over yourself. That was ages ago. She's moved on. Why can't you?'

'What do you mean?'

'Well, you go on and on and on about what a nightmare Saskia was, how she tried to ruin your marriage, how she was obsessed with you for years and you never knew. I think you quite liked it.'

'What?'

'I think, now that you're married and you've got a kid and you live out here in the sticks, you quite like the idea of the beautiful woman who was so, so, so in love with you. It lends a little frisson to your otherwise tedious existence.'

'What?'

'I think you need to get over Saskia. I love her. She loves me. We're getting married on New Year's Eve. If you can't accept that, so be it. I don't want you there. And, by the way, you're too slow.'

And off he ran, my best friend, the bastard, leaving me to hobble home, speechless, wronged and demotivated.

Monday 7 October

The morning after you've been dressed down by your best friend is a bleak one. I had stopped being defensive and started to wonder if he had a point. Not about me needing Saskia and all her associated excitement to cheer up my suburban existence. Not that. Just about whether I was being completely unfair. But then I reminded myself that, even last week, she'd thrust her boobs in my face. Surely she was the unfair one, not me.

Tuesday 8 October

Of course she was one of those people who thrust their boobs in everybody's faces. She was probably given sex education as a toddler. She may even have a Danish mother. I don't know. Maybe I was creating too much of a fuss. Maybe I was trying to make my own boring life more exciting. People always exaggerate the past to make themselves sound more crazy and fun. Maybe I've started to do that myself. Maybe I can no longer separate the truth from my own exaggerations.

Wednesday 9 October

First encounter with member of opposite sex: Sarah 'The Donkey' Philips

How I remember it, officially: I was fourteen. She was blonde and large-breasted. We kissed in the park. She let me feel her breasts. She gave me her number, but I never called.

How I really remember it, honestly: I was fifteen. She was mousy-brown and kept rats. We kissed in the park. She didn't really have breasts. I gave her my number, but she never called, largely because she was renowned for snogging a different bloke every weekend.

First girlfriend: Vanessa Hughes

How I remember it, officially: I was sixteen. She was blonde and large-breasted. Very, very beautiful. She was a year older than me. We dated for six months and then things fizzled out, probably because of all the snogging we did.

How I remember it, honestly: I was eighteen. She was mousy-brown and small-breasted. Quite pretty. Two days older than me. We dated for two months and then she dumped me because Lance Baker had a tattoo and a car with a sunroof.

First and only proper two-timing steamy affair: Saskia

How I remember it, officially: she was blonde, large-breasted and never wore pants, we had alfresco sex two hours after meeting. She was crazy and exciting. Then mad. Then a nightmare.

How I remember it, honestly: blonde, breasts, no pants, alfresco. Crazy and exciting. Mad, Nightmare. Then not a nightmare any more.

Thursday 10 October

So it's definitely all me. She's just a vivacious, spirited woman who's enjoying life and love. And I'm an overanalytical, self-centred arse who's trying to ruin his best friend's relationship by making his own life feel more interesting.

This is what I'm thinking as I walk to the station. But then I reach the station and notice the local newspaper headline screaming out of the billboard: 'Cat murderer strikes again.'

I buy the paper.

Checking that Brenda is not on the train, I open the paper to the page-three splash. Brenda and Bob are staring out at me. She is holding an unoccupied flea collar. He is looking stony-faced. In the background, a croquet mallet is propped up against the hedge. The picture quality is too poor to spot any discernible stains.

The article is written as if this is the biggest story the paper has had in years which, if it hadn't been for the man two villages down from us who chopped up his wife and fed her to his Staffordshire bull terrier last Christmas, it would have been. Brenda and Bob got another cat to replace Smudgie. They called it Smidgie. It refused to go into the garden. ''We thought Smidgie sensed the pain and suffering of Smudgie,' said the tearful city worker,' the article read. And then, yesterday, they found it in the pub kitchen, brutally slain. Just like last time. They think the killer crawled in through the dog flap. A local officer (guess who) described the case as the most horrific he'd seen in his entire career. ''A serial killer is at large,' the policeman explained. 'And he needs to be stopped before more innocent pets get hurt.''

At work, I am halfway through trying to establish how long the effects of Lion Poo last when a delivery arrives. Three huge boxes of aloe vera. Even though I still have two and a half boxes left from my stupid original order.

I phone the aloe-vera area sales manager.

'You signed a contract and a direct-debit form,' he says, unsympathetically.

'Did I?'

'Yes. You agreed to take £400 of stock a month for six months. You can't go back on that now. We'd be stuck with a lot of aloe vera if you suddenly decided you weren't going to take it off us. It's all shipped here from America, you know. It doesn't grow on trees.'

I need to make up with Andy, and he needs to do a lot more shagging. It is my only hope of not being killed by (a) a falling tower of aloe vera or (b) a wife who discovers that not only did I rack up an £8,000 debt from internet gambling but I also then racked up a further £2,400 on aloe vera in an attempt to offset it.

Friday 11 October

'Did you hear a second cat has been murdered?' Isabel is chewing some toast methodically. Jacob is chewing a pen absent-mindedly.

'Yes, except you can't murder a cat. Is he all right chewing that pen?'

'Yes, he's teething.' She always says this. He's been teething for six months. Every time he cries, it's because he's teething.

'What if he fell while he was chewing the pen? He could kill himself instantly.'

'He won't fall.' She has been reading more

286

books which say we must constantly expose our child to danger. It is the only way he will learn. 'He'll only fall if you make him think he might fall.'

I decide to change the subject.

'You know that whole aloe-vera thing? Well, a girl at work's trying to flog it. Just wondered if any of the mums might be in the market for some?'

'I'll ask. Or you can ask tomorrow.'

'Tomorrow?'

'Yes, we're going camping, remember? With the baby group?'

Saturday 12 October

I definitely don't remember us ever having a conversation about a baby-group camping trip. Not one in October. Not with Teresa and Annabel and their difficult children. I certainly don't remember agreeing to it. Why would I ever agree to a whole weekend of mixing their difficult children with our wonderful but also difficult child? And yet here we are in a field near Brighton, in the rain, trying to set up a tent we last used when we were young and stupid and content to spend a whole crappy weekend in a crappy little tent at a crappy little music festival with drunk people knocking out our pegs and not shutting up until 4 a.m.

Teresa has a tent that can only be described as a house. It has a main living space, a vestibule and four bedrooms. I ask if it has a billiard room and she doesn't laugh.

Annabel has a yurt, handmade in Mongolia.

We have a tent with a hole in it which smells of wet dog.

'It got a bit wet in the flood,' says Isabel, by way of warning me not to complain too much since the flood — and therefore everything related to the flood — is my fault for evermore.

The plan, if you can call it that, had been to cook sausages (brought by Teresa, who knows the best butcher in the whole of Europe) and burgers (brought by Annabel, who made them by hand because everything's always best when it's homemade) on the open fire, but the horizontal rain confined us to Teresa's tent hall instead. All we could do was sit there eating cold cheese sandwiches and wait for it to get dark enough to call it a day.

Obviously, Teresa's perfect child was asleep by 7.30 p.m. on the dot. 'Routine,' said Teresa instructively, while the two remaining feral children, wide awake as usual and with no apparent intention of going to sleep ever again, made yet another break for the great outdoors. It was too dark to see, but I swear I heard Isabel's eyes rolling as Teresa then expanded on her theories of infant discipline.

Eventually, we all turned in, and that's when the crying started. First Teresa's (no doubt part of a routine), then Annabel's, then ours. One child after another having its nightly moan. Next time I go camping with other people's children — which will be never — I will pitch our tent in a separate field.

Sunday 13 October

How do you get trench foot? Can you still get it these days or was it something that died out in the 1970s? The field in which we are camping is fairly trench-like. My shoes have been soaked since three minutes after we arrived yesterday. It's still raining horizontally and I'm pretty sure that I have water on the lung as well. Is that also something you can still get? Or is it water on the brain? I've definitely got something on the lung, though, because there's a clicking noise every time I breathe. Sitting in a wet field during a cold October weekend with people whose parenting methods differ wildly from our own is not my idea of heaven. Even when Teresa hands me a fresh coffee made from the finest Jamaican coffee beans money can buy.

But Isabel is loving it. She wants to stay another night.

'Please can we stay another night? Please, please, please, please, please? The others are going home. It will be just us. It will be so romantic. Pleeeeeease.'

'We won't have the use of Teresa's show tent. And it's still raining.'

'Pleeeeeease.'

Jacob's big eyes are also begging. He's obviously very happy in that puddle eating that mud.

'Okay,' I say, because it's impossible not to with all those pleases and, besides, there is nothing at home but Andy not talking to me, Alex telling me the intimate rewards of his new-found hard-ball-playing and a spate of cat murders for which I am, ridiculously, chief suspect.

In the evening, alone in our field, Jacob knocked out early by the gallons of fresh air his little lungs have sucked in, Isabel and I made love in our damp, cold tent. And, for the first time in a very, very long time, it was proper, loving, caring and unrushed. Afterwards, the skies had cleared. It took a while but I got a fire going and we sat beside it chatting. This is what married life used to be like. Time. Sex. Chatting.

'I think I'm going to arrange an engagement party for Andy and Saskia,' I said after we'd finished wittering on about how wonderful everything was. (You have to cover a lot of ground in these rare moments of child-free peace and togetherness.)

'I think that's a good idea.'

'You do?'

'Yes.'

'But I thought you hated Saskia.'

'She's not my favourite person in the world, but she makes Andy happy. And if you don't accept that, you're going to lose him.'

'I know.'

'And by the way, I put a note in playgroup about the aloe vera. You can tell the girl at work we need fifteen bottles.'

'Great. And you know that triathlon practice we did last week?'

'Yes.'

'Personal best by twenty minutes.'

'Well done. We need a new tent.'

'Yes. I'll get one in the sales. Have you sent the form back for the Child Trust Fund thingy?'

'No. A man's coming round to replace the shelves in the living room.'

'Sure I shouldn't do it?'

'Yes.'

'Okay.'

'I love you.'

'I love you, too.'

'Shall we go camping in France next spr — '

And that was it. Jacob had woken up. Global politics, the crack in the car windscreen and the prospects of a general election would have to wait until the next time we had a chance for a proper conversation.

Monday 14 October

Worst Monday ever, including the Monday when I was seven that I broke my arm on a rockery, the Monday when I was nine that I found out there was no afterlife and the Monday when I was twenty-six that somebody told me it was perfectly safe to reheat hot dogs.

REASONS IT WAS THE WORST MONDAY EVER

First, the weekend was over. And even though it was a wet weekend and our tent had a hole in it, it was the best weekend of the year.

Second, we had to get up at 5 a.m., pack up in the rain and race home, and the traffic was so bad I had to leave for work without having a shower.

Third, I was still only five minutes late, but Janice nonetheless complained.

Fourth, she then said, 'Did you hear that a second cat was murdered? Maybe we should look into it for our news pages,' before announcing that she was off to a cat show and wouldn't have time to write her column. Would I mind?

Fifth, I am so pathetic that I felt honoured to be handed my old 'Good enough to eat?' column back for one month only. Until I discovered it was Whiskas Fisherman's Choice. I always hated the fish ones. At least with rabbit I could pretend it was bolognaise.

Sixth, I had to try it a second time because I wasn't paying attention the first time.

Seventh, I e-mailed Andy to ask if we could talk and he didn't reply.

Eighth, due to the wet weather, all the trains are completely and utterly not working.

Ninth, *South-East Today* has announced a £10,000 reward for information leading to the prosecution of the cat murderer. It is a record amount, and although the donor remains anonymous, it is thought to be an eccentric local millionaire who is as appalled as *South-East Today* is pretending to be at the terrible spate of murders. Can two be a spate? Can cats be murdered? Honestly.

Tenth, when I finally get home, Alex calls to say he has had another tiff with Geoff and wants advice on how to be more assertive when it comes to deciding who does which household chores.

HOW TO WIN THE HOUSEHOLD CHORES BATTLE

The divvying up of chores is like picking a playground football team, except that it's more complicated and fraught with greater danger. You don't want to get left with Fatty Jenkins (or, in this case, the washing up), but letting on that fact is a mistake. You need to give the impression that Fatty is someone you really want on your team.

Start by taking on a chore you like and they hate but pretend you don't like it ('I'll put out the rubbish, darling, even though I hate it'). Then allow them to make two choices by way of compensation. As long as you have been ambiguous about your feelings towards Fatty, there is now every chance that they will pick him. Continue in this way until Fatty has been picked.

Note: if you have always been anti-Fatty, you will either get Fatty or you'll have to pay dearly to avoid Fatty (we're talking pairing socks, unloading the dishwasher and being in charge of vacuum cleaner bag resupply combined).

Finally, go for jobs that are unpleasant but rare rather than bearable but daily. Leaf-sweeping is good because it's seasonal. Ditto cleaning out the shed. Hoovering, less so.

'So to not get Fatty, I need to clean out the shed?' asks Alex, wide-eyed, even though we're on the phone.

'Precisely. You learn fast, my boy.'

Tuesday 15 October

'Hellooooo, officer. I notice there's a £10,000 reward for information leading to the killer of those poor weeee cats.' My voice is trembling, but I'm pretty sure my Scottish accent is convincing.

'Yes, who's speaking?'

'I dinne wanteh sey yit, but what would constitute . . . information?'

'Listen, mate, we have a murder investigation in the full glare of the media spotlight here. I haven't got time for prank callers.'

And he hung up. Idiot. How does he know I don't have relevant information?

Friday 18 October

Andy wasn't ignoring me. He was in the Dominican Republic. But he's back now, and now he *is* ignoring me.

'Look, I'm sorry. You were right. I was obviously trying to make my own life more exciting by inventing some sort of frisson with Saskia and her new breasts. But it was entirely subconscious, I promise.'

'They are good breasts.'

'Yes, they are — and I'm happy for you and her and, ummm, them.'

'Really?'

'Yes. Really.'

'Okay, well fine. I know some people find it hard to understand Saskia. Other women, especially.'

'Isabel likes Saskia. She thinks we all need to start getting on. Which is why we'd like to throw an engagement party for you.'

'You would?'

'Yes, we would.'

'That's amazing. Does it have to be in your village?'

'No. Do you need some more aloe vera?'

All sorted, and we didn't even have to hug.

Saturday 19 October

'I've been doing the budget — and I can't work out how we're spending so much.' This is the problem with going camping with other people. Teresa spent the time she wasn't showing off about her well-routined child showing off about her tight control of the family purse strings. Yes, they earned a lot of money. Yes, they could afford a tent that was a house and a Thule roof box to put it in. But, no, this didn't mean they were going to waste money. So now Isabel has become a mini-Teresa.

'What?'

'I've been doing the budgets, and all our money seems to be vanishing. You're transferring money to your account, but all the bills are still coming out of the joint account. I thought you said the transfers were for the bills?'

She's on to me. She's going to follow the trail to the £8,000 gambling debt. Don't panic. Think. Think of an excuse. Think quickly, though, because if you don't, she'll leave and so will Jacob. And there will be no one to monitor him. And he'll be left with pens in his mouth at the tops of staircases, on the brink of tragic toddler death. And a full and balanced understanding of the whys and with-whats of sexual reproduction. Think. Stop panicking. THINK!

'Darling?' says Isabel because I've been trying to think for several seconds now.

'Yes?' Don't say yes. Answer the question.

'Where's all the money going?'

And then I stopped panicking and said, 'I must have got in a muddle. I've got loads in my account. I'll put it back over to the joint account on Monday. Shall we go to that soft-play centre Teresa was going on about this afternoon?'

Brilliant. Ish.

★ ★ ★

Why is it that every time I change the subject, I change it to something else I don't want to talk

296

about? Like going to a soft-play centre. Of course Isabel didn't want to go. Of course it would be a nice idea for Jacob and me to spend some quality time together. Of course I'm now partially trapped in a padded cylinder four storeys up with snotty toddlers throwing not-that-padded balls at my head.

Jacob's eyes are on stalks, though. He can't quite believe the world can be this much fun — and I can't quite believe how wonderful it is to be in a world where pretty much everything is quite padded. If only our house were like this. And then a child who looks like he's been raised entirely on Happy Meals pushes Jacob off a padded stool and into a ball pit. Not counting birth, teething, the time he fell down the stairs and the time we all got Spanish flu in Devon, this is the first time my son has been exposed to the cruelties of the world. He isn't hurt, he's just shocked. He looks up at me from the pit of balls and tries to smile, but his lip is wobbling. And then he starts to cry.

The Happy Meal child sniggers. He's at least four years old, and he shouldn't even be in the Baby Zone. I feel cold rage. He is only four, but he's hurt my son. As he comes around again for another run at the obstacles he's far too big for, I stick out my foot. He flies into the padded wall, jarring himself on a rope ladder on the way down.

'That man tripped me!' he shouts. 'THAT MAN TRIPPED ME!'

'No, I didn't.' Mums are beginning to look up from their *Grazias*.

'Yes, you did. You tripped me, you bastard.'

'That's no way to — '

'You tripped me. I'm going to get my dad on you.'

Only then did I notice a large bald man with tattoos on his face ordering his morning pint of lager from the coffee kiosk. I decided there and then that Jacob had had enough stimulation for one day and beat a hasty retreat.

Sunday 20 October

Another twelve minutes off triathlon time personal best. Andy is no longer patently bored going along at my pace. I think I might even be getting a six-pack. I think I might even subscribe to *Men's Health*. I could become one of those thirty-something fell runners you see in North Face ads. A man who thinks nothing of running a marathon in the snow across a mountain, possibly being chased by a helicopter — and all before breakfast. A breakfast of healthy things like muesli and carrot juice and cabbage and egg yolks.

Isabel isn't sure. She thinks the six-pack might be a little roll of fat that dips a bit in the middle, creating the momentary illusion of a four-pack.

Monday 21 October

No sleep at all last night, and not for any exciting reasons. Jacob had a temperature. I had to do thirteen laps of the block to get him to sleep. So I was not in a good mood even before I got to work and found that Janice had taken all the jokes out of my cat food column. It now sounds like (a) I love cat food and (b) I take this column really, really seriously. As if readers think it's normal for someone to eat cat food. Janice never did this when it used to be my column.

'You never used to do this when it used to be my column.'

'We've found that the readers prefer a more serious approach to the subject,' she replied pompously.

'Nonsense.'

'Not nonsense.' And she threw a bundle of letters, most of them signed by readers pretending to be their cats (scrawly marks, drawings of paws, etc.), saying how delighted they are that it's not just them who loves the taste of cat food.

I have to get out of this job.

On the plus side, just, Alex says we can have Andy and Saskia's engagement party at his pretentious Moroccan-style pied-à-terre. And for the first time in my life, I am pleased that Alex exists.

Tuesday 22 October

Another night without a single wink of sleep. Isabel says Jacob is teething again. Every time she says this, I feel better. Of course it's teething, that's what's wrong. It's not leukaemia or rubella or tuberculosis or some as yet undetected psychosomatic issue that will affect my child for the rest of his shortened life. It's just a tooth. But then you expect a tooth. You need a tooth. For all the crying and screaming and the miserable, desperate looks your poor suffering child is giving you, surely a tooth, an actual tooth, is not too much to ask? And we haven't had a tooth, not since Isabel first suggested teething in April.

'It's not teething. I think it's serious.'

'It *is* teething. Look, his cheeks are red.'

So at 4 a.m., I type 'red cheeks', 'pain' and 'temperature' on a website offering to diagnose illnesses. It says it's teething. You can never believe anything the internet tells you.

Wednesday 23 October

So tired it hurts. Jacob, having slept all day, wakes up fourteen seconds after I step in from work.

'How is he?' I ask half anxiously, one-quarter self-interestedly, one-eighth desperately and another eighth hysterically. And Jacob answers for himself by giving me a pained smile and then bursting into tears.

'It's worse in the evenings,' says Isabel unhelpfully. And so for a third night, we have a crying, grumpy, tetchy, impossible-to-console baby on our hands. 'It's definitely a tooth. Look

300

how swollen his gums are.'

'I think we should take him to hospital,' I reply. 'This can't be normal. This cannot be the normal way people get teeth. Someone would have invented something to stop it.'

'We're not going to hospital. I'm not going to spend all night waiting in A&E with a sick child.'

'Well, you're not going to go when he's fine, are you?'

'He is fine. Mum looked at him this morning. He's teething.'

'She's a retired doctor. Shouldn't we get a current one? There may be new diseases she doesn't even know about.'

'Stop it. You're not helping.'

And I stop it because I'm not.

Thursday 24 October

He finally fell asleep at 5 a.m., the poor sausage. And then he woke at 7 a.m. and his cheeks weren't red any more. He looked at us both. We looked at him, anxiously, the epitome of panicky first-time parents. He smiled and we smiled back because there it was: a tooth.

'I told you he was teething.'

'I can't believe we have to go through this nineteen more times.'

I can't remember how I got to work. I can't remember what happened at work. I can't remember coming home, but I can remember going to bed. At 8 p.m. Bliss.

Saturday 26 October

Both sets of parents over for lunch. *Both of them.* Why do we do this? Why not separate them? Divide and rule.

Isabel's mum: 'Hello, my darlinks. It's been such a long time since we've come over for a proper lunch. And you've cooked? My goodness, we were expecting a cold collation.'

My mum: 'You've cooked? How wonderful.'

Isabel's dad: 'Of course they've cooked. It's lunch, isn't it? They wouldn't have us round here for sandwiches. Just because they've got a child, it doesn't mean the world has to stop.'

My dad: 'Too right. Lunch is lunch. All this fuss these days over babies. It's a wonder anyone eats. I see the builders have done a good job of getting rid of that ridiculous bathroom.'

Isabel and I are in the kitchen arguing over which set of parents is more incendiary when the doorbell rings.

'Afternoon, Mr Walker.'

'Hello, officer. It's not really a good time, I'm afraid.'

'Oh, it isn't, is it?'

'No, it's not. How's the investigation going? Found your murderer?'

'Not yet. Not yet. That's why I'm here. We haven't enough evidence to proceed further with these investigations.'

'That's a shame.'

'A shame indeed, sir. But you mark my words, the case is not closed. And I shall be keeping an eye out until we find the offender.'

'You still think it's me, don't you? That's the only possible explanation for you driving half an hour out of your jurisdiction on a Saturday to interrupt my lunch with my family.'

'Bit of a temper, haven't we, sir?'

'No, I just think it's a bit rich.'

'A *bit rich*, sir? I'm only doing my job, sir. Have a good lunch, sir.'

Isabel's mum: 'Was that the police?'

My mum: 'Goodness gracious, what did the police want?'

Isabel's dad: 'What have you two been up to?'

My dad: 'It's not drugs, is it? Read an article last week. Mums doing the school run on cocaine.'

Her dad: 'Bloody ridiculous. Parents today. What's wrong with the pub?'

My dad: 'Leave the kids in the car. Packet of crisps and some blackcurrant juice. Perfectly happy. Nice pint of bitter for me. Home in time for tea. Never did you any harm. Not like all this class-A-drugs parenting.'

Sunday 27 October

Andy has only now decided to mention that we have to raise £600 each to be in the triathlon. He didn't mention it earlier because he knew I had money problems. But we're doing the triathlon for Animal Samaritans. He thought it would fit in, what with the magazine I work for and the chickens dying. And those poor murdered cats. I don't understand how his brain works some-times.

'So I have to ask everyone I know if they can sponsor me doing something fun for a charity that provides a phone service for suicidal animals?'

'It doesn't do that. It's a last-line rescue shelter. It's where my mum got her chameleon. Twiggy's the patron.'

'And we can't do the triathlon unless we raise £600?'

'No.'

'In four weeks?'

'Yes.'

Monday 28 October

'You still haven't moved the money from your account to the joint account, darling. It's going to go overdrawn.'

'Sorry. Just had to pay the deposit for the triathlon.'

'What deposit?'

'Well, it's a sponsorship thing so I have to raise £600, but Andy forgot to mention it so I've put some of it up myself. I'll get it back.'

I'm lying about lies I already lied about. This is extreme compound lying. Lying cubed. I arrive at work all flustered and edgy.

'How long are all those boxes going to be there?' Janice really does have a knack for getting the little picture.

'I don't know, Janice. But they're right over in

304

the corner. They're miles away from your desk. Is it a problem?'

'It's only that Dennis is in Birmingham again for the next ten days and I'm going to have to bring my cat in and you know how he gets frightened of cardboard boxes.'

'What?'

'Cardboard boxes. They intimidate him.'

For a moment, I think: Just let it go. You're still sleep-deprived. You're stressed. You need to empathise with Janice. She does love her cats. This is *Cat World*, after all.

And then I think: No, people need to stop putting cats before humans.

And then I say, 'For God's sake, Janice. It's only a bloody cat. How can a bloody cat be frightened of a bloody cardboard box? It's only a bloody cardboard box. It's not a bucket of water. It's not a bigger cat. It's not a cat murderer, is it?'

I have perhaps overstated my case and Janice is suddenly a bit tearful. 'When he was a kitten,' she sniffs, 'his breeder kept him and the rest of his litter in a cardboard box. Then, one day, when the breeder couldn't sell them, he chucked the cardboard box in a river. Except the kittens managed to escape when the box hit a log. As the kittens made for the riverbank . . . '

She stops to blow her nose.

' . . . he attacked them with his walking stick, killing them one by one. The RSPCA were on to him, but they got there too late. Too late for all but Snowy. And that's why he doesn't like cardboard boxes.'

'I'll have them out of here by the end of the week.'

Wednesday 30 October

Alex has draped his entire annoying maisonette in deep-red velvet for Andy and Saskia's engagement party. There are lava lamps in every corner (because 'they're trendy again'). There are small coves curtained off and packed with black beanbags (because 'even though they're getting married, it doesn't mean we can't have a sexy party'). The music is dark. The atmosphere is dark. The cocktails are dark red. In fact, the only thing that separates this from an East European brothel is the food (my contribution: canapés from Marks & Spencer).

'Don't you think this is all a bit . . . dark?' I ask as I arrange my sausage rolls on a rubberised tablecloth.

But then Saskia and Andy arrive. 'Oh my God, I love it,' screams Saskia. 'It's so sssssssssssssss-sexy.'

So I guess we're fine. And I can start drinking. And Isabel can start drinking, too. Jacob is at home with his grandparents, nineteen bottles of milk, five pages of written instructions, seven new toys, six emergency numbers and some last-resort Tixylix. We can relax. Or try to.

'Do you think he'll be all right?'

'Yes, he'll be fine.'

'Are you sure?'

'Yes, I'm sure.'

'Are you really sure?'

'Yes, I'm really sure.'

'Good, I'll have one of those red cocktails, then.'

By quarter past eight, we are both drunk and tired. By quarter past nine, we are inebriated and exhausted. This is way past our bedtime, but it's amazing to be out with my beautiful wife again. It's like the old days when we were young and free.

'William. Isabel. Thank you. Thank you for organising this party. I know it means a lot to Andy,' shouts Saskia above the dark throb of music.

'It's the least we could do,' replies Isabel. 'We're really happy for you both. Congratulations.' She's being nice. Isabel is being nice to Saskia. At least, I think she's being nice. She might be doing one of those fake nices women do when they're actually being the opposite of nice.

'Cool music,' says Saskia, by way of disinterested small talk.

'Yes, very cool music,' I reply, because if Isabel is being fake nice and Saskia is making disinterested small talk, I need to interject.

'You said you hated it a minute ago,' says Isabel, who is either just having a bit of a tease or she's getting grumpy because she thinks I'm saying the music is cool to look cool in front of Saskia. If it's the latter, then she's definitely being fake nice, which is bad.

'Well, I did. But this is a good track.' I'm starting to sweat. There's probably no need to

307

sweat, but there might be. I can't tell.

'Hi, guys. Great party. Thank you so much.' It's Andy. Thank Christ for that. It takes four more of the strange red cocktails to recover from what may or may not have been a potentially tricky situation.

Everything is great. I have a second wind. I love this cool party. It's so . . . cool. I'm dancing. I'm still cool. Look at these moves. Check out these shapes.

'I love it when you do your joke dancing,' shouts Isabel.

'My what?'

'Your joke dancing. I've always loved it.'

She kisses me before I can protest. And then she kisses me again. We can get away with it because it's so dark and the music is so throbby.

I have room spin. It must be the sheer excitement of being child-free. I don't know what happened to my Middle-Age Self-Preservation System.

THE MIDDLE-AGE SELF-PRESERVATION SYSTEM (MASPS)

1. You have the power to sense hangovers twelve hours before they start. The more advanced middle-aged person can stop drinking even before he or she has started.

2. You listen to traffic reports before you drive anywhere involving a motorway.

3. You buy shoes based on comfort and durability rather than style.

4. You pack for holidays the day or, in advanced cases, the week before departure.

5. You never arrange to go out more than twice a week or on consecutive evenings.

6. You only make new friends if absolutely necessary.

My MASPS had failed. This is not good, I remember thinking. I was going to feel terrible in the morning. And then, when I should have been thinking about getting a glass of water and having a little sitdown, I set in motion a chain of events that would ruin everything. It began with the words, 'Let's have a lie-down on the beanbags,' whispered saucily in Isabel's ear.

Isabel replied, 'Okay, I'll see you on the beanbags. I need some water.' Her MASPS was already kicking in.

I set off for the beanbags in one of the secret coves, but found Alex and Geoff nibbling each other's faces and did a U-turn. Andy blocked my path, handed me another red cocktail and thanked me again for being such a good friend.

We chatted. I wished him well. He asked whether I still thought he was mad to be marrying Saskia. I said I didn't. He said I could tell him, man to man, because best friends should never lie. I said I definitely didn't. He said he would be more upset if I didn't tell him than if I did. So I said, 'Fine, I don't think you're mad, but I don't think she's wife material.' Then it turned out that Andy was lying: he would be more upset if I told the truth. He looked shocked. So I said, 'Only joking, mate. Hahahahahaha. I can see now that you'll be great together.' And he looked relieved.

Then I remembered my beautiful wife would be waiting for me on the beanbags.

I fumbled my way into the darkest beanbaggy corner and there she was, waiting.

I whispered, 'There you are. Sorry, I got delayed.'

She whispered, 'Hi, darling, I was just taking a breather,' and pulled me towards her.

We started kissing. She smelled different, exotic. Must be the drink. She felt different, exotic. Must be the drink. She was quite aggressive and her breasts were firmer, bigger, bouncier. Must be the —

She froze.

I froze.

I think it was in that order.

A voice behind us said, 'What are you doing?' It was my wife's voice, which was weird because I was holding my wife's breasts in front of me. And then another voice, the one attached to the breasts, the one that was suddenly, obviously Saskia's, said, 'Oh, it's you.'

Then there was a blur. I remember proper lights going on, not bloody lava lamps. I remember shouting, puzzlement, protestation. I remember Isabel storming off into the night and telling me not to come home. And then me telling Andy it was an accident. And then Saskia seeing the funny side and then Andy not seeing the funny side and having a row with her, as all the other guests made their excuses.

Then I remember running wildly into the night, missing the Tube, missing the bus, missing the last available taxi and therefore missing the last fast train home.

The slow train. I remember the slow train. I remember waking with a start one stop before home and thinking to myself, 'Stay awake. It's only another ten minutes. Then you'll be home and you can apologise and sleep and everything will be all right. All you have to do is stay awake.'

And then I remember waking with another start at my station. And jumping out just in time. Except, it wasn't my station, it was the one four stops further down the line. It was the village station. And it was now very late, far too late for any trains to be going back, far too late for taxis in this godforsaken chicken-murdering village. I could call home with my — No, I'd left my bag on the train. My bag with my phone and my money.

I could wait five hours for the first train of the day or I could walk. It couldn't be more than twenty miles. I could have a quick nap in the waiting room. Just a quick one so I had the energy for the walk.

And then I remember waking with yet another start. It was 3 or 4 a.m., I think, and I was in the murky twilight zone between night-before drunkenness and morning-after hangover. I felt sick, I had proper room spin, my face was numb and my brain was throbbing. I started walking, across the village green, past the dreadful pub, past the dreadful village shop run by that dreadful woman who'd automatically taken Brenda's side and refused to sell me basic food provisions, past our house where Louise and Thelma had died and away up the road, north towards home.

Then, I think, it was 5 a.m., and then 5.30 a.m., and cars were beginning to stream past. And then a bus. I could catch the bus, but I couldn't because I had no money and, anyway, this had become a mission and the hangover had taken full hold. The throbbing in my brain was now so acute I stopped to look at my reflection in a window to see if it was visible to the human eye. I couldn't focus enough to tell. Why hadn't I stopped drinking? Why? Why? Why?

And then I was home.

Thursday 31 October

And Isabel and Jacob were still asleep. So I tiptoed into the shower, washed off the night's terrible adventures, shaved, dressed, attempted to regain my composure, wrote 'Sorry — I love you' on a note that I left by the kettle and headed off to the station to (a) report my lost bag and (b) attempt to get through a whole day's work with virtually no sleep and the world's worst hangover. Stupid red cocktails.

'Due to a problem in the Wadhurst area, all trains are subject to cancellation or severe delay.

We apologise for any inconvenience this has caused,' announced the station computer unapologetically.

'I'd like to report a lost bag,' I whispered blearily to the platform assistant.

'It'll have to wait, mate. Bit of a mess today, I'm afraid,' he replied.

'Right, yes. What is it? Leaves on the line? No leaves on the line? The wrong kind of leaves on the line? The late running of an earlier service? Because if it's the latter, that's not a proper excuse.'

'Someone's jumped in front of a train.'

'Oh, right. Sorry. Killed, were they?'

'Nah, just broke a nail. Of course they were killed.'

★ ★ ★

I am an hour late for work, by which time I have ceased to feel sorry for the suicide victim and started to curse their lack of consideration. Why couldn't they jump after the rush hour? Why couldn't they jump on a branch line? Why couldn't they just take an overdose?

Only when Janice has stopped whingeing at me about being late ('This magazine isn't going to go to press by itself') can I call home and begin the long, tedious process of apologising for (accidentally) snogging Saskia. In my two years of marriage and apologising, I have learned that you have to get a lot into the first sentence. That first sentence is crucial.

'Hello.'

313

'Hello, look, I'm sorry, but it was dark, I was drunk, I thought you were her and I didn't realise until — '

'You haven't heard?' I'm in serious trouble here. She isn't even letting me finish the first all-important sentence.

'What?'

'About Brenda.'

'What, now? Another dead cat? Another family hounded out of the village? What?'

'She threw herself in front of a train this morning.'

NOVEMBER

'*I must study politics and war that my sons may have liberty to study mathematics and philosophy. My sons ought to study mathematics and philosophy, geography, natural history, naval architecture, navigation, commerce and agriculture in order to give their children a right to study painting, poetry, music, architecture, statuary, tapestry, and porcelain.*'

JOHN ADAMS,
SECOND PRESIDENT OF THE UNITED STATES
(AND FATHER OF THE SIXTH)

Friday 1 November

Suicide? I mean, she was a nightmare and she made our lives, which were already a nightmare, even more of a nightmare — but suicide? This is partly my fault. I left the Lion Poo in the garden. She deserved it. They deserved it. They deserved Lion Poo in their garden. But suicide? Jumping in front of a train? Hell, I know people love their cats, but that's a bit of an overreaction.

The news has somewhat eclipsed the events of the party. It has also eclipsed the deadline to move the aloe-vera boxes. At least Janice is off on some cat-related assignment. I'll do it first thing on Monday.

Saturday 2 November

Andy and Saskia have decided to postpone the wedding.

That news has somewhat eclipsed Brenda's suicide.

He says it wasn't because of the (accidental) snog — that would be ridiculous — although it did start an argument that hasn't finished. And the argument got him thinking, would there have been an (accidental) snog if Saskia wasn't so . . . Saskia-ish? And now he's thinking that maybe I was right all along. Maybe she isn't the girl for him. Beyond the sex, the continual sex, what is there? Maybe my (accidental) snog of his fiancée has saved him from making the biggest mistake of his life.

I start to point out that he's wrong, but he says he doesn't want to talk about it.

He still wants to do the triathlon training tomorrow, but he doesn't want to talk about it then, either.

This is all my fault.

Brenda getting squashed by a train is only partly my fault, but this one — this one is all my fault.

Sunday 3 November

The thing about the triathlon is that we're doing it to prove that we are still young and are not having midlife crises. Or that if we *are* having midlife crises, we're handling them in a supremely manly, sporty way. The rule, unspoken, was that we never discussed this. Officially, we were doing a triathlon. We weren't trying to prove anything. That was it. Now, Andy has broken the rule. He has burst the bubble. He keeps banging on about how pathetic he is, how pathetic his life is, how ridiculous it is that the only way he can feel good about himself is by doing a pointless triathlon.

'I thought you said you didn't want to talk about it?'

'I don't. I'm not. I'm talking about how sad it is that two men in their mid-thirties can only feel like they've achieved anything by doing a stupid, rubbish triathlon.'

'You know it was an accident,' I reply, attempting to discuss the elephant on the cycle track.

'What was an accident?'

'Me and Saskia snogging.'

'Yes, you said.'

'And that we were all drunk.'

'Yes. So?'

'So, don't you think a drunken heated argument about an accident is a bit of a flimsy reason to call off an entire marriage to the girl of your dreams?'

'You don't think she's the girl of my dreams.'

'I don't think she's the girl of *my* dreams. I do

317

think she's the girl of *your* dreams.'

'No, you were right.'

'About what?'

'She is the Destroyer of Relationships. I thought you were being melodramatic, but she's not the girl for me. I was chasing a dream. She's not a dream. I was blinded by all the sex.'

'I didn't say that.'

'You did, in so many words. You said she couldn't be trusted. She was self-centred. She was impossible to share a relationship with. And you were right.'

'I didn't say all that.'

'You did.' He's right, of course. I did. But it sounds much harsher now he's saying it back. And he shouldn't be basing his views of Saskia on what I think. That would be a disaster. Although I suppose it already is a disaster. I wish I'd never said anything about anything in the first place.

'This is nothing more than a tiff. You're being hot-headed. You two are great for each other.'

'I don't want to talk about it.'

Monday 4 November

The trains are stuffed and the platform assistant is still using Brenda as an excuse, even though that was four days ago ('Yeah, but the late running of these services has been caused by the late running of earlier services which, in turn, have been caused by the late running of Thursday's services — it's butterfly theory, innit?'). By the time I get in to work, Snowy is already looking at the cardboard boxes nervously.

'Oh, God, I'm so sorry. The boxes. I'll get rid of them now.'

But Janice has other cats on her mind. 'Have you seen the news? That woman with the murdered cats? She killed herself.'

'I know. That's why I'm late again. She jumped in front of a train.'

'But that was last Thursday.'

'I know. It's butterfly theory.'

'Poor woman. Losing two cats. It's more than any person can cope with. And her poor husband. Both cats and now his wife. How will he manage?'

'He'll probably be quite relieved,' I say, too busy transferring ninety bottles of aloe vera from perfectly acceptable cardboard boxes into perfectly unacceptable plastic bags to think about what I'm saying.

'What do you mean?'

'Nothing. Sorry. I was thinking of something else. Did you hear about that new breed of cat? Stands up like a meerkat. Big pointy ears. £20,000 a pop. We should do a feature.'

Wednesday 6 November

'Evening, sir. Mind if we have a few minutes of your time? You aren't under formal caution.'

At least these are different police officers, not the local bobby who looks like Bob and couldn't be objective if his life depended on it. These

319

bobbies have been speaking to Bob, though, and he's told them how I attacked Brenda and then mounted a campaign of intimidation against her. Bob claims I was the one who killed their cats and holds me responsible for her tragic and untimely death. What do I have to say to that?

Nervously, I start by telling them how relieved I am that they said 'killed' and not 'murdered' because everyone else, even the local press, has been using the word 'murdered', which is ridiculous because they're only cats, aren't they?

This, of course, is the wrong thing upon which to focus. They look unimpressed.

I start again, explaining that Bob and Brenda were the ones mounting a campaign of intimidation after she completely over-reacted to what was, in effect, an accident in a kick-boxing class. I point out that they banned us from their pub, they threatened us, they abused their positions on the village committee to turn the rest of the village against us and they killed Louise.

'And who is Louise, sir?' asks one of the policemen, raising an eyebrow.

'My chicken. Did Bob not mention that?'

'No, he didn't. And how did he kill it?'

'His cat did.'

'Cats don't kill chickens, sir.' He raises his other eyebrow.

'He trained his cat specifically to kill my chicken.'

'Right, sir.' If he had a third eyebrow, it too would be raised.

'I also saw him kill his own whippet,' I

continue, because I can see how all this sounds when you say it out loud.

'Did you, sir?'

'Yes. With a croquet mallet. I tipped off the local constabulary at the time, but they did nothing to investigate.'

'That was you, was it, sir?'

'Yes. I did it anonymously for obvious reasons.'

'Well, it was in the file, sir, this . . . anonymous allegation. And we spoke to the constable who investigated. He said it was bunkum. The whippet's at the pub, healthy as can be.'

'Well, Bob replaced the whippet. You don't have to believe me, but he did. I'd be looking at him if I were you.'

'At this stage, sir, these are just routine enquiries. Someone has lost her life. There appear to be no suspicious circumstances but, as we say in this business, never say never. Where were you between the hours of 3 and 5.46 last Thursday morning, sir?'

Oh God.

'I was walking home.'

'Very late to be walking home, isn't it, sir?'

'Yes, well, I missed the last fast train from London.'

'So you walked back from London?'

'No, I fell asleep on the train. I woke up four stops down the line. Then I fell asleep again. Then I walked home.'

'Four stops down the line, sir?'

'Yes.'

'So that would be the station just up the track

from where this woman took her life, sir?'

'Yes, it appears so.'

Thursday 7 November

Alex calls. Geoff is being too clingy and it's annoying him. Could I have a word with Geoff and give him some of my Ninja Bastard Relationship Advice?

No, I have other things to worry about like being the prime suspect in a suicide AND being the main reason my best friend has cancelled his wedding AND being in a permanent doghouse with my wife. I'm hardly the person to help with relationships.

Please.

No.

Please. You're so good at it.

Okay.

Friday 8 November

Jacob spent all evening crying.

'It's another tooth,' I say.

'It's not. He's picking up on the tension.'

'What tension?'

'The tension caused by you spending this month's bills money on your stupid triathlon and then snogging Saskia and then being in exactly the wrong place at the wrong time when Brenda jumps in front of a train. How could you be so stupid?'

Right, *that* tension.

Saturday 9 November

I hate November. Cold, dark, miserable. Long slog into work. Long slog back again. Followed by a weekend of relentless baby duties, all with the background threat of being implicated in the death of a ginger midget. Isabel is being entirely unreasonable. How could I have known that Brenda would be jumping in front of a train at precisely the same time I was unverifiably passed out in a waiting room nearby?

And no one will sponsor me.

'Sorry, I sponsored George to do the 10K last week.'

'Sorry, I sponsored Felicity to do the 5K last month.'

'Sorry, I sponsored Dan to do the 1K last year.'

1K? That's a thousand metres. I run that far to catch the train in the morning. Jacob could crawl that far. That shouldn't deserve sponsorship. You wouldn't ask someone to sponsor you to go to the shops, would you? I'm swimming half that, cycling twenty times that and running ten times that. Surely you can bung me a few quid?

'No, mate. Sorry. Now, when are we going for a beer? I need to talk to you about how lucky you are not to still be at *Life & Times.*'

Johnson is such a tight bastard.

Sunday 10 November

And Andy is a miserable one. We were supposed to be attempting a full-distance, we're-not-having-a-midlife-crisis triathlon today, but he calls first thing to say he can't face exercise or me or anything. So I go on my own and get halfway through the swim and give up. I have never felt so demotivated.

Instead, I go to town to buy a chicken. There's nothing like a civilised Sunday lunch with my lovely but slightly peeved family to cheer us all up. But Waitrose has run out of organic chickens. They never used to run out. I know this because we've been buying organic chickens for ages because the other ones, as Isabel never fails to point out, don't taste like chicken; they taste like fish. And then last month, someone did a documentary about how battery chickens have burned elbows from lying in their own poo and suddenly you can't buy an organic chicken for love nor money.

I buy some organic beef instead. Until someone does a documentary about old battery cows being sanded down to make car-seat covers, you can at least still buy organic beef.

I get home and Isabel has already put the rest of last night's macaroni cheese in the oven. She says she's not in the mood for a roast: we can freeze the beef. So depressed.

Tuesday 12 November

Another three boxes of aloe vera have been delivered to the office. I phone the area sales rep and ask if I can pay a penalty to cancel the remaining orders because I'm at risk of losing my proper job because my boss's cat is having flashbacks. He says that's not the attitude to have if I want to get a Ferrari. I say I don't want to get a Ferrari and he has the temerity to point out that I'm in the wrong business, then. I point out that he is. Shouldn't he be selling time share rather than a herbal lotion? I mean, since when do dodgy pyramid-selling and a hippy plant extract go together? And he says my next delivery will arrive in one month — I should change my attitude and get selling. Then he hangs up.

Thursday 14 November

I am in the pub with Geoff on the pretext of getting his advice for a new kitchen. As if we'd ever have the money for a new kitchen. As if I'd ever let Geoff or Alex near any house refurbishment again. After an hour of ridiculous ideas ('You could have a central pod that comes down from the ceiling like a periscope except it's a wine rack.' 'You could have a glass wall between you and your guests that mists up whenever you're making a hash of dinner.' 'You could have a sink that doubles as a sorbet maker.') I manage to cut to the chase.

'Anyway, how are things with Alex?'

'Yeah, great. I love him so much.'

'Oh, that's brilliant. I thought you were having a rocky patch?'

'Oh no, that's all water under the bridge. He was a bit overbearing for a while but when I had that crash in Morocco, and he wasn't there for me, I realised how much I loved him. Now, I

325

can't bear it if we're apart for a minute. No offence, darling, but I'd rather be in bed with him right now than in the pub with you. Not that we normally make it to the bed. Look at this carpet burn. Hahahahaha.'

'Hahahahaha. I'm happy for you. Just make sure you don't do what I did.'

He stops snorting. 'What did you do?'

'I loved Isabel so much, I almost lost her.'

'When?'

'Oh, a while ago now. When we first met. I was showering her with gifts, running around after her like a lapdog, begging her to spend every minute with me. She hated it.'

'She hated it?'

'Yes, hated it.'

'Well, I know what you mean — Alex was like that for a time. But I'm not like that. I'm not like that, am I?'

'No, of course you're not. I was just saying. I don't suppose you'd like to buy some aloe vera, would you? It's very good for burns.'

Friday 15 November

Text from Alex: 'Geoff's been cool and aloof all day. Love it. Thanks. x.' I am Zen Ninja Jedi of gay relationships.

Text from Andy: 'Can't make Sunday' — our last training day — 'collecting my things from Saskia's while she's out, as per your no-contact rule.' I am not Zen Ninja Jedi of straight relationships.

326

Text from Isabel: 'Please transfer money! Have just got charged for going overdrawn. Grrrr.' I am not even Zen Ninja Jedi of my own relationship.

Saturday 16 November

'Can you take Jacob? I need a lie-in.'
 'Yes, but I was going to pop up to the shops.'
 'You can go later. I need sleep.'
 'Okay.'

'Can you feed Jacob while I do some yoga?'
 'Yes, but I was — '
 'My back's about to go.'
 'Okay.'

'Come on, we're going to be late.'
 'For what?'
 'Annabel's Halloween party.'
 'You didn't tell me about that.'
 'Yes, I did.'
 'But it's not even Halloween any more.'
 'It doesn't matter, we're still going. And I want to get there on time. Can't bear Teresa giving me another lecture about routine.'

'We have to leave now, Jacob's getting grizzly.'
 'But I've just got another beer.'
 'He needs his supper. And *Strictly*'s starting in a minute.'
 'Right.'

Sunday 17 November

Repeat, minus Halloween party.

Monday 18 November

Meet Johnson and Andy in the pub. Johnson is moaning about how we never go to the pub any more. Andy is moaning about how the pursuit of a romantic life is not only pointless, but fraught with misery and, ultimately, loneliness. I'm moaning about everything.

Johnson says Anastasia has gone completely mad and is making everyone blog about everything all of the time.

Andy says that's because she's a woman.

I say he should thank his lucky stars he's not at *Cat World* with an ever-increasing supply of aloe vera and a cat that can't stand boxes.

'Oh yes, how is that whole cat thing going?' Johnson asks, pleased, presumably, to talk about someone else's crisis. 'Has *Cat World* found out its star journalist is implicated in a spate of cat killings and the suicide of a kick-boxing midget?'

'It's not funny, Johnson.'

'It *is* funny.'

'It's not. The police came round the week before last.'

'The dodgy bobby?'

'No, proper police. They were following up on Brenda. Routine, they said, but I'm worried.'

'Ahh. That sounds bad.' The look on Johnson's face is even more pessimistic than usual.

'Why?' I ask.

'Well, are you sure there isn't more to this than the police are letting on?'

'How do you mean?'

'Well, back in the old days when I was on the crime desk of the *Manchester Evening News* . . .'

'Oh, here we go,' interrupts Andy. 'Another load of nonsense from Cracker, here.'

' . . . back on the crime desk, we always used to have another look if someone was hit by a train. You see, it's the classic way to get rid of a body. Everyone in the criminal underworld knows that. Was she lying on the tracks or did she jump?'

'How would I know? I didn't think to ask.'

'Well, you should find out. If she was lying down, she was either very, very determined or she was already dead. And don't forget, you're up against an ex-copper, here. That publican will know how to dispose of a body just as well as anyone. I need a piss.'

Johnson really can lend an extra level of bad to a bad situation.

Tuesday 19 November

'How much sponsorship have you raised?'

'Still only £170.'

'Well, I'll sponsor you the rest.'

'How?'

'Dad gave me some money for my birthday. I was keeping it for a rainy day.'

'I don't want to use that.'

'Too late. I've transferred it to the Animal Samaritans. I know how much this triathlon means to you. And I'm tired of being angry with you. I want you to do this, I want you to feel better about yourself and I want us to get on with our lives.'

It's so much worse when Isabel is being nice. At least if we're arguing, I can pretend she's being unreasonable. But when she's being nice, then it really is all my fault.

Wednesday 20 November

And the trouble is, the triathlon doesn't mean anything any more. Not to me. Not to Andy. Jacob's too young to be impressed. Isabel's too tired of my multiple life crises to really care, even though she's pretending she does. My mum has phoned a couple of times to ask, but she's only being polite. What am I doing it for? What's the point? It's a distraction from my real problem — which is money. Money and dead cats. Money and dead cats and aloe vera. And women.

Thursday 21 November

'We haven't seen you for ages at LoseEverythingYouHaveInternetGambling.com. Have you found some other miraculous way to repay the enormous debt you racked up the last time you were here? Or have you decided to pay it off the sensible way — through hard work and toil

330

— while still trying to keep it secret from your wife? You have? Oh dear. That's going to take years — and she's bound to find out. So why not come back for one last flutter? It could make everything all right again. Here's a welcome back bet of £100. Haaaaaaaappy gambling.'

No. I won't.

No, no, no, no, no, no, no, no.

No, no, no, no, no, no, no, no, no, no, no, no, no, no, no, no, no, no, no, no, no, no, no, no, no, no, no, no, no, no, no, no.

Well, maybe.

Friday 22 November

A thousand pounds! I won a thousand pounds! I've got the old magic back. That's the aloe vera paid for. That's me back to square two. And I'm going to stop. If there's one thing I've learned, it's that you have to know when to stop.

Stop, stop, stop, stop, stop. In a bit.

Saturday 23 November

Another thousand. I've found the perfect amount. One thousand a night. No more, no less. I'm not even going to try to work off the whole debt. I'm going to do this once more and that will be it. It will help. I can manage the rest myself.

'What are you doing on the computer? Don't you need to get an early night? It's the race tomorrow.'

Scuppered. Which is fine. I am in control. A thousand a night. Doesn't have to be every night.

Sunday 24 November

I am late due to lack of sleep. Andy is even later because he was talking to Saskia all night. In the last few weeks, she had gone from hysterical to furious to hysterical again, which he could cope with, but last night she had done The Speech. She had told him that she'd loved him and she'd never really loved anyone properly before. That it was a great step for her to trust a man enough to surrender her emotions to him . . . and that as soon as she'd done that, and committed the rest of her life to him, he'd thrown a strop and called off the wedding.

Now he is thinking of drowning himself halfway through the triathlon. This is not an ideal frame of mind in which to start the race, but the Animal Samaritans are counting on us. As we collect our Dalmatian-spotted swim caps with minutes to spare, he's still moping and I find myself sounding all American: 'We can do this. We have to do this. Give me five.'

Then I see the lake we have to swim across.

'Bloody hell,' I say because it's a bigger lake than I was expecting, but Andy only shrugs.

And then I say 'Bloody hell' again because four or five rows ahead of me is Bob. And next to him is the village bobby, the village postman and the village shopkeeper.

Andy thinks we should leave, but I know he's

only saying that because he's lost the will to live. I haven't lost the will to live, not quite, but the last thing I need is a run-in with a cat-murdering psycho who's pretending to hold me responsible for his wife's suicide.

We're halfway back to Andy's car, pulling off our caps and wet suits, when I feel a huge pang of guilt. This is Isabel's birthday money I'm wasting. This is all those weeks of training. And it's not as if I did the cat murdering or had anything at all to do with the midget jumping in front of a train.

'Stop,' I say, all American again. 'We're doing this. We're doing this goddam triathlon. We came here to do it and we're going to do it.'

Andy is clearly stirred by my stirring speech. Looking at me, then looking at his swim cap, he says, 'Fine, whatever.' We will do this triathlon.

It is only after we've survived the swim and hit the bikes that we catch up with Bob and the village cabal.

'Shall we overtake?' I ask. 'They might not notice us?'

'I don't care,' replies Andy ambivalently. I really hope he's not going to be like this for the rest of his life.

'Let's get past them. It's better than being stuck behind them for the rest of the race.'

And as we cycle past, looking the other way to avoid detection, Bob shouts, 'There's that bastard,' and I look around.

'You bastard,' he shouts, his angry red face even angrier and redder than usual. 'What are you doing here?'

'What are you doing here, more like?'

'Brenda. You remember her? My wife? The woman you drove to suicide? She would have been here today. She was racing for the Samaritans. But they couldn't save her, thanks to you, you bastard.'

'We're doing this for her. In her memory,' puffs the postman. 'And you shouldn't be here.'

'Yeah, you bastard' shouts Bob, working himself into an even greater rage.

'Listen, I don't know what you think I — '

'What's that on your cap? The Animal Samaritans? Are you taking the piss?'

And with that, Bob veers towards me. With a sudden burst of adrenalin, I sprint away, leaving him shaking his fist in the distance.

* * *

We finish. We finish the triathlon. Andy manages a smile. I manage a couple of exhausted whoops because finally, in this year of mistakes, accidents and stupid misunderstandings, I've achieved something. And then we leave because, unless he's had a heart attack or stopped to kill some more domestic animals, Bob won't be far behind us.

The two police officers are waiting for me when we get back to the house — and they aren't there to congratulate me on my sporting prowess. A few more questions, but down at the station, they say. Do I have to do this now? I've just done a whole triathlon. Yes. Would I like a solicitor?

334

I'm still not under formal caution, but they would appreciate my cooperation. Isabel looks worried. I kiss her and tell her everything will be all right. It's like a movie. I wave goodbye from the back of the police car. She waves. Jacob waves. Not even one year old and he can wave properly. None of the other babies in the baby group can do that.

And now it's not like a movie. It's like *The Bill*. Not the new *Bill* with all the shooting and chases and love interest and jazzy music. It's like classic *Bill*, a whole episode in the interview room. I am being interviewed under caution, I am told, although I am not under arrest. Just like in *The Bill*.

'Where were you on the morning of Thursday, 31 October?'

'We've already been through this.' I can pretend I'm in *The Bill*, too.

'Once again for the tape.' Ahh, his *Bill* trumps my *Bill*. So I explain, once again for the tape, that I was staggering around the village trying to find my way back home. It doesn't sound very convincing, I say, but it's the truth.

Then I'm asked to explain my relationship with Brenda and Bob. We go through everything in forensic detail and, even to me, it sounds bad. Like I had a vendetta against Brenda and, when her cat accidentally killed my chicken, I plotted my revenge.

They won't accept my version of events. They don't believe that Bob killed his own whippet and replaced it with an identical one before anyone, even his wife, noticed. They are convinced I killed the cats. They say they had several phone calls from the public (all anonymous) implicating me, which I point out was almost certainly the rest of the village cabal or just some nutters attracted by the ridiculous £10,000 reward.

'Ridiculous? You think a reward to track down a cat murderer is ridiculous?'

Now they've started using the 'murderer' tag as well. Enough is enough. 'Look, I'm tired. I've done a triathlon — for the bloody Animal Samaritans, by the way, in case you really think I hate animals. All your evidence is circumstantial and I can't see the point of continuing this interview. I'd like to go home.'

The cop who has until now been quite friendly — almost, you could say, like the good cop — suddenly becomes very, very angry — almost, you could say, like the bad cop: 'The *point* of this interview is to find out who murdered a poor defenceless woman and then dragged her body across a village green and dumped her on train tracks to destroy all forensic evidence. That's the *point*.'

I feel the room start to spin. 'But it was suicide.'

'She was already dead when the train hit her.'

'I think I'd like a solicitor now.'

Monday 25 November

I was released in the small hours after the duty solicitor challenged the police to charge me or

336

release me. He had obviously been watching too much television as well. All their evidence was circumstantial, he'd pointed out, just like I had. I had motive, they argued, and I was in the area with a ridiculous, unconfirmable alibi. But they didn't have enough. They had hoped for a confession, but I kept confounding them by proclaiming my innocence. And eventually, their time ran out.

'Don't leave the country, sir,' said the bad cop — and he wasn't even joking.

Isabel was still awake when I got home. Seeing the look of worry on her face when the door opened made everything worse. She was pale and tired. She gave me a hug. I tried to reassure her that everything would be okay and we went to bed. It took me hours to get to sleep and when I finally drifted off, I dreamed of a man who looked like me sitting in a parked car outside the gates of a prison. He was waiting for someone. I saw my older self step through the gates and realised the man in the car was Jacob, as an adult. He had grown up without his father. I woke in a sweat to find Isabel already awake, staring out of the window across the moonlit garden. She still looked terrified.

When I woke again, it was 10.30 a.m. and Isabel was not in the bed. I would be two hours late for work. Why hadn't she woken me?

'It's okay. I called Janice. I told her you'd caught a terrible cold on your triathlon.'

'But there were more cardboard boxes. Snowy will be terrified.'

'What?'

337

'Snowy. Janice's cat.'

'The police think you're a prime suspect in a murder. I wouldn't worry about a cat.'

'Cats are what got me here in the first place.'

Tuesday 26 November

Another £1,000 last night, right on the nose. I told myself I was only doing it to take my mind off the whole murder thing, but even I didn't believe me. I still managed to stop at £1,000 and walk away from the virtual table. So I'm down to just under £6,000. I'll get to £5,000 and I'll stop for good because this is a streak and streaks don't last. More importantly, £5,000 is manageable. I've got all the aloe and that's paid for. I've got the job. I can keep £5,000 hidden from Isabel and it will be gone by next spring. If I can get past the whole murder thing, keep my head down at work and focus on my lovely family, I can still finish this year well.

Even this is too much to hope for.

'Look, I know. The boxes. Another order came in. I'm so sorry. I'll move them this afternoon.' I say all this to Janice the minute I get in, before she can have her inevitable whinge.

'Right,' she replies nervously. And she continues being nervous all morning, right up until the point where I say, 'Is something the matter?'

'I had a detective on the phone yesterday. Wanted to know what you thought of cats.'

'Oh, right.'

'He wouldn't say why. He just said it was important.'

'What did you say?'

'I said I thought you were ambivalent.'

'*Ambivalent?* I work for *Cat World*. How can I be ambivalent?'

'Well, he was very pushy. He said he knew you worked for *Cat World*, but he wondered whether I'd noticed anything, anything at all, that might make me think you weren't such a fan of cats. He said it must be hard writing about cats all day long. He wondered whether it could get to you. So I told him.'

'You told him what?'

'I told him about you and Snowy. And the outburst about the boxes.'

'Oh, great.'

'And the other outburst.'

'What 'other outburst'?'

'The one about the column. I also mentioned that your tone had become more . . . sarcastic recently. You used to be such a wonderful cat journalist, always coming up with ideas. But lately, you've been rather, well, snide.'

'Snide?! Me? That's ridiculous. It's just been a difficult few months.'

'I want you to take a few days off.'

'What?'

'Paid, of course. I know you're having money problems.'

'Did you tell the detective that, too?'

'He was calling about the cat murders, wasn't he?'

'Yes.'

'Are you a cat murderer?'

'You can't murder a bloody cat.'

Janice looked even more alarmed. I protested my innocence, I told her about the replaced whippet but it didn't help; she has no feelings for dogs. Only cats. And right then, she was two-thirds convinced her former star cat journalist, the founder of 'Good enough to eat?' was none other than the famous cat slayer of Kent. She didn't even know that I might be a proper murderer as well.

Isabel is ashen when I get home. Ashen is the very worst colour a wife can look. Crimson is bad, possibly even painful, but usually shortlived. Ashen is long-term bad. She doesn't even ask why I am home so early. I tell her anyway.

'I've been suspended pending the investigation into the cat murders. I don't know what will happen when she finds out it's murder-murder as well as cat murder . . . What's wrong?'

She takes a few seconds to reply: 'The police came round again. They wanted to know about our debts.' Her voice is frighteningly measured.

My heart is pounding. I feel sick, but there's nothing I can do except listen, with dread, to the terrible words falling from her lips.

'I said we had had the whole flooding incident, but most of that had been insured. Then I explained how you'd gambled on the internet — it sounds so ridiculous — but we'd got on top of that. We'd got on top of that latest little William crisis. It was only a little blip, I told them. And you know what the policeman said?'

She's ashen *and* teary now. 'He said, 'I hardly think £8,000 is a blip'.'

Immediately I know that my next sentence is the most important sentence of my life and that I must, on no account, get it wrong. If I get it wrong, I'm finished. I will be alone and miserable in some bedsit for ever, drinking cheap whisky, staring at an old dog-eared photo of my beautiful son and my beautiful wife and wondering why I threw everything away. That's if I'm not in a prison cell. I have to say something really, really good, something that can sum up in an understandable, non-inflammatory nutshell why on earth I (a) racked up gambling debts of £8,000 and then (b) only told Isabel about £1,400 of them.

But I can't think of a brilliant sentence. All I can think of is how important it is that I come up with a brilliant sentence because I'm only going to get one sentence. And then all I can think about is how I must stop thinking about how brilliant that sentence needs to be and start thinking about what I should actually say because at least eight seconds have gone by and the window of opportunity is closing. And I have to say something. Anything. Now. Say it. Say it now.

'Darling, I've got it down to £6,000 and I can explain.'

This is exactly the wrong sentence. It is the sentence people say when they can't explain a thing. Any other sentence would have been better. 'Darling, you're looking a bit old these days so I gambled to get money to buy a mail-order bride from the Philippines.' That

341

would have been better. Well, it wouldn't but I've still screwed it. I know this because Isabel doesn't wait for the explanation. She says, 'I want you to be gone by the time I get back from the coffee morning,' grabs Jacob, bundles him into the sling and makes for the door. 'I've been an idiot,' she says as she goes.

Do babies remember things? They've done almost all their formative learning by the time they're three years old, haven't they? That's what Isabel read in one of her infernal books. So we've done one-third of that . . . and most of it involves his father being an utter abject failure. On the other hand, the first thing I can remember is an ice cream I had at Harrods when I was four. So when Jacob is thirty-two, he might not remember what just happened. He might not remember his mother asking his father to leave because the police told her about a gambling debt he had tried to hide.

He might though. He might remember that like I remember the ice cream. He is very advanced for his age.

Wednesday 27 November

The friend's sofa. Back on the friend's sofa. I haven't been here for years. Well, a year and a half. And isn't the sofa symbolic of so many things? Failure, self-loathing, misery, rejection, failure, abject failure, total and abject failure, more failure.

Andy would be sleeping on his sofa if he could; such is his own abject misery. While I have been ruining my life, he has had several more tearful arguments with Saskia. Apparently, she's now stopped saying she loved him and started saying she's glad he doesn't want to marry her because she doesn't want to marry him, not while he's friends with me.

'Why?'

'Because you're the Destroyer of Relationships.'

'What?'

'That's what she said, not me.'

'Ridiculous.'

'That's what *I* said.'

'Especially after what she tried to do to me and Isabel.'

'I know.'

We sit there on the sofa watching *Road Wars*. Drinking. Pretending everything will be all right. It won't be all right. Saskia is moving back to New York. Isabel is almost certainly consulting divorce lawyers as we speak.

At least Geoff and Alex are still keeping the thin flickering flame of true love alight. Maybe they can set an example. Maybe it is possible to re-ignite the passion.

Thursday 28 November

Alex and Geoff have split up. After my little chat with Geoff, it was great for a few days. Both of them were treating each other mean and keeping each other keen. But then neither of them was returning each other's calls. No one was talking. No one was even texting. Everyone was being all cool and aloof.

Alex, who I now realise has phoned up to shout at me, says he always knew I was wrong. You shouldn't play games, he rants, which is rich, coming from him. You should be true and honest and speak with your heart.

'I never wanted to advise you.'

'Well, you shouldn't have done. Look at the mess it's got me in.' He's crying now, which is embarrassing. In any case, he's the least of my worries.

'Look, mate. I'm sorry, but I'm not doing particularly well with my relationship, either.'

'What?'

'Isabel's thrown me out.'

'Why?'

'Because I lied about the extent of my gambling debts, because 2 per cent of her thinks I might have killed some cats and a ginger midget, because of bloody Saskia and because I've probably lost my job.'

'You see, you idiot,' he cries hysterically and, I have to say, unexpectedly after all I've done for him. 'Why do you ruin everything?' This is the original Alex, the Alex I knew before he became new gay, nice Alex. I hang up.

I call Isabel, but she doesn't answer.

I call Andy at work and he says he'll be home in an hour. I sit there watching Noel Edmonds attempt to make a ridiculously tedious game of chance seem tactical. I watch a man with £15,000 on the table throw it all away for 1p.

He's an idiot. Who would behave so stupidly? Then, of course, I realise that I would. I am the loser on *Deal or No Deal*. I switch it off in disgust and stare at the blank wall. If only the blank wall was my life. A nice blank wall. With Jacob on it. And Isabel. But nothing else. A clean slate.

Friday 29 November

Johnson pops round. He starts by telling us both that he warned us. Marriage. Women. Life. All impossible. If only we were gay, then we wouldn't have any of these problems.

Andy points out that Alex and Geoff have just split up.

I point out that it wasn't Isabel who ruined everything.

'Ah, yes. How is the cat murdering going?'

I had been hoping not to mention the latest developments to Johnson because the thought of having to digest his alarmist interpretation of events is almost more than I can bear. And I was right.

'I told you the train thing was suspicious. Didn't I tell you?'

'Yes, you told me.'

'This is bad. This is very bad. What the hell are you doing about it?'

'Nothing. I'm innocent. It was only an interview. They didn't arrest me.'

'What? Are you crazy? You're in the frame. You can't just sit there and let justice take its course.

345

What if it doesn't? You've heard of the Guildford Four? The Birmingham Six?'

'It's hardly the same thing.'

'You idiot. Don't you see?' Johnson is unusually fired up. Normally, he spouts his opinions with an air of superior resignation. He's older, he's wiser, he's been around the block, but he knows no one will take his sage-like advice. This is different. He looks genuinely worried.

'No, I don't bloody see. What can I do? The police are investigating. They can't prove I did something I didn't do.'

'You're mad. You don't know anything. Who do you think killed Brenda?'

'Bob.'

'And what is Bob?'

'A publican?'

'No, an ex-policeman. He thinks like a policeman, he speaks like a policeman, he plans like a policeman. And do you really think if he's killed his wife, her two cats and a whippet, he's not capable of putting someone else in the frame for it?'

'You've watched too much *Bill*.'

'Is it worth taking the risk? Are you just going to sit there feeling sorry for yourself while someone else ruins your life?'

'Yes, I bloody am.'

'You need to take Bob on. You need to beat him at his own game.'

'No.'

'Yes.'

'No.'

Saturday 30 November

In the cold light of morning, despite not sleeping a wink because of the sofa and the thought of having to take on a murdering ex-copper at his own game, I feel better. Not better-better. I still feel terrible and I miss Isabel and Jacob dreadfully, but I do feel a tiny bit more positive about the criminal justice system. This is the twenty-first century, after all. The police don't routinely throw innocent people in prison. Sure, Bob might have been able to dodge the whippet tip-off. And he might have been able to knock off a couple of cats without anyone pointing the finger of suspicion. But this is murder. Surely the police will pursue every line of enquiry. I will be fine.

Then my mobile rings. It is Isabel. I feel nervous — hopeful but nervous. This is a second chance. I need to get this first sentence right. I can't spend the rest of my life on a sofa without her.

'Darling, thank you for call — '

'They're coming for you.'

'What?'

'They're coming for you. They've found incriminating evidence.'

'What do you mean?'

'The police. They found a baseball bat at our house in the village.'

'Right.'

'It was covered in blood.'

'What?'

'It was cat blood. And they've got new CCTV

film. It shows you on the village green an hour later than you said you were there on the night Brenda was killed.'

'What?'

'They wanted to know where you were. They said it was best for everyone if you came in again. I told them where you were. I told them. They're coming.'

The walls close in. Shadows race across the room. I feel dizzy. I feel sick. And then the doorbell rings. I look down the stairs and see the shadows of two familiar figures. One of them moves forward and I see the face of the persistent sergeant peering through the glass. I jump back, whisper goodbye to Isabel, open the back window, scale down the drainpipe and run for it.

DECEMBER

'To become a father is not difficult, but to be a father is.'

UNKNOWN

Sunday 1 December

'What in God's name did you do?'

'Johnson, I panicked.'

'You're telling me you panicked. You ran away from the police!'

'They didn't know I was there. They didn't know I ran.'

'Well, they'll be looking for you. You should go straight to the station and hand yourself in.'

'You said I shouldn't leave things to them. You said I was up against Bob. You said I had to beat him at his own game. Well, his game is murder. And I'm losing. If I hand myself in, I might never see my wife and son again.'

'That's a bit melodramatic, isn't it?'

'They found a baseball bat covered in cat blood at our old house.'

'I know, you already said. And I know it doesn't look good. But just because you killed a couple of stupid cats, it doesn't mean you killed Brenda.'

'Johnson, I didn't kill the cats. Christ!'

'Right, yes. 'Course you didn't. It must have been Bob. Bob planted the bat. Jesus. You're in trouble. You need to keep a low profile until we can prove you're innocent.'

'That's what I've been saying.'

'Where are you now?'

'I'm in a Travelodge near Bracknell.'

'Why?'

'Because whenever hitmen go on the run, they stay in a motel.'

'Right, nice. Well, don't use your credit cards and don't use your phone.'

'I'm using my phone now. You called me — '

'Jesus. Hang up. They could be tracking you. Give me a couple of days and I'll see what I can find out.'

Monday 2 December

Am I a fugitive? Not technically. I haven't escaped prison. I wasn't on bail. We don't even know for sure that they were going to arrest me. I have, of course, checked in as Mr Smith. This is the sort of thing amateur fugitives do. I should have thought of a better name. Mr White. Mr Pickles. Lord Lucan. But it only occurred to me that I should be using an alias as I was filling out the registration card. This is the trouble with not

350

being a proper fugitive. You have the wrong mind-set. With any luck, the receptionist will have assumed I'm having a seedy affair. Or that I'm actually called Mr Smith. Some people have to be.

'Isabel? It's me . . . no . . . no . . . no, I'm not crazy . . . no, I'm not a fugitive . . . for all they know, I could be away on business . . . Oh right, they checked . . . Well, I'll be handing myself in as soon as possible, but I'm being set up here . . . no, I can't . . . no . . . it's my only chance . . . I need time to prove it . . . no . . . no . . . Yes, Johnson is involved, but he's my best bet. He knows people . . . okay . . . I know, okay . . . Right . . . I know. And Isabel? . . . I'm sorry. Okay . . . And Isabel? . . . You do believe me, don't you? . . . Are you sure? Thank you. I love you. Kiss Jacob for me.'

She does believe me . . . I'm pretty sure she believes me. It would be pretty ridiculous if she didn't. You couldn't marry someone, have a child with them and then immediately believe they bludgeoned people to death and left their bodies on train tracks to destroy the evidence. Mind you, if I did bludgeon people to death, I'm not sure I would have told Isabel. I couldn't even tell her I'd lost £8,000.

Tuesday 3 December

'Johnson, it's me.'
    'Hi, Frank. How are you?'
    'No, it's me, William.'

'I don't know anyone called William. How are you, Frank?'

'Is that Johnson?'

'Yes, Frank.'

'It's not Frank, it's William.'

'Bloody hell, William. I know. I'm calling you Frank in case anyone's tapping this call.'

'But I'm calling from a payphone.'

'Oh, right. Well, you can never be too caref — '

I have to insert another pound.

'Johnson?'

'Hi, Frank.'

'Have you found anything out?'

'Yes, you're in loads of trouble. They think you've done a runner, which you have. And they've put out an APB.'

'An *APB*?'

'An All Points Bulletin. Don't you watch *The Bill*?'

'Have you found anything out about Bob?'

'Yes, but not enough. Call me in two days.'

'What am I supposed to do in the meantime?'

'Stay where you are, Frank.'

Wednesday 4 December

I have, quite possibly, only a few days of freedom left, so why did I check in to a Travelodge near Bracknell? The hitman anonymity thing would have worked just as well in a Sheraton or a Hilton. Possibly even a Hotel du Vin. Less anonymous, I'll admit, but if I'd holed up in a Hotel du Vin I could at least have had steak and red wine. All I have here is a Little Chef, and not even the one that Heston Bloody Blumenthal improved. I am eating petrol-station sandwiches and Little Chef Olympic breakfasts. I am growing a beard in an attempt to disguise myself, but it's itchy and patchy. I have been wearing the same clothes for four days. This is not glamorous. I don't even have access to the internet, so I can't continue my winning streak and prove to Isabel that the gambling isn't as terrible as it seemed. I can only sit in my Travelodge room watching daytime television and worrying.

How could they have new CCTV evidence? Wouldn't they have got all of it when they decided Brenda had been murdered? Aren't murder investigations supposed to be comprehensive these days? And regardless of how they got it, had I really been on the village green a whole hour later than I said I was? I know I was drunk — thanks, Alex, for those stupid red cocktails — but I'm sure I was off home when I said I was. I couldn't have covered the distance otherwise. I would have had to run.

Did I run? Maybe I did. Maybe I ran drunk through the night, desperate to get home to say sorry for snogging Saskia. But I would have got tired. Or would I? Maybe the triathlon training combined with the Ninja Daddy Power meant I could run fifteen odd miles drunk. But then surely I would remember that? Or maybe the Ninja Daddy Power also allows my body to switch to autopilot, like it does when I'm pushing the bloody Bugaboo round the block thirty-eight times. Maybe I can now zone out when I have to. Maybe I can zone out when I *need* to.

It is at least possible. It is therefore also at least possible that I lied to the police about the time I left the village. And if that's possible, could I have bumped into Brenda? I mean, why else would I blank out a whole part of the night and then run fifteen miles home? Could we have rowed? Oh my God, what if we rowed?

What if I killed Brenda?

What if she came at me with her midgety fists and her frightening beaky face and, in my drunken state, I panicked, defended myself, killed her by accident, panicked again, dragged her body to the railway track and then ran, in record time, all the way home? If I did, then I'm pretty sure I would have been having some sort of psychotic episode. A sort of Jekyll and Hyde thing. Maybe I was Hyde. And now I'm Jekyll.

My God, maybe I am the killer.

My God.

There's a knock at the door. I freeze. This could be it. This could be the end. I have, at least, a chance to claim manslaughter on the grounds of diminished responsibility given that I can't remember killing anyone. My lawyers can mention the sleep deprivation, the stress, the provocation. No, not the provocation. That would suggest premeditation. Premeditation isn't good.

There is another knock, more insistent. They're not going away.

I could climb out the window. I could run

again. But I'm in my pants and it's December and I probably wouldn't get far. No, I'll just —

The key is in the lock. The manager has been summoned. Saves smashing the door in, I suppose. I am rooted to the spot. I can't think. I need to think but —

The door opens.

It's the cleaner. She looks at me in my pants. I look at her in her cleaning outfit, her Santa hat signifying that this is the season of glad tidings.

'Cleaner,' she says, festively. She's seen it all before.

'Right-o. Sorry, I'll be out in a moment,' I reply, throwing on my clothes, grabbing my last few pounds and pence and heading out to find an off-licence.

Thursday 5 December

There's only one thing in the entire world worse than being holed up in a Travelodge near Bracknell, and that's being holed up in a Travelodge near Bracknell with a terrible, terrible hangover.

'One Olympic breakfast, please. And do you do Bloody Marys?'

Friday 6 December

Of course, I might not be a murderer. Or manslaughterer. Or womanslaughterer. In which case, there's no point drinking myself into

355

oblivion. I need to keep calm. This time next week, I'll be back home — or at least back on Andy's sofa — and I'll be going to work, earning a living, supporting a family and everything will be — Oh shit, work.

'Janice, hi. It's William.'

'William, umm, hello. Umm, hold on a second . . . '

What's she doing? Why is she putting me on hold? Is she tracing this call? Are the police monitoring all calls to known associates? I should hang up. I should hang up and keep a low profile like Johnson says.

'William. Sorry to keep you. Where are you?'

I hang up. I walk away from the payphone. I walk back to the payphone. I phone Johnson.

'Whatever. Leave a message.'

'Johnson, it's Will — It's Frank. I'll call back.'

I have no job. I have no hope. I have only alcohol.

I love you, Isabel. I love you, Jacob. I love you, I love you, I love you. Hiccup. I miss you so much. I can't go to jail. I won't go to jail. We won't be apart. I'd rather die. I'd rather die in a Travelodge in Bracknell than never see you again. They'll never take me alive. Never. Especially not before I have another whisky.

I'm going to call Jacob. I'm going to speak to him. He's probably even speaking by now, he's such a quick learner.

A man dressed as a giant chicken is standing in the Travelodge car park when I emerge, drunk and miserable, into the cold December sunshine.

He rattles his collection bucket at me aggressively. 'Money to re-house battery chickens. Spare a quid, guv'nor.'

'Not interested,' I reply and walk past. I am not in the mood to be hassled by a giant chicken. The chicken tells me to go fuck myself.

'Welcome to the O2 messaging service. The person you are calling is probably trying to move on with their life. Please leave a message if you must, though there's very little point. To re-record your message, press the hash key at any time. Loser.'

'Hi, Isabel. It's me. I love you. I love you so much. I love Jacob. Tell Jacob how much I love him. I'm sorry. I'm sorry for everything. I love — ' Beep. Beep. Beep.

My last coins are gone and the payphone can't even give me enough time to leave a proper message. As I am considering smashing the stupid payphone to stupid pieces, a police car rolls on to the garage forecourt. I look away as calmly as possible and then look back. Two officers are coming straight for me. They're running. They're shouting. I can't hear what they're shouting because I'm drunk and surrounded by Perspex, but it doesn't look good. I'm pretty sure this is it. I'm ready this time. They can take me alive after all. I've had enough. I step out of the payphone box and start to raise my hands.

The officers run straight past me. I look around and see the man dressed as a giant chicken scaling the wall at the back of the Travelodge, his charity bucket fallen to the ground. The first

357

officer vaults the wall after him as his colleague runs back past me, jumps in the car and skids away to head the chicken off.

I take a deep breath of relief.

And then I look at the bucket, lying abandoned in the bushes. It's probably evidence, evidence required to convict the bogus sweary giant charity chicken. I can't take it. It would be criminal. But I have no money, no money for the Travelodge, no money to phone Johnson, no money to phone my wife and child before I am arrested and spend the rest of my life in jail . . . or, if I'm lucky, an asylum. I have no choice.

Back in the room, I count out the money: £144 for imaginary battery chickens is now mine to fight for my freedom. I am taking it as a sign.

Saturday 7 December

'Johnson, it's William. Sorry, Frank. Can you call? You know, about the thing.'

Sunday 8 December

'William. Jesus. There you are. Why didn't you call?'

'I did. For the last three days.'

'Your number didn't come up.'

'I was phoning from a payphone, like you said.'

'Oh, right. Well, you should have left a message.'

'I left messages!'

'Oh, right. Sorry. I never check my voicemail.'

'Oh, for God's sake, Johnson. I've been sat here in a Travelodge all week. I'm going crazy. If I have to eat another Olympic breakfast, I'll die. And you can't even be bothered to check your messages?'

'Calm down, my fugitive friend, I have good news.'

'Well, tell me, then.' And I have to wait several seconds, as Johnson takes a deep, dramatic breath.

'They only went travelling for one year.'

This doesn't sound like something that's going to get me off the hook for murder, but then Johnson begins to explain. Bob and Brenda's official story, the story the village has corroborated to the police, is that Bob retired from the force, they went travelling for a couple of years and then they came to the village and bought the pub. But they only went travelling for one year. For the second mystery year, they were in County Durham trying to set up a new business.

'Another pub?'

'Nope, a pedigree pet-breeding company.'

'How did you find this out?'

'*Durham Gazette*, 17 July 2002. They're in it, launching their new business. *Posh Pets*.'

'Stupid name.'

'That's clearly what the good people of County Durham thought. Bob and Brenda were trying to flog pets for hundreds of pounds. Nobody was interested. And then Bob was caught.'

'What do you mean 'caught'?'

'*Durham Gazette*, 12 March 2003. RSPCA caught a local breeder killing kittens. And guess who the kitten killer was?'

'Bob?'

'Yes, of course, Bob.'

'You're joking?'

'I'm not joking.

'You're joking?'

'I'm not bloody joking! A whole cardboard box of them. Chucked them in the river. And then, when they escaped, guess what he did?'

'He finished them off one by one with a baseball bat and the RSPCA only arrived in time to save the last one.'

'How did you know that?'

'Lucky guess. How come the police don't know about this?'

'Well,' replies Johnson, taking another self-congratulatory breath, 'I spoke to an old mate on the job. He did some checking. Bob was never formally charged. It was a first offence. He claimed he was killing them painlessly. He was an ex-copper. He knew a few people. He pulled a few strings. The deal was that they shut the business and leave in return for no official recording of the incident.'

'Amazing. Can I come home now?'

'No, it's not enough.'

'What? He's been hiding the fact that he killed kittens with a baseball bat. Surely that's enough to make the police re-evaluate him.'

'Probably. But we need to be sure. We need to find that whippet.'

Wednesday 11 December

'This is exciting, isn't it?' says Johnson gleefully. He's only gleeful when he's out snooping, digging through people's bins, uncovering crimes of passion, mucking about. I think I prefer him when he's being middle-aged and grumpy, which is the rest of the time. It's less disconcerting.

'Calm down, Johnson. This isn't a game.'

'We're going to nail Bob like we nailed Alex.' Pure glee. Of course, we *had* nailed Alex. We'd exposed him for the marriage-wrecking, wife-stealing maniac that he was. And it had all been thanks to Johnson going all investigative journalist. But this was quite a bit more serious.

'Alex was only trying to break up my marriage. Bob is a murderer. Not only that, he's trying to frame me for it. And when we were nailing Alex, I didn't have to spend ten days going mad in a Travelodge because you needed time to plan the operation.'

'We had to wait until today. The pub's closed today. We've got a better chance. And besides, it's the first time I could get out of the office without Anastasia noticing.'

'We really, really shouldn't be here at all,' says Andy who looks like he's been dragged all the way here by Johnson. Which he probably has. 'It's not going to help. It will make things worse. Which is typical of life. Every time you try and make things better, they get worse.'

'You tried to patch things up with Saskia?'

'Yes, and she won't have any of it. She says I'm pathetic.'

361

'Yadayadayada,' says Johnson. 'Now can you two cheer up? Look, he's leaving.'

From our hiding place in the scrub off the side of the village green, we watch Bob walk to his car, look suspiciously in both directions and then drive off.

'Don't you think it's going to look bad if we're found with a murder suspect ferreting around in the garden of the murder victim?' asks Andy, scrabbling around in a box hedge.

'Shut up and keep looking,' replies Johnson. 'We don't know how long he'll be gone.'

'I *am* looking, but I can't find anything. How do we even know he didn't get rid of the body?'

'Ninety per cent of killers fail to dispose of the bodies properly,' says Johnson without the slightest hesitation, kicking a hydrangea.

'He's right, though, Johnson,' I say. 'If I get caught here, I'm in serious trouble.'

'You already *are* in serious trouble,' says Johnson. 'Now, look behind that wagon wheel.'

Five worrying minutes later, we have searched the whole garden and found no bludgeoned whippets. Andy and I reconvene by the gate while Johnson tips out a fertiliser bag. You have to admire his dedication, but this is plainly hopeless.

'Come on, Johnson. I think I'd better take my chances down at the police station.' I look down at my feet. It is only then that I notice that the patio stone under my foot is loose. I lever it up to find a thin crust of poorly laid concrete. Just the sort of botch job you'd expect from a cold-hearted whippet-smasher. The crust crumbles

as I prod it with a stick. I feel more excited than
you'd expect at the prospect of finding the
bludgeoned remains of a whippet and start
scraping away, whippet-like, at the hole. Andy
drops to his knees to help, but before we can get
much further, Johnson hisses, 'Hide!'

There is only time to throw the patio stone
back down. I have to leave the dirt and concrete.
Even then, I only just manage to dive behind the
barbecue with the others before Bob strides
angrily through the gate, straight over the newly
disturbed patio and into the pub, slamming the
door behind him.

'We have to make a run for it,' I whisper.

'We're staying put. He might go out again.'

So we wait. And Johnson starts telling Andy
how he made a lucky escape.

'Marriage is never a good idea,' he whispers.

'Married men live longer,' Andy whispers back.

'That's only because they're forced to eat
vegetables and they're banned from going to the
pub. Being married means being nagged and
nagging makes you die slower. The more they
nag, the longer you live and the sooner you wish
you could die. I should know. And so should he.
Look at the mess he's in and only half of that is
to do with the whole murdering thing. Just be
glad you're not him.'

They're both looking at me now and Andy is
nodding in agreement. I'm about to tell them to
stop making each other feel better by being glad
they're not me when the gate opens again. A
ferrety woman with a headscarf, a neat fringe
and dark glasses tiptoes across the patio, kicking

the pile of dirt. She looks familiar, but I can't place her immediately . . .

Bob opens the door, looks even more suspiciously in both directions and lets her in.

'Who was that?' asks Johnson.

'I don't know.'

'Right, let's make a run for it,' says Andy.

'Well, wait a minute. Those two were acting a bit strange, don't you think? Shouldn't we hang on and find out what's going on?'

'No,' we reply in unison, but Johnson says he's not moving. This is his chance to prove his friend is innocent. He'll stay. We can save ourselves. So we stay.

Twenty minutes later, the woman comes out again, her scarf now loosely over her ruffled fringe. I peer over the barbecue as she makes for the gate, but her face is turned away from me. Bob is closing the door when the woman turns and runs back. He looks angry but then smiles and kisses her as passionately as a man called Bob could kiss a woman with a headscarf. And as she turns, I finally recognise her.

Bob has been shagging the village shopkeeper.

'It's the shopkeeper,' I whisper, shocked at Bob's infidelity and at how one man could sleep with the two most spiteful women in one village without getting himself into trouble, when I can't even sleep exclusively with one lovely woman and not get into the worst trouble of my life.

'I've got the evidence,' says Johnson and, for once, one of his gadgets — his 3G, nine-billion-byte video-phone, the one he regularly strokes like a beloved pet — has come in handy.

The door of the pub is about to close when Bob steps out on to the patio again. His eyes narrow as he takes three further steps into the garden. A ceramic gnome looks unperturbed as Bob crouches down. He has noticed the loose cement. He looks around suspiciously, lifts the stone a little, looks around again and then heads back indoors.

'We have to go now,' I say, determined.

'Okay.'

We're just getting off our knees when the door opens again. Ducking down, we watch as Bob comes out with a pickaxe and a shovel. He works quickly, digging down through the cement and then he stops. He stands straight, peers around again and then stoops down towards the hole. With his hands, he clears away the dirt and grabs something.

Johnson is tapping me on the shoulder, miming that he's still recording all this on his phone, and I'm miming, 'I know, shut up and stop tapping me,' when Bob pulls a whippet-shaped clear plastic bag from the ground. For the first few seconds, it's hard to make out anything distinct from all the gunk. Only when Bob turns to carry the bag indoors does it spin round and the three of us gasp. There, squashed against the side of his plastic-bag coffin, is the skeletal grimace of an ex-pet.

Then Johnson's phone rings.

'Shit,' he whispers, pulling it down and under his shirt, but it's too late. The Girls Aloud ring tone ('It's ironic, honest') has alerted Bob to our presence.

★ ★ ★

In the worst horror films, the killer comes at his victims slowly, usually dragging a leg, growling a bit. The harder the victims try to escape, the more of a hash they make of it. They trip. They stumble. They get their clothes caught in barbed wire. They run stupidly down dead ends when they could quite easily have gone in a more sensible direction. They jump in cars they don't have the keys for. And all the while, the killer, dragging his leg, gains on them. It's the hare and the tortoise, with axes.

Bob wasn't slow at all. Within seconds, he'd grabbed the pickaxe and was sprinting towards us. We split up, running back through the garden. Of course, he went for me first. We did four loops of a pub bench before I made for the pergola, shouting all the time for him to calm down. But he took one swipe — and the pergola was gone. I grabbed a garden fork as he bore down on me, deflected a blow and fell against the kennel of one of Bob's earlier victims. Before I could fully comprehend the grim irony, I saw the pickaxe swinging down again. All I could think was, 'You idiot. You've made a right hash of your first year of fatherhood and now you're going to get killed by a mad pickaxe-man. How disappointing.'

I didn't die. Andy flew at Bob, and the pickaxe crunched through the roof of the doghouse rather than my head. Between the two of us, we wrestled the weapon free, but Bob was like a

366

crazed animal, shouting, spitting, furious with rage. We really needed another man to help hold the maniac down. We needed Johnson.

Where *was* Johnson?

'I'm getting all this on my WAP phone!' he yelled excitedly.

'Help!' I yelled back.

'Oh, right,' he replied before jumping on Bob as well and then pointing the phone back at himself from arm's length.

'Stop videoing and call the police!' yelled Andy breathlessly.

'Oh, right,' said Johnson again, but a voice came up from the other end of the garden. 'That won't be necessary. We're here already.'

They had been on to Bob for days. Even before I had fled to my Travelodge, they were pretty sure I was innocent. They had to follow all lines of enquiry, though, given that this was a murder hunt. It hadn't helped my cause when I had vanished, but my wife had convinced them that when confronted with a sensible option and a stupid one, I often chose the latter. It didn't make me a murderer.

Bob, on the other hand, *was* a murderer, but he'd been so confident he could get away with it that he'd treated it almost like a game. 'He's not talking much now,' the detective had confided. 'But the shopkeeper's telling us everything.' It turned out that Bob and Brenda had had a terrible row the night she died because he'd told her he was leaving her. She'd threatened to tell everyone in the village about Bob's animal killings if he did. So he lost his temper and Brenda went the way of the whippet.

Not only had he then convinced the besotted village shopkeeper to give him an alibi, but, together, they had then doctored her security camera to show me staggering across the green an hour later than I said I had. How did they even know I'd been in the area? The village policeman had let it slip in the pub. (He had now been placed on desk duties at another station. Serves him right.) After that, the planted baseball bat was easy.

The shopkeeper was also responsible for the anonymous tip-off implicating me in the whippet murder. It was another part of Bob's swaggering plan. He had told her they could spend the £10,000 on their honeymoon when he finally divorced Brenda. When he murdered her instead, the promise of the honeymoon kept the shop-keeper from running to the police.

'You're in the clear now, mate,' the detective had concluded, hours after I'd arrived at the police station to give a statement. And that's when I knew everything would be all right.

Everything, of course, except my marriage.

I'd already called Isabel to tell her that it was over and that I would be home soon. She had said, 'Okay.' And after a few seconds of silence and me asking if she was still there, she'd said, 'Yes,' in a strange, high-pitched voice. Followed by, 'I can't talk. Jacob's waking up. Call when you're out.'

This meant one of two things: she couldn't talk because Jacob had woken up or she couldn't talk because she was furious with me and Jacob's waking was a convenient excuse. And now here I was, hours later, standing before our front door trying to work out which one it had meant.

Even with the whole horror of the murder behind us, the situation didn't look great. I was still technically in thrown-out mode. Isabel might have phoned to warn me the police were coming and it sounded like she'd done a lot to convince them that I wasn't a murderer while I had been on the run, but that didn't mean all was forgiven. It still left the flooding, the gambling, the (accidental) snogging, the resigning and all the other horrible things I'd put her through. In her first year of motherhood. On reflection, it didn't look great at all.

I took two steps back off the porch. Perhaps I should go back to Andy's and take up my rightful place on the sofa. It was late now. I hadn't called because it was too late, but turning up on the doorstep was hardly any better. I could talk to Isabel tomorrow. That would be the sensible thing to do. But then I wouldn't see her. And I needed to see her.

I took a step forward and paused. No, tomorrow was almost certainly another day. Better to come back then.

It was only when I'd again turned to walk away, resolving to come back tomorrow, that I heard the door open. I stopped and looked round to see Isabel standing in the doorway in my dressing gown.

'Hello,' I said.

'Hello,' she replied. This was not good. Even

though she was in my dressing gown, which suggested that at the very least she hadn't chopped up all my clothes and burned them, she didn't sound or look happy to see me. And in that moment, I realised that I had probably lost her. No one could blame her. She had had to cope with all the pressures of being a new mother while her husband had done everything he could to make that even harder. There was nothing I could say to make that better. There was no killer first sentence. No Hollywood password to a happy, schmaltzy ending.

I looked into her eyes and saw great tiredness. I saw anger and hurt, and I saw that she was sad. These are not the things you want to see in the woman you love. And at that same moment, I wished I were a million miles away, ruining someone else's life.

Then she said, 'Come in.'

After a few seconds, I walked to the doorway. She stood aside to let me past, but as I stepped into the hall, she took my hand. I looked back and saw that she had tears in her eyes. Suddenly, so did I. I put my arms out and we hugged. For a long, long time. And I vowed to myself that I would never let go. This thing I had — this wife, this baby, this family — was more precious than I had ever imagined and I would never let go.

Friday 13 December

Anastasia has resigned. She's off to work at *Life & Times*' arch rival. She's such a social climber.

370

Johnson is to be the next Editor. He wants me to be his deputy now that I don't have a criminal record. Deputy and head of blogging.

'I'll think about it,' I tell him. 'I have to clear away a few boxes first.'

Janice says she's sorry she ever doubted me. She's sorry for what she told the police. She's delighted the man who killed Snowy's brothers and sisters is finally going to get his comeuppance. She wants me to have my 'Good enough to eat?' column back. Because I'm better at it than she is.

I am pretty good at that column.

Wednesday 18 December

The pub. Andy.

'Andy, I have learned something in these last twelve months and I need you to hear it. Everything I've ever advised anyone about women and relationships is wrong. The only reason I'm still married is because my wife knows, if she ignores the things I say and do, that I love her and I am probably the right man for her. Everything would indicate otherwise, but she's smart enough to ignore it. The secret to the perfect relationship is for the man to do as few stupid things as possible and the woman to realise that when he's doing those stupid things, he doesn't mean to.'

'Why are you telling me this?'

'Because the woman who was destined to ignore the stupid things you do is Saskia. It was only the stupid things I did and said that have put that in jeopardy.'

'It's too late.'

'It's not too late.'

'It is. She's going back to New York.'

Thursday 19 December

The coffee shop. Saskia. Her breasts aren't looking quite as pointy this time. The jab, she says, is wearing off. She's going to be reinflated before she leaves London. I tell her Andy loves her. I tell her he made a mistake. 'He shouldn't have listened to me. He shouldn't listen to any bloke. Blokes are always wrong, particularly this one and, secondarily, that one.'

'Why isn't he here telling me this?'

'Because he now thinks you're better off without him.'

'But I love him.'

'I told him that — but only after I'd told him never to believe anything I told him. So he won't believe me. He's a bloke, you see. He's an idiot. We're all idiots.'

Friday 20 December

The coffee shop again. Alex and Geoff.

'Why is *he* here? I thought you wanted to talk about your bloody kitchen.'

'And why is *he* here? I thought I told you I hated him and never wanted to see him again.'

'Right, you two. Stop talking and let me speak. You love each other. You are great for each other. But you have a problem. You are both blokes and blokes, as I have learned in the last twelve months, are rubbish at lots of things, but mainly relationships. Usually they have a sensible, level-headed, rational woman to ignore their stupidity but, in your case, there is no woman. You've both been asking me advice about relationships over the last few months. This, I now realise, is a terrible idea. You should be asking a woman.'

'This is all sounding a bit sexist, Will.'

'No, it's practical. I am to blame for you two breaking up. If I hadn't advised you, you'd quite possibly still be together. You need to ask women about relationship longevity and, if they're not available, ask each other. You love each other. You're great together. You have a lifetime of ruining other people's houses ahead of you. Only an idiot couldn't see that. Now, I'm going to go back to work and you two are going to talk. And from now on, you're going to stick to Isabel's advice, not mine.'

Wednesday 25 December

Christmas Day

'Breast or leg, Dad?'

'Leg, darling. Always like a bit of leg.'

'Daaaaaad, don't be minging.' Isabel has reverted to her teenage self.

'Pass the cranberry sauce, Mum.'

'Oh, look. Jacob's smiling,' replies Mum and I realise I have no hope of getting the cranberry sauce any time soon. I fold my arms crossly, and Isabel gives me the stop-being-a-teenager look.

'Look at his lovely teeth.' Isabel's mum is getting involved, too. 'Polish teeth are always strong. He must have Polish teeth.'

'Hasn't he got lovely eyes, though,' says Mum. 'South Africans always smile with their eyes.'

'He's got your nose,' says Isabel's dad to Isabel's mum.

'He's got proper hair now, hasn't he?' says Isabel, by way of interruption.

'Let's hope it doesn't turn out like William's,' says Dad.

'Hahahahahahahahahahaha,' says everyone, including Jacob, the cheeky little chap, and Isabel squeezes my hand under the table.

Tuesday 31 December

Tomorrow my son will be one. He'll be two this time next year and then he'll be going to university before we know it. Probably Oxford. Or Harvard. Or he'll drop out because he finds the constraints of formal education tedious. That's what Isabel would like — an education conducted largely under oak trees, using dandelions to explain gravity. And he'll become a great actor or philosopher — or none of the above.

I don't mind. I don't mind what happens to

him as long as he's happy like I am. Yes, I am happy. I don't know why I think I'm not half the time. Overall, looking at the big picture, I am happy. I might not be able to stay up to see in the New Year because my son, my beautiful son, woke up and wanted to play the bouncy bed game at 4.30 a.m., but who would trade the bouncy bed game for some boring TV fireworks? I may still have nine boxes of aloe vera at work, and plenty more to come, but the fact that my four best customers, Andy, Saskia, Geoff and Alex, are all busy giving each other sex injuries again should mean I'm clear within the decade. I may also have a £6,000 gambling debt, but, you know, how important is money, really, when you're happy? Which I am.

'Morning, darling, would you like a coffee?'

'Yes, please. Can you take Jacob while I have a bath?'

'Of course, darling. No problem at all.' (Even though I was about to sit down and read the paper.)

'And you haven't forgotten that we're seeing the baby group for an early New Year's party, have you?'

'No, of course not, darling.' (Bloody hell, I'm sure she never mentioned that. I thought we were having a quiet night in.)

'And you are going to put those babygros up in the loft later, aren't you?'

'Yes, sweetness.' Satisfied, she turns to head off for her bath and I realise then that this is normal. Everything that just happened there is normal. And I like normal. I like it a lot.

'I love you,' I say suddenly as she turns up the stairs. She stops, turns round and comes back into the kitchen, eyeing me suspiciously.

'Why are you being so nice? What have you done now?'

Acknowledgements

Phew. That's that out the way. A few thank yous and I'll be gone.

Thanks, firstly, to Annabel Wright, my editor at HarperPress, who despite still insisting on being Canadian, is very, very good at English. Thanks to Katherine Josselyn, Taressa Brennan, Ben Hurd, Clare Smith and the big cheese, Bond, John Bond. They work tirelessly, some for doughnuts, some for not even doughnuts.

Euan Thorneycroft, my agent at A.M. Heath, has never asked for a doughnut. He's in it for the love of it. Sort of.

There are lots of other people who have supported or tolerated this latest writing adventure: my massively put-upon parents and parents-in-law, the good people of the *Sunday Times*, the less good people of our baby group, Mehmet, the coffee guy on Platform 1 of Sevenoaks railway station, and many other friends and family members. Except, of course for Martin, who continues to contribute nothing, absolutely nothing.

But gratitude to overshadow all other gratitude goes to Harriet. Not only has she been a co-conspirator and improver of plot once again, but she has also become a mother twice-over since I last wrote an acknowledgements page. One thing you don't necessarily need when you're a mother of two young boys is a husband dodging nappy duty in order to finish a novel. Particularly a novel full of jokes about parenting.

She has not only endured the disruption but encouraged it, madwoman that she is. This is much more than I deserve.

Finally, thank you to the two boys, without whom none of the jokes about parenting would have been quite so hard earned.

We do hope that you have enjoyed reading this large print book.

Did you know that all of our titles are available for purchase?

We publish a wide range of high quality large print books including:
Romances, Mysteries, Classics
General Fiction
Non Fiction and Westerns

Special interest titles available in large print are:
The Little Oxford Dictionary
Music Book
Song Book
Hymn Book
Service Book

Also available from us courtesy of Oxford University Press:
Young Readers' Dictionary
(large print edition)
Young Readers' Thesaurus
(large print edition)

For further information or a free brochure, please contact us at:
Ulverscroft Large Print Books Ltd.,
The Green, Bradgate Road, Anstey,
Leicester, LE7 7FU, England.
Tel: (00 44) 0116 236 4325
Fax: (00 44) 0116 234 0205

WILLIAM WALKER'S FIRST YEAR OF MARRIAGE

Matt Rudd

William is a happy man. He has just married Isabel, the girl of his dreams, and is confidently sailing along on a sea of wedded bliss. Things couldn't be much better. Sure, there are a few bumps in the road, but life on the whole is good. That is until Isabel's 'best friend' Alex starts to intrude on their wedded bliss. And when William's ex-girlfriend Saskia — aka 'the Destroyer of Relationships' — appears on the scene, things go from bad to worse. For marriage, William quickly discovers, has its own set of rules. And though falling in love is easy, staying in love can be a whole lot trickier . . .

THE IMPORTANCE OF BEING A BACHELOR

Mike Gayle

George and Joan Bachelor are the proud (albeit slightly disappointed) parents of three grown-up boys whose lives aren't quite what they had hoped for . . . Adam is addicted to TWKGs (The Wrong Kind of Girls); Luke bears the scars of a savage divorce; and 'baby' Russell's love life contains nothing but heartache. When, months shy of his fortieth wedding anniversary, George Bachelor announces he's leaving the family home to try his hand at the single life, everything is thrown into turmoil. Now as well as sorting out their own love lives, the boys have got to sort out their parents' too . . . or face losing the one thing they could always count on.

A SUMMER FLING

Milly Johnson

When Christie blows in like a warm wind to take over their department, five very different women find themselves thrown together at work ... Anna is left reeling after her fiance's departure with a younger woman. Then there's Grace, trapped in a loveless marriage after falling for her husband's motherless brood. Can she prevent Dawn, engaged to love-rat Calum, from making the same mistake she did? And Raychel would seem to be the happiest, with a loving husband, Ben. But what dark secrets lurk behind this perfect facade? Under Christie's kindly hand, the girls have difficult choices to make. Yet none of them quite realized how much they needed the sense of fun, laughter, and loyalty that abounds when five women become friends.

DAYS OF GOLD

Jude Deveraux

Scotland, 1766. Angus McTern's grandfather had lost the family's land and castle in a card game, but the young laird takes his duties seriously. Respected by his clan — he has everything he wants in life. But then the legal heiress to the castle — the beautiful Edilean Talbot arrives. Angus resents her privileged upbringing and his clan's worship of her. Then suddenly, when Edilean's inheritance is stolen, Angus finds himself accused of snatching the inheritance *and* the heiress. To escape prosecution, he boards a ship to America with Edilean, during which a love grows between them. In America, however, freedom eludes them. Edilean's money-hungry fiance forces Edilean to return to Scotland with him. That is, until fate draws Angus and Edilean together once more . . .

THE FOUNTAIN

Mary Nichols

Melsham, in Norfolk, 1920. Barbara Bosgrove looks forward to the annual Harvest Supper and Ball. There, George Kennett seeks her out for a dance, having had his eye on her since spotting her punting on the Cam with her friend Penny, and Penny's charming brother Simon. George vows to win Barbara's hand in marriage — a woman of her prestige would raise his prospects considerably. And, despite George's serious manner — unlike Simon with his great sense of fun — Barbara agrees to marry him, believing him to be reliable. But marriage to George, with his constant infidelity and his callous and ruthless business plans, wears Barbara down. Meanwhile Simon, who has always loved her, reawakens Barbara's passion and fighting spirit, but at what cost?